Praise for *The Sealwoman's Gift*

'A remarkable feat of imagination'   *Guardian*

'An evocative, striking new novel'   *The Times*

'Richly imagined and energetically told, *The Sealwoman's Gift*
is a powerful tale of loss and endurance'   *Sunday Times*

'An epic journey in every sense: although it's historical, it's
incredibly relevant to our world today'   *Zoe Ball Book Club*

'A really, really good read'   *BBC Radio 2 Book Club*

'A novel that moves gracefully between what is known and what
must be imagined'   *TLS*

'A rich, captivating work'   *Mail on Sunday*

'Engrossing, atmospheric'   *Sunday Express*

'Compelling'   *Good Housekeeping*

'From the first, it leaps from the page . . . I enjoyed and admired
it in equal measure'   Sarah Perry

Praise for *The Ninth Child*

'A memorable, riveting, page-turning story. I savoured it!'
Alistair Moffat

'Extraordinarily vivid. Few books have this impact on me'
Michelle Gallen, author of *Big Girl Small Town*

'An absolute triumph. I loved the lively intelligent heroine and the brooding sense of menace throughout'
Sarah Haywood, author of *The Cactus*

'Wonderful. One never messes with the faeries'
Melanie Reid, *The Times*

'An engaging mix of folklore and Victorian history'
Sunday Times

'Pacy and accomplished, with a supernatural chill'
The Herald

'A dramatic and magical novel told with enormous zest and wit'
Les Wilson, author of *The Drowned and The Saved*

'A very impressive piece of work, drawing on a strong sense of place and a rich seam of history and folklore for its power'
Donald Murray, author of *As the Women Lay Dreaming*

'An accomplished piece of writing, cementing Magnusson's place as one of Scotland's leading writers' *Scotland on Sunday*

Music in the Dark

Also by Sally Magnusson

Where Memories Go
The Sealwoman's Gift
The Ninth Child

Music in
the Dark

Sally Magnusson

JOHN MURRAY

First published in Great Britain in 2023 by John Murray (Publishers)
An Imprint of John Murray Press
An Hachette UK company

1

A CIP catalogue record for this title is available from the British Library

Hardback ISBN 978 1 529 34593 3
Trade Paperback ISBN 978 1 529 34594 0
eBook ISBN 978 1 529 34596 4

Typeset in Hoefler Text by
Palimpsest Book Production Limited, Falkirk, Stirlingshire

Printed and bound by Clays Ltd, Elcograf S.p.A.

John Murray policy is to use papers that are natural, renewable and
recyclable products and made from wood grown in sustainable forests.
The logging and manufacturing processes are expected to conform
to the environmental regulations of the country of origin.

John Murray (Publishers)
Carmelite House
50 Victoria Embankment
London EC4Y 0DZ

www.johnmurraypress.co.uk

To Lisa Highton
With thanks for the Two Roads years

Contents

She could write. She could count. She could think. She could parse a Latin sentence and decline a Latin noun. She could hear melodies in the white wind and the restive waters and the pulse of rain on leaf, and make songs of them in Gaelic and English. She knew that people condoned inhumane practices and that words could persuade them to recognise it. She was Jamesina Ross.

Part I

The Kitchen Bed

Late evening

Wednesday, 23 July 1884

I

There he goes, giving the embers in the range a last stir, which is a thing he does every night. To keep the warmth going, he says, though they could do without it this time of year. On hot nights this bed is a cauldron. Cold nights too, come to that, now that her body has started firing up for no reason at all, which, heaven knows, she could have done without too. He'll be getting soot over the place if he's not careful, though he usually is, right enough, being in most respects a careful man, tidy and precise. She liked that about him from the start. Those long, deft fingers whisking his tools away, arranging his pelts and his felts –

pelts felts,

felts pelts –

his movements quick and neat.

Just let the ashes be, she has told him more than once, but where's the point? He'll get his own way, as he always does. Comes across so mild and compliant, but the next thing you know he'll be doing whatever it is you said not to and your head will be birling at how he has managed it. That's how they ended up in a train last week, wheeching up to the Highlands before she had time to catch her breath, the hills getting higher and balder, sunlight on the great firths, lagoons of wren's-egg blue in the firmament, which is just the kind of word Mr Aird would have used. She had made it plain as plain that she did not want to be dragged back to Strathcarron. Not the slightest interest did she have in peering at glens with their souls ripped out and wailing over the field she was carried from on a litter thirty years ago. 'Come on,' says he. 'It will do us good to go back.' Well, maybe it did (and this is the trouble she's got here, because he was right in the end that good came from it), though she'll likely not get a wink's sleep thinking about everything that visit has left in her mind. They got back to Anne Street, yesterday was it? and they've been quiet with one another since, their minds full and their hearts too. He was affected by that trip more than he thought he would be. Said it made him feel as if he had been leading his life backwards since the day he knocked at her door nine months ago.

But this knack he has of getting his own way. Not an inkling of that wily determination did she get when he turned up on her doorstep out of the blue last Halloween, doing that apologetic wee stroke to his lip that she recognised right away. She had him down then for being diffident, shy even, which was all to the good. He would not be the kind of lodger to push himself forward and get in her way, but could be relied on to wipe his shoes on the mat, make his bed and keep himself to himself. Now look at him. He went off and bought those rail tickets without so much as a by-your-leave, and that was that: they were off the next day, she in her wedding hat and a bad temper. It's infuriating (*in* plus *furia*, into fury) to have to go round wondering what he is going to produce next that you have explicitly told him you want nothing to do with. A mirror, for instance. He's been on about putting one up since the day they were wed, which was how many weeks ago? not many. He could do with one for trimming his moustache, he said. Dear lord, that moustache. Started mentioning how nicely it would fit over the mantelpiece in the parlour.

'Do you think I want to see this?' she had demanded, jabbing a finger at the broken cheek. 'Or this?', slapping at the cavity in her forehead with the heel of her palm.

'I don't see why not,' he said, calm as you like.

Well, if he ever does bring a mirror into this house, she will smash it. She'll hurl one of his precious shoes at it, toss it out the window with her eyes shut if she has to. And maybe he knows it, because he hasn't smuggled one in yet, although he does make an unnecessary exhibition of standing in front of the kitchen window when the sun is slanting in just so, jutting his chin from side to side and making an awful palaver about locating his lip in the glass.

She watches him bending over the fire, noting the way his hair has started to creep over the collar of his nightshirt. Still plenty of black in it, curtain-straight. He was taken once for an Algonquian Indian, so he says. Algonquian: now there's a word. Urchin hair is what she used to think. She'll get the scissors to it in the morning.

To be truthful, he's quite a bonnie figure to look at in this light. Which she will certainly not be telling him, since he is not as far removed from vanity as he likes to think he is. He's lean and graceful as he rises to his feet there, his face just that bit mysterious and unknowable. Mind you, everything is beautiful and mysterious in this light. Look at the way it has softened the edges of the room and draped all her ordinary bits and pieces in dove-grey shadows. It wouldn't take much to imagine that table ready for a banquet, never mind that not so long ago they were eating a couple of haddock fillets off it, Brodie's best, and a switched egg. A starched cloth is upon it in her mind's eye, freshened in an orchard breeze and perfumed with, let's say, soap. Oh, and apples. Candles on their way, tall, white candles, not the old stub she keeps on a chair by the bed in case anyone, usually her, is taken short in the night.

Where was she? A banquet. A feast of meat and sweet wine. That's from *The Odyssey*. The fruit of the lotus, whatever that is, did she ever know? but it gives her a sleepy feeling yet. Honeyed Migdale sunshine pouring through the manse window and over the pages of Mr Aird's book. The long walk home with the sun drooping into the Strathcarron hills, storming her mind with poetry.

Evening light.

Vespera lux.

Funny to have Latin words and ancient stories popping out without even trying. Mr Aird would be proud of her: the Reverend Gustavus Aird, who has also come back this evening exactly as he used to be, trotting beside her on his pony or pushing books under her nose in his bright study. Words and scenes and stories, clear as a rinsed morning. And yet was she not in and out of Brodie's twice this morning before she remembered she was there for haddock? How do you explain that? How do you explain why it's so hard to think about some things and not others? One minute she can be remembering with such clarity; and not just remembering but thinking through and working out; not just having a thought but analysing it along the way. She can revel then, just revel, in the words arranging themselves in her head. She can observe her mind as if she is outside it, rejoicing in the poetry of silent sound, the beautiful mystery of meaning.

The next minute hour day week it's different. She tried explaining this to the old doctor. Sometimes it's like being inside a bad colour, she told him. Or maybe she didn't. Maybe she is just telling him now. My mind struggles sometimes, Doctor, to get out of this colour. What colour, my dear? An off shade of white mostly, but it could be any colour that shouldn't be there. Nothing with a dazzle, Doctor – that's the main thing to understand. It's not a pure white like fresh snow in the sunlight, or a bleached sheet, or the rim of an egg fried just right. More like a stained handkerchief you can hardly bear to wash, knowing who's had a nose to it. And right enough he did seem to understand, that doctor, if she could remember his name.

Damage, he said. There is ancient damage.

A tweak to the curtains now, same as always. It never makes the slightest difference how much tweaking he does, because the evening light leaks right through them at this time of year and that's that, but he does it every night anyway: a tug to each side, a wee pat, a quick eyeing of the hem which he likely thinks he could have sewn better himself. He's light on his feet too –
evening light, foot light,
that's a pun –
and on the slight side for a man in his forties. Slight, light. Light, slight. Something feline in his grace.

Feles. A cat.

Felicity. Happiness.

Mr Aird glancing down from his pony. A pearly morning sky. Brambles draped in spider gauze. Autumn berries bright as blood.

'What has happiness to do with cats, sir?'

'Not a thing,' Mr Aird said, and his eyes creased that way they used to when he was pleased. She liked to please the minister.

'The English word *felicity* – take note of this, Jamesina; I shall ask you next time – is from the Latin *felicitas*, which is derived in its turn from *felix*, which means "happy". *Feles*, a cat. *Felix*, happy. You have it?'

She had it. She skipped after him as the beast picked a nimble path among the stones along the water's edge.

Felix, felicitas, she sang to herself.

It's as if a cupboard in her mind has been yanked open, memories spilling everywhere. Or maybe not a cupboard. 'Construct your metaphors with exactitude, Jamesina.' Might be a drawer, a chest, trunk, jar, box. Pandora's box. Might be a barrel. Barrel of fun, barrel of memories. Or a bunker, like the one under the dresser there that you can't let the coalman fill too high or there will be an almighty mess. A mess of memories gleaming black over her clean floor.

When the knock came last year, she thought it was bairns wanting something for their Halloween. She always had something in for the guisers when they chapped her door, even if it was just the wee ones up the stair hopping around in an old sheet. She liked to reward their thin voices and tell them it was good to know poems, good to sing songs. But not a thing did she have in for them that night.

She was sitting by the kitchen range with her back to the bed, usual position, so she could pretend to herself that Archie was still in it, right there behind her if she only chose to look, sleeping soft and gentle with the fever gone and the tight, violet skin beneath his eyes fair again and smooth. She was feeling angry with herself for not having an apple in the house to give those bairns when she had meant to get a bag of them in that afternoon. She sat on. The bairns would take themselves off soon enough.

But no, the knocking came again. And then again, bolder this time, cheeky besoms. They'd be scuffing her good step. So she took herself off to answer the door.

Slim-built man standing there, dark hair greying in places, neatly dressed if a mite threadbare about the seams. Polite. Introduced himself in an American accent by a name she had not heard in years and years and years.

At first she thought, who's to say it's him? There are Munros all over Scotland and there must be plenty gone overseas as well. Nothing to say that some stray shoemaker at her door with a name anybody could have was going to be one of the Strathcarron boys.

She knew, though. There was a lot that was different, right enough – dear heavens, the moustache – but there was a moment when he did that patting thing to his lip, that flick of a forefinger to one side then the other, that she knew. Scales fell from her eyes, as Mr Aird would say, like Paul, or was it Saul, in Damascus, and what were scales doing there anyway, because it sounded awful sore.

Eye scales
skin scales
fish scales
leaf scales
music scales
kettle scales
tooth scales
justice scales
Brodie's scales
Pinkerton's scales
MacPhail's scales.

Anyway, she knew who he was. In that moment she knew exactly who he used to be.

2

He likes to see her wrapped like this in drowsy shadow. Darkness takes hours to claim the room at this time of year, especially with the kitchen curtains being so thin and inclined to meet more hesitantly in the middle than a stickler for straight lines and neat stitching generally likes to see. But there is something severely hopeful about Scotland's summer light that he deeply appreciates. Even so far south of the place he first encountered it, even in a town of smoking chimneys, there is a bracing northern quality to it. It feels to him now as if he has missed this light, although if he is honest he never gave it a thought before. The skies over the Passaic river were filled with storm light, golden light, brown industrial light, hazy yellow heat light, but there were never skies like these.

He enjoys feeling her eyes on him from the bed as he goes round making the room ready for sleep, straightening the breadbin as he passes the dresser, checking the latch on the door through to the lobby. There is safety in detail, safety in order. 'Do you always do that?' she asked on their wedding night, a shade querulously. He had smiled at that. 'Well, there wasn't much to check on when I was sleeping in the parlour,' he said.

He slides into bed and stretches on his side to face her, head propped on one arm. Leaning closer, he rakes his fingers through the wiry waves that are escaping her nightcap in the usual fashion. Why does she insist on wearing this abomination when there is always more hair out than in?

Smoothing a few strands aside, he puts his thumb to her forehead, pressing gently in the hollow of the old injury, stroking her warm skin. She likes him to do this, although he took his life in his hands the first time, oh boy he did, and if not his life, his tenancy for sure. Sometimes it still strikes him as extraordinary that he is here in her bed at all.

Her hands are clasped across the front of her nightgown like a plaster-cast saint in some dusty cathedral. The saint in question has also begun fanning her face with small but ostentatious blowing motions, which is not encouraging either.

He places a light hand on one breast, the degree of lightness precisely calculated to leave the impression of a chance alighting. Should retreat become advisable, the hand can be just as casually removed and forces reassembled. It depends on how the marital wind is blowing on any given night and in particular on whether Jamesina has unaccountably, and in the space of about three seconds, become too hot. In the latter event he has been known to murmur, 'In that case let's get this nightgown off you then.' An eminently practical solution, as anyone would agree. But, 'No, that won't help!' she is liable to snap back. Experience suggests that the demure approach is the wiser one.

Cupping her breast a fraction more purposefully, he sets about the gentle squeezing which experience assures him is the place to start when approaching a garment so formidably impenetrable, so determinedly tied at the neck, so snugly shrouding the feet. Whether his hand can proceed further, on a cautiously judged path southwards towards an ankle and then up the more hazardous route of the inside leg, remains to be seen.

He might try singing as he goes. She likes that sometimes.

Part II

The Shoemaker

Autumn 1883

3

He arrived in October, making his way curiously along the snaking length of Rutherglen's Anne Street between two rows of tall stone buildings, each joined to the next. The thoroughfare was nowhere near as wide as the Main Street he had walked along to reach it, which could give Newark's Broad Street a run for its money, but this was no slum alleyway of the kind the word *tenement* had led him to fear either. Copious autumn light reached the cobbles from a sky less thickly clogged with smoke than many he had known, and there was a decent expanse of sidewalk, for which he offered up a small prayer of thanks on behalf of his laboriously patterned brogues.

The buildings were four storeys high, made higher still by a crown of tall chimneys. Along one side of the street the tenements curved outwards in a series of rather striking bay windows. Number 13, its soot-stained frontage disappointingly blank, was on the other. This was the house that a friendly woman on the omnibus from Glasgow had suggested he try for lodgings: 'If I'm no' mistaken, the Widow Bain has a room to let. First floor, turn left.'

The soles of his shoes sent echoes of his arrival up the spiralled steps that led off the stone passageway of the tenement close. Someone had drawn a border of chalky patterning along one edge of the passage and up the stairs. It was scuffed in places, but pretty all the same. He followed a swirl of leaves and trailing petals to the first landing and straight to the left-hand door at which, checking the name BAIN on the plate, he knocked.

There was no reply.

'She'll be out with the laundry,' a blowsy woman with untidy hair shouted down to him from above. A row of small children gazed at him through the railings.

'I'm told she's looking for a lodger,' he called up.

'Aye, so I hear,' the woman bawled back, launching herself and her small flotilla down the stairs to join him. The children pummelled each other languidly while their mother inspected the stranger with the keenest interest.

'Aye, she'll have plenty of room in there now, poor wifie. Mind, she's a fiercesome character when she feels like it, I'll be warning you, and daft as they come other times. If I have to go traipsing after her for that wash house key one more time—'

An arm swung back to make contact with a small ear behind her left thigh, while her eyes continued to travel up and down the stranger. 'Did I not tell you to stop that, Kenny!'

'Well, I'm grateful to you for the warning, ma'am.' He doffed his cap, winked at the diminutive Kenny, now working up a theatrical whine, and turned to go. The movement disturbed the veins of a leaf design at his feet. A cloud of white particles rose in the dim air and settled on his polished toe.

*

He whiled away the rest of the afternoon in one of the public houses with which the Main Street was abundantly speckled. There he received instruction from a group of devoted drinkers on the unarguable superiority of the Scottish town in which, thanks to Mr John Wilson, formerly of J. C. Wilson Boots and Shoes, Broad Street, Newark, he found himself opening a workshop.

First and foremost, the patrons of White's public house insisted that he would be wise to remember that Rutherglen was far older than Glasgow, its upstart neighbour across the Clyde. Rutherglen had been a settlement of medieval trading importance when Glasgow was still in nappies. It remained a matter of solemn grievance that over subsequent centuries Glasgow should not only have outgrown Rutherglen in a showy fashion quite uncalled for, but had had the cheek to commandeer the lower reaches of their very own River Clyde for its ships and, even more gallingly, go on to become the second merchandising city of the British empire after London. Rutherglen had found itself left behind, a village of country weavers in whitewashed cottages.

'But look at us now,' one rheumy old chap confided. 'Folk can't wait to get out o' Glasgow and flit here. We've got posh houses and fancy new tenements and our very ain shipyard making ferry boats. And we've got plenty o' factories' – moist-eyed, he sat back to deliver the clinching argument – 'that smell just as bad as theirs.'

As it happened, the stranger knew a thing or two about factories. When they asked where he had got himself an accent like that, he could have spun them a tale till closing time. But he was never a man to talk much, and the answer to where he came from was complicated.

By the time he left the tavern, gaggles of waifs in fancy dress were roaming the dark streets. He had forgotten it was Halloween. The gaslights along Anne Street shone on sallow faces plastered in chalk, small heads in scarves and oversized flat caps, flaps of bed-sheet above baggy shorts, scrappy skirts over insect legs and shoeless feet. Not so fancy dress really, and not a patch on the ghoulish cavalcades of his own youth.

Up the stairs at Number 13 nobody answered his knock this time either. Noticing a line of light beneath the door, he tried again. No sound from within. One more sharp rap. Perhaps the Widow Bain was deaf.

The door was wrenched open. 'Would you sto—'

The woman sucked in an exasperated breath. 'Yes?'

Greying hair combed high off an oddly shaped forehead. Startlingly lopsided face. Eyes raking him from head to immaculate foot.

He swept off his cap. 'I beg your pardon, ma'am. I believe you have a room for rent?'

He watched her assessing him and immediately felt rumpled. True enough, his coat and trousers had seen better days. But then, judging from that face, so had she.

'Who are you?' she demanded without civility.

Newly arrived in the country, he blurted, and wondered why he was talking so fast. Shoemaker by trade. Workshop on Stonelaw Road. In need of lodgings. Had been given her address.

The woman's eyes narrowed. He touched his moustache with his forefinger and delivered a reassuring pat to one side, then the other. He only did this when he was nervous. He was hardly ever nervous.

'What's your name?' she asked.

He told her. She stared longer, too long for politeness. Then she turned and stalked back inside, leaving him to follow if he would.

'Close the door if you're staying,' she said over her shoulder.

4

He followed the Widow Bain into a small lobby. A long black coat and a shapeless black hat (made, as he could not help noticing, of inferior felt) hung from a wooden stand. A furled black umbrella stood to attention beneath. From the lobby he pursued her through one of two doors into the kitchen, a square, high-ceilinged room plainly also serving as the main living quarters. It was rank with the smell of some nameless boiled vegetable. That pot should have been off the hob ten minutes ago, he thought.

The black range on which the pot was bubbling with such ardour took up most of one wall. There was an oven inside the range, a kettle resting on top and a fire slumbering in the middle. Three irons rested in their cradles. From a drying pulley above hung an assortment of female garments from which he hastily averted his eyes, although not before observing a prodigious array of lace, ruffles and frills. He shot a curious look at the woman in her dowdy apron. She was explaining in brusque tones that the house consisted of a front room and a kitchen. The kitchen here was where she slept – she nodded to a set-in bed in a recess along the back wall – and she would thank him not to go thinking he could wander in and out whenever he felt like it.

Across from the bed was a high sash window. In the night-blackened glass he caught the image of her figure standing next to his: the piled hair raising her height to just above his shoulder, the distorted slope of cheekbone mirrored back as grey shadow. When she saw him looking, she marched over and tugged the curtains shut.

He noted a sink under the window, a dresser of dark wood thinly arrayed with plates, saucers and cups, a shelf above with milk jug, sugar bowl, teapot and a serving dish or two. The modest accoutrements of a small life, he thought, with a sideways glance at the woman, whose demeanour, all spikes and elbows, suggested she knew exactly what he was thinking and dared him to say it.

On the surface of the dresser stood a large jug brimming with scarlet berries in a spray of foliage.

'Hawthorn,' she said, acknowledging his glance. 'There's a hedge of them in—' The sentence drifted away.

In the centre of the room a slender wooden table was set for a meal for one. Knife, fork, plate, cup and saucer. He wondered what she would be dining on tonight, or what he, heaven help him, would be dining on tomorrow if he stayed. The reeking vegetable had yet to be put out of its misery. Perhaps she had a pie in the oven.

She led him back across the lobby and into a much chillier room, meagrely furnished, which she designated the parlour. The gaslight on Anne Street cast a dull glow through another dark window. The fireplace grate was empty.

'You can have this room,' the Widow Bain said, snatching the curtain across. 'It's not been used in a while, but you'll not find cleaner.'

She looked at him in that appraising way again, amused, he might have reckoned, if such a humourless face could be said to manifest amusement. What had she seen? He stole a glance downwards: coat buttoned correctly, shoes clean.

I need to go somewhere else, he thought. I'll not be able to stand this. Thought next, I'm too tired to go anywhere.

He gave another quick pat to his moustache, this side, that side, as he debated what to do. Months later Jamesina told him that this was the moment she knew for sure.

'I had an idea you were a guiser,' the woman said suddenly, still studying him with disconcerting attention. 'That's why I didn't answer the door.'

'Well, there are a lot of ghosts out tonight, ma'am,' he said, emboldened to risk a tame joke. 'But I'm not one of them.'

Another long stare.

He tried again. 'You find it a nuisance, then, having kids come to your door like that?'

'A nuisance? No. They're good bairns up the stair. I usually have something in for them – apples, sometimes some nuts – but this time I didn't.' She added vaguely, 'I don't know why I haven't got anything in for Halloween.'

He made to speak, but she had already collected herself and the brusqueness was back. If he was minded to stay, she would thank him to remember a few things. There was a bed in the closet, where he would be fine and comfortable. She had slept there herself while her son was in the kitchen bed. (He opened his mouth to ask a question, but she held up a peremptory palm.) She was not in the habit of receiving visitors, so the parlour was never used for entertaining. (Just as well, he thought, with a glance at the sole chair before the fire.) She would bring him a jug of warm water and a bowl for washing when required. She would not tolerate drunkenness: she had had enough of that in her time and would smell his breath halfway up Anne Street if he ever tried it. (He eased his upper body back a fraction.) However, she did keep a tot for medicinal purposes, if applied for in a proper manner. Breakfast and a knife-and-fork tea would be provided. (The murdered vegetable rose to mind and he nodded carefully.) He could get his dinner here at the weekend. Rent to be paid promptly one week in advance. He would have to see to it that she was well up and about before he came through to the kitchen for his breakfast. He would find a privy downstairs in the back court and the whole stair using it, and if he felt like complaining he could try his luck in the new tenements across the road and pay the difference. And he'd better make sure he emptied his own chamber pot while he was at it down there, because she wasn't his servant to do it for him, nor his wife either.

The speech was delivered with a concentrated belligerence which rocked him somewhat, although the note of effort in it was interesting. So was the pleasant, musical lilt to her voice, which also had the effect of undermining her manner. Since docking in Glasgow he had heard this accent already in the conversations of strangers on the street or the omnibus. The city seemed to be full of migrant Highlanders who had lived there long enough to speak their English with the idioms of the Lowland Scot but laced with the intonation of their native Gaelic. Every time he heard this accent he had strained to listen, because in it was something of his mother.

He thanked the woman. He was working up to asking if she

would be so kind as to make up the parlour fire, so that he could take his coat off.

'That's where you'll be sleeping,' she said, indicating a door at the back of the room. 'You'll find plenty of space underneath the bed for your things.'

Opening the door with some misgivings, he found himself at the mouth of a high-ceilinged closet entirely filled by a narrow bed. Thank God, it did look long enough to sleep a man in comfort. He felt her eyes on him as he peered in. Such a craving he had to crawl into this cupboard and fling himself down. The sheets smelled faintly of lavender.

He turned to her, struck by a thought. 'Did you make the patterns on the stairs, Mrs Bain?'

Her eyebrows snapped together. They were long and thick, and darker than her hair, which was well threaded with white. Although so industriously engaged in scowling at him, these brows intrigued him. It was not that he recognised them – not the slightest notion came to him that he might know this woman – but there was a prickle of familiarity all the same. The eyes beneath were harder to look at. Handsome eyes in a ravaged face. They made him think of broken glass. They made him want to look away. They made him want to look again.

'Was it you that scuffed them?' she was saying. 'The alder leaves along the landing?'

He gathered himself hurriedly. 'Well, not deliberately, Mrs Bain. I guess I'll take more care in future.'

'Well, if you're to bide here, don't you go bringing the pipe-clay in on your feet.'

'No, ma'am. I won't.'

So he was staying, was he? When did he make that decision?

'But I wonder, Mrs Bain, if I might prevail on you to let me carry through some coal to get a fire going in here?'

Later, when she had retired to the kitchen, he put his travelling bag on the bed and flicked open the clasps. He took out three shirts, neatly folded, one brown waistcoat, four pairs of socks, a few undergarments packed around a china shaving mug, one shaving brush, one razor folded inside its handle and secreted for further safety within another pair of socks, one leather strop for sharpening it, one partly used bar of soap, one towel and two slim books. His tools were stowed at the workshop.

And whose life, the Widow Bain might be entitled to enquire of him, did he think he was calling small?

It was unlike him to be gloomy, but tonight had been unsettling. What kind of landlady had he fetched up with here? What was going on behind the hectoring? And that disfigured face: he hoped he had not gawped too rudely. Ah, but her voice. Those *sh* sounds, like the wind on the moors, reminding him so powerfully of his mother speaking English in America, although naturally hers had borne no hint of Glasgow and she never did manage to say much anyway, which was hardly to be wondered at in a woman who had to be carried on to American soil on his brother's back and pushed down the eastern seaboard in a wheelbarrow.

In the slightly damp, sweet-smelling bed in which his landlady had unbent far enough to deposit a porcelain bed-warmer, he lay listening to Anne Street settling for the night. Stones skittered about the pavement below as an irritated stick stumped past: *tap, tap, whack*; *tap, tap, whack*. Further along, a merry fellow in full voice was taking an inordinate time to locate either his note or his front door. Every now and then a barrage of shouts descended from above, where young Kenny seemed to be in trouble again.

Nearest of all, from the recessed bed in the kitchen, directly through the wall from his own, there came a sound like a muffled howl.

Part III

The Kitchen Bed

Dusk

Wednesday, 23 July 1884

5

She is getting hot. Insects of heat are creeping across her chest, her arms, and there goes her neck now. What does a woman do to deserve this on top of everything else? Oh, to plunge into ice, call on the four winds of Strathcarron to blow on her body, throw every stitch off – which, right enough, is the one thing she could actually do, but that will just give him ideas, and she doesn't want him having ideas because, because, well, because it's such an effort, everything's such an effort, he's such an effort, except he's not, not always, only think what she felt the time he asked her to, the night she said she would. That fugitive shock of desire. The joy of it. The joy of him. Gone fugitive again. (*Fugere*, to flee.) A man in your bed is just a trouble when your body is burning up for no good reason and your head is full to bursting with where you've been these last few days and all you want is a bit of peace.

That's him started singing now. It's quiet enough to make it sound as if he is just having an innocent sing to himself while he gets on with a bit of fondling, but she knows fine what he's up to. He's hoping that she will sing along too, because it's what he is always on at her to do. It gives her a reeled-in feeling when he does this, like the perch he caught on the river in

New Jersey with the Indian name that she liked when he told her because it meant 'peaceful valley'. She said she was glad somebody's valley was peaceful, and he said it probably didn't stay peaceful very long after the settlers moved in, and that gave her a damp feeling because there is not a new experience under the sun.

How deep his voice is, though. Even now she gets a wee tremor about the throat when it rumbles into a silence like this, the air empty but for a last sigh from the range fire and a giggle outside the window from some lassie doing what she shouldn't in the back court. Maybe the surprise is that such a neat and slender man has not got a lighter voice. Maybe it's that he is a man at all.

'Don't sing that, would you.'

'Why not?' he says. 'I like it. It's been in my head since we got back.'

And off he goes again. *'Glencalvie, my Glencalvie, that the people left.'*

'Well, I don't. Jingly thing. I never liked it.'

And that is true. The making of that song was hard and she never got it right. Mining words out of feelings was hard, especially English words, and they needed to be English because she wanted others to understand them, those folk beyond the Highlands who had let Glencalvie's tragedy happen. She wanted a melody that would make people cry, and make them remember, and she had thought maybe a chorus would do it. He cannot see how troubling it is to hear it sung, so much in the song and so little, the rhythm too pat.

'But you composed it,' he is saying. 'And I took it away with

32

me, which makes it mine too in a way, don't you think? We sang it in the factory and Michael Reilly – you recall I told you about Michael Reilly? – he cried every single time.'

He's away again. '*Glencalvie, oh, Glencalvie, where the waters meet.*'

'I'm telling you I don't like it.'

All right, that was a bit sharp. Now he is not saying anything. Sometimes he doesn't say anything because he has not got anything to say, and sometimes it's because he has and he's trying to stop himself saying it, which she can tell by a sort of quiver in his jaw. And that was one there.

'All right, then, what is it? Why do I have to like my own song?'

He still won't say anything. Just lies there, eyes gleaming like lamps. He's always at his most irritating when he does his speaking in silence.

'It's sad,' she says at last. 'I think that's what's wrong. The song is too sad.'

And Glencalvie wasn't sad, was it? It wasn't a sad place for a bairn to grow up. Not until the very end. Not until the folk were lying cold in the graveyard beside their colder ancestors under a sky the blue-black colour of Mr Aird's ink. No, Glencalvie is new words and childish poems in the making. Glencalvie is her grandfather, dry-spoken and courteous, a gaunt figure parcelled by the fire. Glencalvie is the water and the cloud-shadowed hill, the homely place they shared with the wood thrush and the mountain thrush, the green linnet, the kite, the silver salmon flopping up the falls in July, the hooded crow that was still patrolling the bare trees in December, screeching into the morning's quiet.

In the 1840s it was one of three townships inhabiting the broad valley of Strathcarron in Ross-shire. There was Glencalvie at the western end, the small settlement of Amatnatua between, and as you walked eastwards you came to Greenyards, the largest, which sprawled along both sides of the Carron river until the valley tapered towards the village of Ardgay and the river neared the sea.

Strathcarron was so remote a Highland glen that the government had paid for a church to be built near Glencalvie, to make certain that its people would hear the preaching of the Word and get their sins attended to. Remoteness is only a matter of perspective, though. The folk living there did not feel themselves remote at all, but exactly in the middle of what mattered to them in a township bounded by water, bountifully bounded by water (that's assonance) and full of the bounteous bounty they were not supposed to enjoy but did anyway when the gamekeeper's back was turned, because a fat salmon leaping home under God's sky from God's own sea was surely meant for all of God's people. Inverness was remote, Glasgow and Edinburgh were remote, and London, where the laws were made that ruled them, was the most remote of the lot.

Glencalvie, oh Glencalvie, where the waters meet. See, this is how he gets her. The words start running through her head and the song gets tasted before she can stop it, melody entangling itself in thought, the words shaping themselves into memories whether she likes it or not.

Here is the Water of Calvie pottering past her house. Afterwards it gathers enough force to crash into the River

Carron in a frenzy of froth. And here comes the Carron itself, scooping up the Black Water next and chivvying both tributaries through glistening ravines and lumpy moorland and on between the cultivated rigs of Greenyards to the firth. All along the strath houses are hummocked into the lee of the braes. In the brown seasons they breathe with the moor itself and when the winter snows come they slouch into the tufted white slopes like sheltering beasts.

She can see herself in the doorway, watching the Calvie dawdle into dark pools and around shallow islets of stone where the alders have taken root, those spreading trees where honey bees seek out catkins to load up with early pollen when the winter is hardly gone, and the moths spin their haze of white silk when summer is nearly past.

'Never let anyone disparage the turf-house,' Mr Aird said to her once. It was a shivery day at Glencalvie: weak sky, wet air, the clouds plumped with rain. She squinted the question up at him.

'*Disparage*. To represent the way your people live as being of little worth. Your grandfather's hearth, let me tell you, child, is of more worth to me on a February afternoon than that mausoleum of a manse. Your house, Jamesina, while a trifle eye-watering as to smoke and its egress, is designed exactly to its purpose.' He winked. 'And is of especial worth if the fire should chance to contain a potato or two, which your mother can usually be relied on to invite me to partake of if I present to her my most boyish smile.'

'*Disparage*, sir?' Never mind the minister's boyish smile. He could not have been thirty yet in those days, but he was an antique figure to her already in his voluminous black cloak, the effect enhanced by the ornate English he insisted on addressing her in. For the good of her education, he said, although the Gaelic came to him just as easy.

'Ah yes. *Disparage*. The idea behind the word is a breaking asunder of respect for what makes one person equal to another. Remember *par* is Latin for "equal" and *dis* the prefix that expresses a negative. We have spoken about prefixes before, have we not?' Disguise,

distress,

dispossess,

dismember,

disremember,

misremember,

unremember.

Remembering this. The wind blustering down the strath until it exhausted itself over the Dornoch Firth. Mr Aird asking, 'What does that wind sound like?'

He liked doing that when they were out together, getting her to observe minutely, the way the Gaelic bards did, and describe what she saw. The sun freckling the lochan over there. 'Freckles of light. Yes, very good.' The round December moon bobbing along the treeline in time with her steps, its surface scratched by branches. 'Well observed, my dear.'

The game was to say the first word that came to mind.

'White,' she said.

He glanced down from his pony, which was a sturdy beast and just as well with the size of its owner. Its mottled cream and grey coat looked dirty even when it was not.

'I was looking for a sound not a colour, Jamesina.'

She stopped walking, obliging him to rein in his mount and

wait. Which – what patience he had when you think of it – he did. And what a dramatic play she made of tilting up her chin, closing her eyes and furrowing her brow.

'It's a white wind,' she pronounced. 'It sounds white and thin, like Grandfather's cheeks.'

The minister had a particular way of tipping back his head when he was thinking about something, sending his nose into the air and fixing his eyes on the horizon. It was a long, broad nose, and his hair flowed off his face in flaxen waves like the lion in one of the Sunday school picture books about poor children in Africa who needed her prayers. Later she would learn that *leo* was Latin for 'lion' and this was a leonine gesture.

He flung his head back in that exact way as he considered her description of the wind.

'You know, I believe you're right,' he said. 'The wind is blowing very white today. Well done, child. Climb up beside me and we'll make haste to be back before it takes a turn for the blue.'

His church was a little way along the Black Water at Croick. It was a plain grey-stone kirk with a belfry and lattice windows and a walled graveyard guarded by sycamore, horse chestnut and black ash, which bowed their backs to the wind from the hills. It wasn't a big church compared with the ones you see in the towns, but it was always full, which goes to show how many folk were in the glen yet in those days. Mr Aird towered over the pulpit, a big physical presence with a big voice, the way Highlanders liked their ministers. Croick was his first charge, and the people of the Strathcarron townships were his first parishioners.

*

A January blizzard the night Mr Aird was ordained. Waking on her pallet bed in a shower of ice crystals as her grandfather flurried and stamped through the door.

He was just back from the new minister's ordination service, which had gone on later than it should because of the weather. The officiating clergy and elders of the Presbytery of Tain had been forced to abandon their carriage in a swollen drift and labour along the banks of the Carron on foot. They had staggered into the kirk with wild hair and matted whiskers, and with half the hats and at least one wig departed for ever.

Dots of snow melting on her face. Her mother banking up the fire and her grandfather stretching out his hands to the heat as he described the service. The black huddle of wet dignitaries around the communion table. The chorus of hoarse blessings and violent nose-blowings. The struggle one elder had to turn the frail pages of the Bible with his cold hands. Gustavus Aird puffing out his vows in clouds of grey-white breath, then wallowing through the snow-lit darkness from the kirk to the squat stone manse nearby that was to be his home. Grandfather thought the young man had borne up very well, all in all.

As a Gaelic-speaking Highlander himself, this minister was an acceptable figure of authority in Strathcarron. He was a farmer's son from not so far away in Easter Ross, who had taken his turn with the thresher before he went to the grammar school in Tain and then the university in Aberdeen. He had wanted to be a churchman all his life, so he said, and as a bairn used to practise preaching to the beasts in his father's cattle shed, wagging his forefinger at their patient heads and shaking his own in sorrow at the depths of their depravity. Along the educational way he also absorbed the classical literature of Greece and Rome. Thinking about it, Homer and Virgil and the like can't always have been the most comfortable companions of Holy Scripture and the principles of temperance in that capacious mind of his. Forty years it's taken her to wonder about the nimble swerves that must have been required when it came to classical deities and carousing Greeks.

It was considered to the minister's credit that his Christian name came from a king, a Protestant king, naturally, passed down from a Scottish nobleman who fought for King Gustavus Adolphus of Sweden in the seventeenth century. Munros had been the first family to bear it, which was good enough for the folk of Strathcarron because Munro was a fine Ross-shire name, second only in ubiquity to the Rosses themselves.

Glencalvie liked it that their new minister did not need telling about how they depended on each other in the township; how four heads of families were bound for the rental and everyone else contributed according to their means and their share of the grazings; how they grew their oats and barley and potatoes in the ridges of earth that shadowed the slope behind the houses, peat heaped into them for depth and drainage, old thatch dug into the soil too so that nothing was wasted; how the black cattle they raised for cash were fattened together on the grass higher up. Nobody had to explain to Gustavus Aird how attached folk were to the life there, for all that the soil was stony and the weather brutal and there were times, awful times, when the potato crop was diseased or the grain harvest spoiled or when the cattle prices slumped and there was barely enough food to see them through the winter. Community was a thing too hard to put across in words to anyone who did not feel its value in bone and heart: the value of having your people around you, not just the living neighbours you sang and argued and gossiped and laboured with but the generations before them, still alive in your songs and your stories, who had worked that same land themselves, made the clothes, ground the grain, cooked the food and shaken the frost from their hair in the morning.

Township folk thought of the land as belonging to them in a way that had nothing to do with exchanging title deeds in a lawyer's office in Edinburgh or managing the land as a business. That was a thing she came to understand as she grew up. The land was theirs because their ancestors had gathered its stones for their homes and worked the earth with care in ways that gave everyone a share. It was theirs through ancient ties of kinship to the clan chieftains, who these days were running up debts in large London houses or had already sold on their birthright to others. The new lairds wanted a return on their investment, not an extended family: this she also came to understand.

Mr Aird spent his early days as minister ambling on his horse from one township to the next to hear catechisms and conduct funerals and draw attention to misdemeanours and whatever else he found to do that would keep him from having to return to the draughty manse beside the Black Water. She thought she was the bee's knees when he let her skip beside him. Likely her company diverted him, blithe bairn as she was then, eager to attach herself to older folk the way young ones will when their father is dead before they're born and there was never a brother or sister.

Her father had been James Ross. His name sat inside hers

and she was proud to be carrying something of him, although she has wondered since if she only got it because her mother could not be bothered thinking up another. There was hardly a man's name in the Highlands that someone had not had the bright idea of burdening a baby girl with by adding an -*ina*.

She grew up quick and clever and full of herself, which must have pleased the teacher in Gustavus Aird. On their excursions he taught her bigger English words than she had from the Glencalvie school, and some fairly advanced Latin grammar. Thinking back, there was quite a hunger in that glen for book-learning, and a big effort made to teach it too, since it meant the folk would know their scriptures and right from wrong. There were all sorts came to the school when she was there: girls and boys, older people too. Folk still talked of a man called Iverach, who used to wade to the schoolhouse through snows and swollen rivers when he was well over a hundred. The school-master in her own time knew some Latin and taught them that as well as English. Mr Aird took it upon himself to rectify any deficiencies.

The minister even let her practise her songs on him, though he could hardly keep to one single line of a tune himself. What she liked best when they were out together was to put her own words to old Gaelic songs, those melodies you heard sung so often they grew right into you: the mournful laments the old folk liked so much, or the jaunty melodies the women waulked to outside in the summer, beating and stretching the woven cloth around the table.

Make me a song about this here, or that there, Mr Aird would say with a whisk of his cloak, the dark hat clamped on his yellowy hair. He would be pointing to something, a young willow maybe that was stirring in the breeze off the river. Or he would say, See you that spit of rain striking the lochan yonder? What does it make you think of?

And she would ponder the question, trying out words to herself, seeing if she could fit them into a rhythm. Sometimes he would give her time by slowing the pony so much that the poor beast had to be dissuaded from plunging its head into a hopeful clump of clover. (That's a transferred epithet.) And there was the minister hauling away at the bit, because he probably did have somewhere he actually had to go.

Latin lessons went according to the thought that had struck him last. When he became tired of her songs once, he held up a hand and boomed, *'Nox erat concubia, et omnia canentia sub sideribus muta errant.* Which means, child: "It was the first sleep of night, and all singing things were silent beneath the stars." You may take that as a hint. Learn it, if you please.'

It was not night at all, this scene she is remembering, but a watery autumn morning. Vapour was feathering the tops of the hills, and the tall grasses inclined their necks under pearls of moisture. The air smelled of turned earth.

She must have looked crestfallen, because he went on with an air of kindly munificence, 'If singers are to be silent, they may like instead to hear about the third declension of nouns, eh?'

She waited. He was not seeking her assent.

'You notice there the noun *Nox*. It will change its shape in a sentence according to its relation to other words. *Nox* is used if "night" is the subject, as in *Nox erat concubia*. You follow me?'

She nodded uncertainly, knowing fine well that the lesson would continue at pace whether she followed or not. 'The word becomes *noctem* when it is the object of the sentence; *noctis* to indicate the possessive, "of the night"; then come *nocti*, "to the night", and *nocte*, "by the night". From the root is grown the English word *nocturnal*, a most elegant word.'

And here she is forty years later, night gathering around the kitchen bed and all the ways *nox* can disport itself in a Latin sentence still snug in her brain, while panic paralyses her if she has to add one and fourpence to ninepence ha'penny to work out the change from half a crown.

'Decline *nox* for me, then, Jamesina. Pay heed to the change in consonant between vocative and accusative.'

'I will, sir. *Nox, nox, noctem, noctis, nocti, nocte.*'

'And the plural?'

'*Noctes, noctes, noctes, noctium, noctibus, noctibus.*'

'You have it. We call this the third declension. We shall look anon at how other nouns behave in this declension. We might begin with *lux*.'

Nox and *lux*. Night and light. Words learned and words practised, words behaving, words in order, words with relationships, words in a list, words attempting a rhyme, words acting on one another to make a purer sense.

Words remembered, the beat of their rhythms soothing in her damaged head.

Words tethering her to thoughts when they start to fly.

Was there not a thought she had before her husband started singing there, his hand fiddling about in that apologetic way that makes her wish he would get a move on?

Fleeting is what you call that sort of thought. A fleeting, fleeing, flying thought. A flying swiftly thought. Swifts darting across the braided sky, the scream of them in the white winds of Glencalvie.

A thought she was going to examine. Maybe say it aloud to see what he made of it, watching his mouth for the clue, the funny thing it does at the edges. No, it's away.

Flown thought.

Fled thought.

Fugitive thought.

Glencalvie, though. Clear and fresh to her tonight as a Highland burn. Sunday services on a hill by the Black Water, the grass tickling her ankles and the river's homely melody. The pages of Mr Aird's Bible lifting in the summer breeze. What were they doing outside? Why were they not in the church? Something to do with the Disruption. (*Disrumpere*, 'to break apart'.) The Church of Scotland broken apart over who had the right to appoint a minister: congregation or landowner? Mr Aird was for the people's right. Christ was head of the Scottish Kirk, said he, and it mattered not how much money you had or how much land you owned, no man should be allowed to go foisting his own choice of minister on Christ's own people. Just about every family in Strathcarron followed him when he left Croick to join the new Free Church. Her grandfather said Highlanders had control of nothing else, so was it any surprise they were all for the Free Kirk? She worried for Mr Aird, though. What if he got burned at the stake? Would she have to watch? Would his insides melt before his hair caught fire? Her mother said what kind of mind did she have that could imagine such things, and her grandfather said not to worry, it wasn't as if God's servant had become a Catholic.

What he was, Mr Aird said, was a seceder. He and hundreds of other ministers were withdrawing from a church in which the state had taken on powers in areas it had no business in.

'*Secedere*, Jamesina. *Se*, "apart", and *cedere*, "to go". Practise it.'

A farmer beyond the strath offered him a place to stay and some pasture for his cow and his horse, and he preached to his flock in the open, no roof between them and heaven and skylarks singing in the praying's pauses when it wasn't raining. Once they opened their eyes to a glisk of sunshine through a parted cloud. Mr Aird brought it into his word that day and said it was a sign of something or other.

He could get angry sometimes, though, Mr Aird. Usually in the middle of a sermon or when he was working himself up about the evils of drink. Or that time he asked the Sunday school class where our Saviour was born and she piped up, 'Inverness, sir?' to make the other bairns laugh, which not one of them did, just as well for them, and neither did he. Too big for your boots, my girl, she is thinking now. He made her write out the Gospel of St Matthew. 'In its entirety, mind, although I bid you pay particular regard to the geographical references in chapter 2, verse 1.' For a while after that she was banned from accompanying him anywhere.

There will likely have been more scoldings over the years than she can bring to mind, but it feels to her now, lying here, that the approval of Gustavus Aird enveloped the whole of her childhood like a blessing. His encouragement of her poems gave them value. His praise for her learning made it worth pursuing. His pride in her became her pride in herself.

45

Come to think, it is maybe what lets her march down Main Street to this day with a basket of other women's bloody sanitary rags over one arm and her nose in the air like a lion.

'Where are you now, Jamesina?'

Swimming deep in another place is where she is. Let me be.

She looks at him, looks through him, hauls herself back to the surface. Irritation is rising too. Sometimes the pulse of her irritation thunders so loud she can hear nothing else.

'Come back,' he is saying. At least he's not singing.

When did her emotions become so.

So.

Irritation, sadness. Sadness, irritation. Sadness.

Limited, that's the word. Stripped down.

'What are you thinking?'

'That I wish you would go to sleep.'

He chuckles. Leaves his hand on her breast. No doubt it will be off exploring in a minute, and after that she'll maybe get some peace.

She lays her hand on his and helps it on its way.

Part IV

The Man from *The Times*

May 1845

6

Thomas Langton Esq., The Inn, Ardgay, near Tain, Ross-shire
To Mrs Elizabeth Langton, 4, Willow Terrace, Shepherd's
Bush, London

15 May 1845

My dear Mother,

*You will be relieved to learn that I arrived in the Highlands of
Scotland without mishap and neither froze, combusted or starved
on any of the trains that bore me north, nor met with the tragic
accident you were so convinced would befall me. The railway guard
who was reported to have been decapitated by a bridge while
checking his passengers' luggage was indeed an unfortunate case, but
as I explained at the station I could foresee no circumstances in
which I would personally be called upon to mount the roof as the
train was entering a tunnel; and so it transpired.*

*The woollen rug and footwarmer came in handy at all times, for
which I must thank you again. In declining your further invitation
to avail myself of a travel cap with flaps to ward off earache, it
was ungracious of me to refer so flippantly to this being May not*

January. The laugh was firmly on me. Indeed the draughts were firmly on me, and they blasted in through every crevice of every railway carriage in which I spent every uncomfortable hour. An elderly gentleman opposite did place on his head just such a cap as you attempted to press on me and I must confess to thinking wistfully in that moment, and certainly more generously, of your maternal forethought.

There is as yet no rail connection between England and Scotland, and those few routes already opened beyond the border take the traveller nowhere near the Highlands. This meant I was obliged to endure a long coach journey thereafter along some of the most dreadful roads imaginable. However, I must honestly report that after some hours I was paying little heed to the discomforts of the journey, so compelled was my attention by the changing scenery as we left the towns and rolling arable fields of the Lowlands behind and the hills became craggier and the moors more empty and desolate. Every now and then a gully would open beneath the window with such dizzying suddenness that I thought we must surely plunge from the road. I hasten to add, Mother, that there was no reason to fear for the driving of our coachman, who if truth be told, rarely seemed in a hurry to get anywhere.

Truly I cannot depict for you the bleakness and the beauty that opened before my eyes as we travelled ever further north, although it is a skill my pen must discover if readers of The Times are to understand the situation in Strathcarron and the events that are proceeding there. It is easy to forget that within a few days' travel of London our kingdom encompasses a landscape so different, and a mode of living so rooted in the ancient forms of relationship and social organisation this landscape has bred, that those of us in the south have no more idea of it than life on the moon.

The final lap of the coach journey took me and my fellow passengers along the southern shore of the Dornoch Firth at a high old spank (at last) towards the hamlet of Ardgay, where there awaited us one of the few reputable inns in the area. Ardgay consists of naught but a few houses and untidy plots of land. It lies across a fine metal bridge from the small port of Bonar, where vessels up to 60 tons arrive with supplies of coal, lime, meal and so on and carry back down the firth wood, wool, oak-bark and grains. The bridge spans a water known as the Kyle of Sutherland, which at that point opens into the firth. I am told the metal arches are a source of much curiosity and wonder throughout neighbouring counties. Indeed, I was informed of a county man hereabouts that his only dying regret was that he had never seen the Bonar Bridge! All this goes a deal too far for the well-travelled southerner, but it is certainly an interesting specimen of the work of Mr Thomas Telford. The River Carron, along the banks of which I have been spending much time since I arrived, falls into the Kyle at Bonar. The river rises in the hills on the west coast of Scotland (the land mass being exceedingly narrow here), not far from the head of Loch Broom, and flows hither in almost a straight line to the east coast.

I hope I have given you a picture of the area in which I am now residing and have allayed your fears that I was off into the uncharted Unknown, where I was certain to be captured by marauding clansmen. These days, Mother, are long gone. The Highlands are really quite civilised, and although the communities of the Strathcarron valley are so remote, even they may be reached without too arduous a drive.

Glencalvie, at the far end of what is termed the 'strath' (which is to say a broad mountain valley), is one of three simple communities that are here called 'townships'. Eighteen families have each a cottage in the Glencalvie part of the valley, which is extremely rough and bleak. Hills close in on all sides, leaving a gentle declivity of poor arable land which is dotted over with cairns of stone and rock, not more than 15 to 20 acres in extent. For this piece of indifferent land, with a right of pasturage on the hills impinging on it – and upon which, if it were not a fact that sheep do live, you would not credit that they could live, so entirely does it seem devoid of vegetation beyond the brown heather – the almost incredible rent of 55 pounds 10 shillings has been paid by the people together. I am convinced that for the same land no farmer in England would give 15 pounds at the utmost. This is a matter I intend to address in my first report.

I am told, by the by, that the tenantry have always paid their rent punctually and were indeed prepared to find more. They have no one on the poor's roll and have always helped one another over the winter. I am further informed that not one resident of this valley has been charged with any offence for years back. By this you will begin to understand the dismay at their treatment. The threat of eviction has hung over these law-abiding people for many years, promises to them have been made and broken, and now they are obliged to leave.

My main informant is a local clergyman, the Reverend Gustavus Aird, who has been striving with exceeding energy to ameliorate the unfolding tragedy. He is the gentleman who organised the Fund for the relief of the cottagers being removed from Glencalvie. You may recall that it was a notice submitted to The Times *concerning this Fund which piqued the interest of the editor – not least the intention of practically the whole township to seek asylum in a local grave-yard. The editor was minded to satisfy himself as to the facts of the case, which were on the face of it dramatic.*

I am even now somewhat dazed to have been entrusted with a commission of such importance, and am determined not to trifle with Mr Delane's faith in me. The editor believes that my legal training will stand me in good stead in assessing the evidence, and I am doing so, I believe, diligently, mindful that what is happening in Strathcarron is but the latest in a long and widespread series of such removals. Indeed, the owners of the great estates across the Highlands have been replacing the resident peasantry with more financially productive ventures for well-nigh a century now. The land issues are in some degree complicated, although, as I begin to think, less so morally. I am excited and – only to you would I confess this – a little nervous, not least because I find growing within myself, as I become familiar with the facts of the case and the people themselves, an indignation which I must strive to keep in check.

Pray take care of your chest and give my greetings to Father. I must make a start now on my first submission. Look for it around the nineteenth or twentieth of this month.

Your affectionate son,

Thomas Langton

Ps The inn here is reasonably comfortable and the food adequate as long as you like oatmeal. The sheets, if I may assure you before you ask, are clean.

Part V

The Kitchen Bed

Before midnight
Wednesday, 23 July 1884

7

They are lying close and nourished in the darkness, the bed curtains drawn tightly around them, sealing them into the recess. This is a procedure upon which, no matter how hot she is, his wife insists during their times of intimacy. If he understands this precaution correctly, it is in case a neighbour should chance to catch them at it, unlikely as this might prove behind a locked door on the first floor.

He reaches out an arm to enfold her again, wondering if she is sleeping yet. She made love to him with such gratifying haste that he thought she would be off any minute. He is drifting pleasantly himself.

No, the sheet is whipped aside.

'Too hot again,' she declares, flinging herself about the pillow.

Not asleep, then.

Tomorrow is going to be a busy day. Mrs Montgomery will be in for her pumps. He will have to brace himself for a difficult explanation about shank pieces, which she will not understand. And there is still the problem of Miss Elspeth Taylor. Neat ankle, three soft corns on the inner sides of the smaller toes on both feet. How to persuade that young lady out of a sharp point? Making what she wants will be less trouble, but that kind of shoe repels him. Toes already so crushed and crowded they are on top of each other.

Try to deflect her with some decorative ideas.

A satin bow would work.

Silk mix good with kidskin.

Buttons might be.

Don't start on buttons.

Go to sleep, man.

'I'm sorry,' she says. His eyes are closed, but anyway. 'Am I keeping you awake?'

'No,' he mumbles back. Which is nice of him, because likely she is.

It is taking her a while to know how to be with a considerate man, how to respond to his carefulness with her body and her feelings without the impatience that is as likely to be called forth as gratitude, thankless woman that she is. Yet she could weep sometimes with a kind of wonder when she remembers what it was like before with Willie Bain. She used to think she could not bear that man on her, over her, in her, for one moment longer. Could not bear it. Would scream if she had to endure any longer, although she knew what would happen if she did that, because she understood by then that Willie Bain was a vicious man. Whereupon, of course, she did bear it.

In those days she used to summon – yes, this is what she did – she used to summon Thomas Langton to her rescue: the wholesome and infinitely pleasing memory of portly Thomas Langton, early infatuation (*in* plus *fatuus*, 'into foolish', which is about right) of Jamesina Ross of Glencalvie. Dear goodness, she has not thought about him for such a long time.

He came to report on the eviction of the Glencalvie folk, and his arrival in Strathcarron was so wildly exciting that at the time it almost overpowered the drama of losing her home and having to live for days in a graveyard.

Mr Aird was the one who enticed the young man to the north from London, or so he was always boasting. The minister had been called to a new kirk at Bonar by then, part of the new Free Church that was setting up everywhere. His kirk was being built away over at Loch Migdale, up the hill from the Bonar bridge, but he still kept an eye on the townships of the strath, which he had taken to doing in a battered-looking phaeton with that same old pony. When the time came to leave, he was on hand to help the Glencalvie folk work out what to do.

The laird of Kindeace had been trying to get them out of Glencalvie for long enough. A good three years earlier the local sheriff had arrived at the bridge on horseback with a handful of young-looking men, boys most of them, to deliver the first notices of eviction. It was the women of the township stopped them that time. She would have been how old then? Ten, maybe? Watched it from behind a clump of soggy reeds, hugging her knees for warmth.

She can see the women yet, fanning out with the bridge behind them, the clashing rivers below, a fire smouldering at their side and the smell of wet peat in the air. Can see flame-haired Donalda Vass out in front, in the position where

Donalda Vass, so her mother used to say, always had to be. Funny the things you start remembering your mother saying, even the waspish ones you would rather forget, because that bairn liked Donalda Vass, admired her flounce and her verve and the air she had of being ready for anything. Chest thrust forward and what you might be calling a leer on her face, she lunged for the main man at the front and the women around her all cheered.

She can remember being transfixed by the theatre of this. Young as she was, she could sense that the women's ferocity was largely fabricated; and that awkwardness rather than aggression was what was coming off the men, jiggling about on their horses there in front of the narrow bridge.

Donalda was just grabbing hold of the man's plaid to pull him off the horse, which was a black one, huge beast, when Mr Aird, wasn't it? – that's right, he was in the middle of it, too – Mr Aird roared out in his loudest pulpit voice, 'Let go, woman! He's the sheriff. Lay hands on that one and you're in trouble.'

She can see the sheriff dismounting then, dark, irritated-looking character, and shouting to the women to make way so that he and his men could walk across the bridge and deliver the notices to the homes of the four Glencalvie tenants. She can see Donalda Vass thrusting her breasts at his face and refusing to move.

'Right, that's enough,' he barked. 'Bring forward the notices.'

A group of young men shuffled to the front and were promptly set upon by the women. She can see Donalda clasping the first lad in a bosomy embrace while yelling bantering endearments in his ear. Can see her seizing his wrist before he had time to think what to do with his rolled-up summons. Can see another of the women holding a smoking peat to the other end of the paper while someone else was busy grabbing at the wrist of the next lad and another woman was stabbing a stick in the fire to secure the next peat. Can see eager flames scurrying up the papers as one by one the constables, if that is what they were, let go. Can see the angry expression on the sheriff's face. Can see him hesitate a moment then turn on his heel, leap back on his mount under a battery of taunts, toss his plaid over his shoulder and start leading his bedraggled force back the way they had come. Can hear the jeers that followed them. Thinking back now, it was an ugly noise. Some of these lads in their scrappy uniforms would not have been much older than Archie.

How sweet, all the same, was the hot and sickly pleasure of seeing authority humiliated. She recognised it at ten. Has never forgotten the taste.

'We won, Mr Aird. We won,' she said to the minister after.

Those hungry little flames, the men jerking their fingers away, the flecks of black paper fluttering in the wind, the women raising their arms in triumph.

The minister sounded weary. 'Thanks be to God that sheriff is a sensible man,' he said. 'You've won for now, Jamesina.'

The old laird ailed and died and it was three years before his heir's factor had another go. Three years' grace is not to be discounted. But the notices were delivered in the end, handed straight to the four tenants in person this time. They thought they had been invited to Tain to sign a new rental agreement and got writs of removal shoved across the table at them instead. They had till the following May to flit and remove with their families and dependants.

And here's the exact date, come to her just like that, though she would be hard-pressed to say what day of the month today is and won't be trying. They had to be out before Sunday, 25th of May 1845.

Gustavus Aird and her grandfather, John Gillespie, discussed what should be done in the low voices the grown-ups reserved for serious matters, her grandfather whey-faced on his pallet by the fire, the minister spilling out of their best chair the way he always did. There would be stock to sell and a sum to be divided among the families for going peaceably, but nothing could be sold or claimed or shared until they were out of their homes. Where were folk to go on the 24th?

The graveyard, said either the one or the other. They could go to the graveyard at Croick. They could sleep beneath the budding trees and above the polished bones of their ancestors. There was nowhere else.

The night frosts could still be deadly in May, so Mr Aird said he would try to raise some money for tents. He wrote to some gentlemen he knew, asking if they would join a fundraising committee to buy tarpaulins and help tide the poorest folk over. The Free Kirk ministers at Ardgay and Dornoch came on it, and a few others. Then he drafted a letter for the committee to send out to the newspapers.

Such a letter it was. He went round for ages carrying in a pocket inside his cloak the printed version he had cut from one of the papers, and he showed it around with a shy, pleased look which, now she thinks of it, might be described as boyish right enough, though all she was interested in then were the words, which are inside her yet. They were angry words, passionate and full of capital letters. They told how ninety folk, possessed of immortal souls and created after the divine image, were being driven out of home and fatherland to make way for fir and larch plants, deer and roes and moorfowl and partridges and hares and goodness knows what else that could be shot and bring in some money, not to mention sheep.

'Always have an eye to the particular when you write, Jamesina.'

It talked of blameless people finding themselves in want of so much as one foot of soil to lay their heads upon, save the place of the sepulchres of their fathers. She liked the rhythm of that line and memorised 'sepulchre' for future use, although they both knew fine that her ancestors did not have memorials of that kind at all. There were words about the Glencalvie folk not blaming their landlord for the SYSTEM of clearing the Highlands of human beings, which the law allowed, and being grateful for being given TIME to look for other places. Which they weren't, as far as she could tell. Her mother was not very grateful anyway. 'What use is time when there's nothing to spend it on?' Elizabeth Ross wanted to know. Which, to be fair to Mr Aird, he did say in his letter as well – a point about those who could work not being able to find any, and others being so aged and infirm that they could not emigrate even if the most ample provision were made for their passage to America. 'Which it won't be,' Elizabeth Ross sniffed, once she heard what *ample* meant.

Mr Aird had it in mind to get readers in Scotland and England feeling sorry for Glencalvie. What he was hoping for was donations. What he was not expecting was *The Times* to send their own man north to check on the facts, although he was awful pleased with himself when they did.

'My humble notice was of considerable interest to Mr Delane, the editor,' he said. 'He appointed a commissioner at once.'

'What's a commissioner, sir?'

'Oh, *The Times* likes these titles. He is some kind of journalist, man of letters, reporter. A pleasant fellow at any rate. I called on him at the inn in Ardgay – he has taken a room there – and I can tell you I expect great things of him. Great things. He declares an intention of interviewing everyone he can and seeing for himself. I believe he will report truly.'

'Will he come to Glencalvie?' She held her breath. She is practically holding it now as the scene floods back.

'Without a doubt. I shall accompany him myself when time spares. It's not everyone has the English to talk to him.'

'Let me help. I can translate for him. I can show him what he needs to see. Do you think he would like to hear a poem?'

'Wheesht, child, that's enough.' Mr Aird mused a moment. 'Although I do wonder if you could be of assistance here. How old are you now?'

'Thirteen? Fourteen?' She was never sure how old she was. 'Old enough to be trusted with this.'

'Well, I may let you help me. But only if you promise not to talk the man's ears off. He has hired some conveyance or other, so he and I will likely drive out tomorrow, although I fear it has not occurred to him that you cannot just drive along a road and descend at the front door of a township dwelling.' He winked. 'I think I'm going to have to lend the fellow a pair of stout shoes.'

It was torture to wait for the Adonis to appear (Adonis being a mortal youth of remarkable beauty, which Thomas Langton was not, thinking back, but he did have curls and lovely pink cheeks). She idled all morning at the point where the road to Croick could take you no closer to Glencalvie and anyone travelling by carriage must leave it, until she had worked herself into an agony of certainty that Mr Aird and the commissioner were not coming. The visitor had been urgently called back to London. The visitor was still in the area but had found more important people to interview. Mr Aird had mistaken the visitor's intentions in the first place. The visitor had been taken suddenly ill – this was more like it – but had been granted just enough time before expiring to gasp to Mr Aird (stooping over his bedside in the Ardgay Inn to whisper a last, anguished prayer) that the local lassie the minister had just been describing to him in such glowing terms should pen a report in his stead. Yes, much better. Soon an essay of miraculous eloquence would be winging its way to London from an unknown genius, the Bard of Strathcarron. The country would rise up in protest at such a heartless SYSTEM (she would be sure to remember the capital letters). The folk of Glencalvie would keep their homes. And lo, the name of Jamesina Ross would be blessed among women for ever. Which was likely a blasphemy, but anyway.

The pony and trap rounded the bend on wheels like twin moons, and the minister, surrendering the reins, leaped to the ground and turned to encourage a pink-looking young man, who adjusted a pair of round spectacles and peered closely at the grass as he stepped down. She can see him now. He is smaller than the minister, although so is everyone, and somewhat more padded than anyone she has met before, granted that she has not met many folk at all. The Glencalvie men tend to be lean; the schoolmaster is distinctly angular; the minister is broad of chest and shoulder but lithe in his movements. This man is not fat exactly, but the strain about these buttons does convey an impression that is not thin. It suggests a life spent reading with your feet on a desk, which she caught a mortified Mr Aird doing in the Croick manse once and has since considered a mark of leisured intellect.

'This is the lassie I was telling you about, Mr Langton,' said the minister, beckoning her forward. 'Jamesina Ross. I know she seems young, but she's a fine scholar and knows every inch of the glen.'

Did he have to say young?

'Pleased to meet you, Miss Ross,' the young man said, sweeping off his gentleman's hat to reveal a head of riotous light-brown hair.

He called her Miss Ross.

His English was less melodic than the minister's, more flat, the words trim and harder-edged. She would practise that. His face was fair and smooth in the areas devoid of whiskers and he had a warming smile, which she returned with enthusiasm.

'I am very pleased to meet you too, sir.'

The three of them walked over the Black Water bridge and on across the tufted moorland towards the township, Mr Aird explaining what sort of folk lived in Glencalvie and how hard everyone there worked, her thinking they had better not be taking him to meet Willie Ross then, who never lifted a finger for anyone. Fancy remembering Willie Ross after all this time, sleekit-looking character with big teeth. It was a disgrace, said Mr Aird, that folk like these should be so unjustly expelled.

Expelled was a new word. *Ex* would be 'out' and she would ask later about *pel*. *Pauper* was also new. Old Jessie McCulloch's name came up there. Right to this day it is still Jessie McCulloch she sees in her mind's eye when she hears that word, the bunched fists clutching the sides of the cart that carried her away, the awful keening in the wind.

Mr Aird became more and more exercised as he talked. Mr Langton questioned him closely, sometimes coming to an abrupt halt to listen. He looked exceedingly intelligent with those glasses on. Mr Aird was telling him that over the whole of Strathcarron there were twenty-seven paupers, and before he had had to leave Croick everyone had contributed to a collection every Sunday to help look after them. That was right enough; and her mother was always fretting at her grandfather for putting too much in the collection ladle, saying if he wasn't careful they would be needing it themselves. But the lairds hereabouts lived elsewhere and gave nothing to the poor, Mr Aird said, and it had taken a visiting Englishman to shame them, some colonel from Kent, who came every year to shoot and had always left ten pounds with the minister to distribute.

Mr Aird was getting himself so worked up that his nose was going that red way it did.

'So an English gentleman and a stranger, who gets no rental from the parish and has no tie to bind him to it, gives out more to support the aged and the feeble out of pure humanity than the whole of the parish, including the proprietors who derive two thousand pounds a year from it.'

Mr Langton nodded. 'Perhaps, good sir, you would be kind enough to place these facts on paper, that I might have them before me in calm order?'

'With pleasure,' said Mr Aird. 'And you must forgive me if I become passionate, sir. These are grave matters and your readers should know of them.'

Thomas Langton smiled. 'Indeed they will. Now, Miss Ross, might you be so kind as to tell me a little about the people I am to meet here?'

'With pleasure,' she said, stealing a glance at the minister, who inclined his head a fraction and squeezed his eyes together, which meant he had noticed.

Her mother wafted the visitor through their own house in a fluttery manner that was most unlike her. Asked if he might examine the construction of the cottage, she pointed at the timber crucks set in the ground opposite each other to support the roof. She invited him to inspect the walls with their base of stones and the courses of turf that reached to the height of his head. He nodded gravely, asked a question or two and then commended her on the cleanliness and tidiness of the house, which his own mother would heartily appreciate, he said, being a rigorous housewife herself. Elizabeth Ross flushed right the way down her neck to hear him.

Next day the young man returned alone and she led him down the south bank of the Carron as far as Greenyards, where she introduced him to old Lizzie Ross, a second cousin of her father, or was it third, who introduced him to another ten folk, who did their best to explain to Thomas Langton how it felt to be wondering all the time when the laird of Kindeace, who owned their land as well as Glencalvie, would get round to evicting them too.

As she recalls, the Greenyards folk told him there was nothing to be done but get on with your life, although many were anxious. They knew all too well what had happened elsewhere, and not just in their own strath but all over the Highlands and Islands. The older ones remembered what had gone on a generation ago in the Sutherland family's lands next door, the folk there ordered from inland straths like their own to the bald North Sea coast and expected to change from being farmers to fisherfolk overnight. By now the Strathcarron lands were like a solitary leaf left behind by the autumn winds and ready for a winter falling.

That will have been the kind of poetic thing she told Thomas Langton anyway. She was not shy of adding a word or two of atmosphere to the more boring replies he was offered at Greenyards, or an occasional 'as one of our bards has said' when the story lacked colour.

On the way back to the road she chose the least lumpy paths and looked out for the most decorous spots for him to catch breath and press a handkerchief to his smooth and really very handsome brow. It was a warm day, full of the heady scents of May. The braes were golden with broom and small white butterflies flitted among the grasses. She drew to a halt beneath a blossomy rowan and indicated an almost dry rock.

'Would you care to rest a moment, sir?' she said in her careful English.

'Thank you, Jamesina.' He had dispensed with Miss Ross, which she felt on balance to be a good sign, indicating a progression of intimacy. 'I see it has not escaped your attention that I have indulged in one or two dinners too many of late.'

This being precisely true, she shook her head in mortification. 'No, no, no. I only thought you looked hot.'

'Well, you're right. I am hot.'

He set his hat on the ground and the unruly curls sprang to attention. She wondered what it would feel like to bounce her hand on those curls. He unbuttoned the tweed jacket and slipped it over his arm to reveal a waistcoat so busy with patterned blues and blacks that he could have disappeared without comment among the grouse. The arms of his shirt were the opposite: white, impossibly white, almost too white to believe in without touching, and stroking, and possibly burying her face in. She felt her cheeks flaring again.

If Thomas Langton noticed her confusion, he made no sign of it. Laying his jacket over the rock, he eased himself gingerly on top of it and looked about him.

'"Rolled round in earth's diurnal course with rocks and stones and trees,"' he observed, almost to himself but not quite, because he seemed to be waiting to hear what she made of it.

She did not know what to make of it. 'What is "diurnal"?' she asked.

'It means during the daytime. This is a diurnal conversation we are having, you and I. The words are from a poem. Did you guess?'

She shook her head.

From the Latin *dies*. Must be. She would try it on Mr Aird.

'The poet means that the girl he is writing about is back among the natural world, among stones like these around us, and rocks like this I'm sitting on, and trees like the one we are under. This girl is part of it all.'

70

He looked suddenly doubtful about where he was going with this. 'The girl has, um, died, you see.'

'Died?'

'But she's still living in a sense. That's what the poet is saying, I think: that she is part of something greater or bigger than death.'

'Tell me the poem, sir,' she said, settling herself in the grass and gazing up at him, likely enough frowning, which was a thing her mother said she did too much of. These eyebrows of yours, Elizabeth Ross was in the habit of stating sorrowfully, could not be laid at her feet, nor the feet of anyone in the Gillespie family. Makes her smile even now to think of the floor strewn with eyebrows.

'The poem is very short,' he said, 'and it goes like this.'

He spoke the lines slowly, forming each word with exaggerated care in case she struggled to understand. Which was good of him, although it made her feel a bit humiliated because the words were not all that hard.

> *A slumber did my spirit seal;*
> *I had no human fears:*
> *She seemed a thing that could not feel*
> *The touch of earthly years.*
>
> *No motion has she now, no force;*
> *She neither hears nor sees;*
> *Rolled round in earth's diurnal course,*
> *With rocks and stones and trees.*

He waited for her to speak, but she kept staring at him, knitting and kneading her eyebrows.

'It's thought,' he said, 'that William Wordsworth was writing about a young girl called Lucy. He wrote a number of poems about her.'

She nodded slowly. 'Who is William Wordsworth?'

'He's a poet who is elderly and rather grand now, but he wrote some very exciting poems when he was young. I think they're exciting anyway.' He paused for a reaction, but she stared on. 'He doesn't shy from using simple words rather than poetic ones, and he wants us to hear voices from ordinary people, such as, I mean, country people, er, milkmaids, shepherds, um, beggars . . .'

He petered out a bit there and dabbed at his face with his hanky. Likely remembered he was talking to one of the ordinary folk.

'Anyway, not many English poets had done it so well before. And these poems about Lucy are very beautiful.'

'And sad,' she said.

His glance lingered on her. 'Yes, sad. Because dying is sad, isn't it? And Lucy's dying made Wordsworth especially sad, because not many people knew about her life or would ever be aware she had gone. She lived so far from everywhere.'

He stopped again. Probably thinking this time, dear God, what have I said now?

'Not like you, Jamesina,' he said in a rush. 'You have many people to love and praise you. Lucy was—'

'Tell me another one,' she commanded, quite rudely if she is honest.

'Not if it's going to make you sad. We are having a happy day and the sun is shining.'

'It's all right to say sad poems when the sun is shining,' she explained patiently. 'I tell them to Mr Aird all the time.'

'Oh, I see. Very well then, here is the other I was thinking of.'

He pushed his spectacles further up his nose with his middle finger, folded the milkily clad arms and squinted past her into the blue distance.

> She dwelt among the untrodden ways
> Beside the springs of Dove,
> A maid whom there were none to praise
> And very few to love:
>
> A violet by a mossy stone
> Half hidden from the eye!
> —Fair, as a star when only one
> Is shining in the sky.
>
> She lived unknown, and few could know
> When Lucy ceased to be;
> But she is in her grave, and, oh,
> The difference to me!

'Well?' he said.

She can remember the wash of relief.

'Oh, that one's not sad. She made a difference to the poet, didn't she? He's sad about her being in the grave but that means she matters. She's like a violet – that's a flower, isn't it? – and it's all right that you can't see it. The poem makes—'

'On you go,' he said softly.

She was brimming with eagerness. Oh, to be brimful of eagerness again.

'The poem makes her life worth something,' she said.

He smiled and began to pull on his jacket. 'You have a good feeling for poetry, Jamesina. I am going to think of more poems to share with you. Would you like that? I have a great deal of work to do here and further afield, but I'll put myself to consider what you might enjoy. Wordsworth understands children very well.'

Well, that stung. 'I am not a bairn,' she declared and sprang to her feet. 'I have no need of being understood.'

'Of course not,' Thomas Langton said, 'you are a clever, thinking young woman. Very clever. Clever enough, I hope, to lead me back to the road before my horse gives up its driver for lost and returns to Ardgay without me. I plan an excursion out of Strathcarron tomorrow and I really must get back to prepare.'

'Are you leaving?' She looked up at him, aghast.

'Only for a day or two. I want to see for myself how the poorest people beyond the strath are living. It is not enough to report hearsay.'

'But you'll be back?'

'I shall return to bear witness to the clearance of Glencalvie. That I promise you.' He clapped the tall hat back on his head and stepped aside for her to walk in front of him. 'Now, lay on, Macduff.'

She had no idea what he meant, but it did not matter because he was coming back and she was clever and thinking. *Thinking*, present participle as an adjective. Was that different from thoughtful? Also, she was not just clever, she was very clever.

She skipped ahead so fast that he had to call to her to slow down and please to avoid all thistles.

At home she went over the scene. Those dark-blue eyes behind the spectacles, studying her as she talked. Kind eyes, interested eyes, interested-in-her eyes. She put herself to sleep with a story that would have made her cry if she could have managed it. Jamesina Ross, who was about to become homeless, would not live unknown, for here was someone who would know her. When she ceased to be, he would weep at her grave. He would hurl himself upon the brown earth to sob out her name: Jamesina, my love, oh, the difference to me. He would write a poem about her, or failing that a notice in *The Times*, which would do very well too. They would be married by then, of course.

8

Croick kirkyard. She walked through it again last week and little, it seemed to her, wandering down the quiet path with her husband, had changed in forty years. Of course there was no encampment lining the walls. No fire. No excited bairns, no anxious parents. No mother birthing or aged person dying. No human sounds. No human smells. But for all that, the place was as she remembered: a simple walled enclosure around the grey-stone kirk, sheltered by a few bent trees.

When they visited last week the trees were all exuberantly leafed. In the final week of May 1845, a few slow buds were still to open and it was cold as they settled for their first night under the tented roofs that Mr Aird had produced from somewhere. The Black Water was streaming away nearby, and there was comfort in that low gurgling when you were lying on the ground wondering if there might be a dead person underneath you and whether that dead person was in the habit of walking in the night or would be put off by a crowd.

A few gravestones were poking up from the grass around them, small ones mostly, listing a bit. They all faced west up Strath Cuileannach, up and up to where the Black Water began in the mountains amid shattered rocks and freezing winds. She remembers a convoy of clouds streaming towards them through the dusk-light, spits of rain gusting down the glen and being flung on to the tarpaulins with a drumming noise.

She remembers pulling a blanket over her head and breathing in the smoke from the fire that had been built in the middle of the graveyard, trying to pretend it was rising from her family's own hearth, from their own Glencalvie fire, the one her mother had grimly doused before they left.

But there was no pretending that night. The fire's drowning still hissed in her head. The last breaths of their old life refused to yield to imaginings.

She tried thinking about Thomas Langton instead, snug in the Ardgay Inn, maybe dreaming up the best words to tell their story right now. Except he might not be able to concentrate tonight because he would be thinking about Jamesina Ross, such a clever and thinking lassie with such beautiful eyes, as everyone says, mainly her grandfather, and quite nice hair.

She shut her ears to the howls of Donalda Vass, half lying against a screened gravestone by the far wall to endure the most public of labours. Her mother said giving birth in the middle of a churchyard was the best that woman had managed yet in a lifetime of drawing attention to herself. It was a mean thing to say, but the part of her that had passed beyond childhood and could hear the thrumming of adult despair along the grassy earth understood that her mother was afraid, and that her tongue sharpened when she was worried, just as Grandfather became ever more dry and morose. She tried to take comfort from John Gillespie's presence on the ground beside her, and to ignore the shivering he had been doing for hours, the deep and fevered shivering that blankets did not help and was too frightening to think about.

In the kitchen bed a verse comes back to her.

> *Glencalvie, oh Glencalvie, where the waters meet,*
> *Glencalvie, my Glencalvie, that the people left.*
> > *We slept beside cold slabs of stone,*
> > *warmed by generations gone*
> > *who loved this place and thought it theirs*
> > *and ours for aye.*

She moves her lips but makes no sound. The quiet breathing goes on at her side. Maybe he is sleeping right enough.

It can only have been days that the Glencalvie people lived in the kirkyard, but it seemed to go on and on. She has a memory of watching to see where folk went to relieve themselves so that she could be sure to avoid them, because it was her bleeding time. Old Jessie McCulloch in the next tent did her business right there, and her mother said not to look and what was the old soul supposed to do. Which was kinder than she was about Donalda Vass, whose baby kept them all awake with its quivery newborn crying. Everyone was waiting for some money to come, or news of a place to move to, or a job, or a ship, or a miracle, or the Lord's return, whichever came first.

Her grandfather was too weak to sit up, and her mother

knelt beside him with his head in her lap, saying things like, what's going to happen to us when he's gone? Which was embarrassing when likely he could hear every word.

Next morning, watching from her blanket as dawn pinked the pale stone of the kirk, she made herself a promise. One day she was going to bear witness to this. That was a phrase Thomas Langton had used. Telling was what words were for – in songs, poems, books, letters, reports in newspapers. It was what being good at English made you capable of. You had to tell folk that you were here, that real, thinking, sorrowing folk were sleeping in this graveyard, human beings made in God's image, as Mr Aird was always saying.

We are the people who have dwelt among the untrodden ways, she thought to herself as she listened to the murmurings and groanings of neighbours waking up in the morning's chill. We are the Lucy who lived unknown. We are the folk who are ceasing to be.

The man from *The Times* visited them, as he had said he would. He wanted to observe the Sunday service on the hill above Croick first, and asked if she would explain what was being said and sung as they went along. It was necessary to stand very near him for this, because she had to whisper. His skin smelled lovely up close: salt and soap and some sweat from the little bit of climbing he had to do to get up there. Likely she didn't smell very lovely herself, which did not occur to her at the time, and just as well. Nobody thought much about washing in those days, although she's made up for it since all right.

Afterwards he came to meet them at the kirkyard. Everyone clustered round to thank him for his help, pressing in on him, seizing his little plump hands and saying, '*Taing mhòr, taing mhòr.*' He knew he was being thanked and was fair glowing with pleasure.

When he spied her watching, he waved. 'Jamesina! I'm glad to have found you again. Come and talk to me.'

They sat down a little way up the slope. Thomas Langton was not nearly so wary of where he put his feet these days, although he did flap his hat at the midges and inspected the grass before committing himself.

'It touches me very much to receive the thanks of your people like this,' he said when they were settled. 'There is now a great deal of sympathy in the country for their plight and there have been several offers of help, including from a gentleman with land in Ross-shire who has offered a number of homes and potato-grounds. Rent-free, I may say.'

He whisked his hat about. 'And his wife and daughter in Bath have collected no less than thirty pounds for the relief of others.'

Likely she remembers this part because Bath was such a funny name for a town. He explained that Roman legions had been there once and liked to keep themselves clean; and since she knew all about the Romans from Mr Aird she was able then, blissfully, to say something clever that had him nodding admiringly.

'And I must thank you in my turn for all the assistance you rendered me,' he said, turning to look at her. She felt the usual blush on its way and lowered her head.

There were tiny blue flowers in the grass, which she nudged with her toes. The sun was warm on her bare neck, the grass smelled of summer and the broom was more extravagantly yellow than she had ever noticed before. Everything in the whole world was perfectly itself.

'I have a gift in mind to express my gratitude,' he said. 'No, I'm not telling you what it is, but I think you'll like it. Very well, since you look at me so imploringly, it's a book of poetry. I'm going to ask Mr Aird to make sure it reaches you.'

Now she did dare to look at him. 'Is Lucy in it?'

'Yes, it's a volume of Mr Wordsworth's verse and Lucy is in it. But there is a poem that is not there – it's one he wrote later – and I've been thinking I would let you hear it. If it's to your taste I can write it down for you to learn. It's about a river. Or at least it was composed on a famous bridge in London with a great river running beneath. You have so many rivers here, I thought you would like it. Will you hear it?'

'Yes,' she whispered. Thomas Langton had been thinking about her, imagining what would make her happy, planning this moment. Her heart would burst.

'Very well, then, let me see if I can remember it. And then I must be on my way before these infernal insects complete their meal.'

And so he began, gazing out over Croick to the hills beyond in a poetic manner which did not involve looking at her in the slightest degree, a detail she was happily able to correct in the future when he strolled into her imagination in a poky room in Glasgow, proclaiming his passion in a milky-white shirt (quickly removed, along with his spectacles and his trousers), and stopped her thinking about Willie Bain for many minutes at a time.

Earth has not anything to show more fair:
Dull would he be of soul who could pass by
A sight so touching in its majesty:
This City now doth, like a garment, wear
The beauty of the morning; silent, bare,
Ships, towers, domes, theatres, and temples lie
Open unto the fields, and to the sky;
All bright and glittering in the smokeless air.
Never did sun more beautifully steep
In his first splendour, valley, rock, or hill;
Ne'er saw I, never felt, a calm so deep!
The river glideth at his own sweet will:
Dear God! the very houses seem asleep;
And all that mighty heart is lying still!

'What do you think, then?' he said, turning to her at last with his sweet smile.

'There is very much to think about,' she said gravely. And there was. 'But mainly I am thinking how much I would like to stand on that bridge. Maybe I'll do that when I go to London.'

'You would like to go to London, Jamesina?'

Head down, frowning fiercely at a lone daisy, she nodded. There was no possible way to hint at the role she envisaged for him in this ambition.

'Will you be coming back one day?' she asked instead. She did not add, 'when I'm older', but likely the question still sounded a bit pointed, because he blinked very fast behind his glasses. He said he hoped his editor would permit him to pursue his investigations in the Highlands further in the course of time, in which case he might indeed find himself in the bosom of the Ardgay Inn again one day. *Bosom* covered her in more confusion.

'Perhaps we shall meet again, if your family is still in the area,' he said, adding gently, 'Do you know where you will go?'

'I am to go to Greenyards,' she said. 'We have kin there.'

He stood up and dusted his trousers. Then he bowed a farewell to her very formally, which was thrilling, and bade her convey his warm regards to her mother, which was not.

The families trailed away from the graveyard encampment at last, pushing their frailest folk in carts, their mothers, fathers, aunts, uncles and the others like Jessie McCulloch who belonged to nobody and to everybody. The old woman clawed the sides of the jolting cart, her face as grey as the blanket she was wrapped in. As she was borne away she opened her mouth wide and cried out a farewell lamentation to the air and the waters and the dear green places of her youth. It was a sound as forlorn as the cry of the evening lapwing or the most plaintive curlew that ever glided like a London river through the boisterous Strathcarron skies. And yet it was like neither of these, because this was a human sound. It went so deep into her own bones that it lies here yet. She has made it since herself, this noise, keening for Archie in the night when there was nobody to hear.

Her grandfather was not among the folk who left. If a man can will himself to die, he did it. While rugs and blankets were being pulled down around him, bedding gathered and bairns collected, John Gillespie begged his Lord over and over to take him, that he might not burden any man or any woman longer with his presence on this earth. He did not go joyously from this life to the next, but sorely and bitterly.

He was laid to rest beneath the wall at the furthest corner of the kirkyard, where the sodden remains of an older season's leaf-fall mingled with the earth and slid into the ground after him in a coppery paste.

'*And all that mighty heart is lying still*,' she said to the wind that took his soul.

That afternoon she and her mother left Croick. Mr Aird slung their bedding over the back of his pony, hung pots and kettle from the saddle and placed the family Bible in a woollen bag which he carried on his own person. Together the three of them walked down the south bank of the Carron and away.

> *Glencalvie, where the waters meet,*
> *Glencalvie, that the people left,*
> *Glencalvie is no more.*

This time she is singing aloud. Not so very loud really, and she wasn't meaning to do it at all, but there you are, the song has found its way.

She can tell he is listening, because his sleeping breath, which it turns out is not his sleeping breath, has paused. When she reaches the end he says, eyes still closed, 'Not too sad for you after all, then, that song?'

No, not sad exactly. What it does is remind her that by putting words to a thing, and a melody to hold them fast, you are saying it mattered, even if you are always going to think you could have composed it better. That girl in the kirkyard knew something that the years with Willie Bain, the years of grieving, the years of interminable scrubbing, made her forget. Old Jessie McCulloch mattered. That is what she knew then. Her grandfather dying on the cold earth of a graveyard mattered. Donalda Vass and that homeless bairnie of hers mattered. Her words themselves mattered. Words in a song, words in a poem, words caressed until at last they speak a truth, one soul to another, they all mattered.

And maybe they matter still. Which is a thought she cannot get her mind to fold around properly but is starting to feel tonight, if you can feel a thought.

Part VI

The Man from *The Times*

May 1845

9

Thomas Langton Esq., The Inn, Ardgay, near Tain, Ross-shire
To Mrs Elizabeth Langton, 4 Willow Terrace, Shepherd's
Bush, London

27 May 1845

My dear Mother,

It is done. The Glencalvie people have left their homes at last in most pitiable circumstances. You will recall that some 90 people in 18 families had given bond to leave peaceably on the 24th of May. The following day I came on these people assembled on a hillside to take part in a service of worship. They were seated in a circle on the grass, listening to one of their elders read to them in their native Gaelic. A talented child with good English whispered a translation in my ear, and I recognised from her account the great Psalm, 'If I take the wings of the morning and dwell in the uttermost parts of the sea, even there shall thy hand lead me, and thy right hand shall hold me.' *As I surrendered to the haunting rhythms of this alien tongue, the Psalm spoke powerfully to my own soul. In that moment I understood, I who have wanted for little in this life save to afford a better tailor, the comfort of feeling oneself held safe when an earthly home no longer exists.*

I drove on to the Established Church of Croick, which serves a remnant of the pre-Disruption congregation. The service there was partly in Gaelic and partly in English, but the congregation was miserably thin: there were but ten persons besides the minister in the church. Behind the building and within the churchyard, a long kind of booth had been erected, the roof formed of tarpaulin stretched over poles and the sides closed in with horse-cloths, rugs, blankets and plaids. This was the refuge of the Glencalvie people. They had kept their promise to leave and saved their bondsmen. A fire was kindled in the churchyard, around which I later counted 23 children. Two cradles, with infants in them, were close to the fire, sheltered by the mothers. Others busied themselves in dividing the tent into compartments, by means of blankets, for the different families. Most affecting to me, as I had opportunity to study the scene, were those children. While the older people looked uniformly gloomy and dejected, the children were playing happily around the fire, pleased with the novelty of all around them, as indeed I could readily imagine myself having been in such a situation. I shall describe this scene to the best of my ability in my final dispatch to The Times, *which I mean to send with this letter on the afternoon mail-coach.*

Yesterday a group of the Glencalvie people walked over to Ardgay for the purpose of receiving the value of their stock and a shared amount for going out peaceably. They were met by Mr McKenzie of Tain, the law agent employed to settle with them, which painful duty the gentleman executed with much kindness and consideration. Among the dozen men and women that I saw, there was not the least noise or disturbance, and cruel as was their position, not a murmur escaped them. I believe their spirit is broken. Each family had on average about 18 pounds to receive in all, which is evidence that they were respectably supporting themselves before, but it will soon be spent. I say to you, Mother, that it is a moral certainty that most of these men and their families will be reduced to pauperism. This is the benefit the country derives from such proprietors and factors as have owned and managed this glen.

I am pleased to say that my reports have already alerted at least one benefactor who declares himself in a position to ameliorate the plight of some. But supposing no material help had been forthcoming, I cannot but think I would still feel gratified that this Glencalvie clearance, one among so many that have taken place in the outer reaches of our Great Britain, has not passed unnoticed, uncensured or unlamented. It is what permits me to sleep at night.

Since writing last, I have also travelled further afield. You will have gathered from my reports my mounting dismay at the situations I have encountered almost everywhere I go. I continue to be disturbed by the condition of the Highland poor, whose plight has been greatly exacerbated by the Disruption of the Church of Scotland two years past. Since that period, when the great mass of Highland people went over to the Free Church, the Sunday collections, which were the principal aids to the paupers, have become wholly inadequate. The poor have no choice but to depend on the heritors, which is to say landowners, who are not only failing in their duty to support them but, as I discover, in some instances exacting punishment on those fellow beings who take pity on the impoverished souls.

You will forgive me, Mother, for pouring out my feelings the moment a fresh sheet of paper presents for duty and a pen secures *itself in my hand, but my mind is overflowing with all I have heard and seen. What burdens me is not only the events of dramatic moment such as I have witnessed at Glencalvie, which have about them the element of sensation which appeals to the taste of the modern readership. What I am also sensible of is the toll of small tragedies, although not small to them, among overlooked individuals, which I see everywhere about me. It is not the infamy of house-burnings I hear of, although the older people here in Strathcarron still recall with horror the burnings that did take place on the Sutherland lands within their memory; yet in terms of human cost these present removals of the 1840s strike me as no less reprehensible, even if they come cloaked in less egregious wickedness and are in some cases carried through with patience from the authorities and even a degree of sympathy. These people live under a system that allows the powerful to justify the casual eviction from home and hearth of the powerless. Yes, some with youth and energy on their side may find the wherewithal to emigrate and make a better life far from these shores. Yes, the fortunate may find work in the south. But the majority will not.*

I have no wish, and I say this truly and hope my writings in The Times *have reflected it, to fall into the stupid error of accusing the whole gentry of a county of natural meanness and tyranny. No doubt there are good and humane men among them, as in all communities. I have looked closely, you may believe, into the circumstances which may have caused better-intentioned men to resort to the mean shifts of which I am informed at every turn. What I hear is that many of the heritors and large farmers, having been led into expensive habits from the higher rents and prices obtained during the war, have got into embarrassment, and very many of the estates are now in the hands of trustees for the benefit* of their creditors; others are shackled by debts and expenses which they have not always the means to meet. I believe that to this may be traced the greater part of those oppressions which shock humanity today, and of those meannesses which make us ashamed of our common nature.

Mother, I have gone on too long. I have not even thanked you for your own loving letter, which arrived by this morning's mail. I am glad to have it safely in my hand, as I am departing Ardgay tomorrow. I am relieved to hear that your cough has eased, and that Mrs Halworth's daughter was safely confined, which must be a relief. Since you ask, I do agree that Tabitha is a highly suitable name, with impressive biblical associations, and that Mrs Halworth need have no fears of its being considered un-English.

If I may ask a favour, I would be pleased if you would send to this address my volume of William Wordsworth's Lyrical Ballads, which you will find third from the left on the second bookshelf from the bottom in my chamber. Pray mark the package for the attention of Miss Jamesina Ross. She is the young girl who acted as my interpreter. I have been struck by her lively mind and imagination, and would like to reward her efforts with a gift she will appreciate. I shall alert Mr Aird to keep an eye open for its arrival, as I am assured he will be taking note of where the people go.

I look forward to seeing you and Father before long and to partaking again of some good English fare. How I have yearned for one mouthful of Mrs Halworth's jam roll! Expect to hear by telegraph the date of my return.

Your loving son,
Thomas Langton

Part VII

The Lodger

Winter 1883/4

10

Lodger and landlady established a household routine with more ease than the uncomfortable first evening at 13, Anne Street had led the shoemaker to fear. As he was the first to reassure himself, even the most exacting of landladies could not take exception to one so regular in his habits, so reliable with the rent, so tidy, quiet and abstemious. More abstemious than she was, he soon noticed. Medicinal purposes, indeed!

On waking he made sure to listen for morning sounds from the kitchen and enter only when, ear to the door, he heard the kettle being filled at the sink or banged down on the hob, an exercise invariably invested with a grumpier energy than he could see a reason for. After breakfast he would collect his tools and bid a cheerful goodbye, leaving Mistress Bain to do whatever she did in the course of the day with other women's laundry. By then he had been enlightened about the frills on the kitchen pulley.

'How do you think I've been paying the rent all these years?' she wished to know. 'Inherited wealth?'

He considered this an unfair tone to take. Den of vice? he thought about suggesting.

'Do you take in laundry perhaps?' he asked instead, as blandly and inoffensively as it was possible to deliver a bland and inoffensive question.

'Yes, I do,' she snapped back. 'And if you look down on someone who washes other folk's clothes for a living, you can march straight back out and find another place to stay.'

He swallowed. 'No need for that, I assure you, Mrs Bain. And do you have many' – good grief, what were they called? – 'clients? You know, customers?'

'Enough. I collect from up Stonelaw way and put everything through the wash house in the back court on a Monday, which is my day. I dry what I can on the line, but the rest comes into the kitchen. When it's raining you can hardly see the length of yourself for washing in here, so I'll thank you to save me the trouble and keep your shirts clean.'

'You'll be glad I'm not a miner then, ma'am,' he said, and was rewarded by a quick, lopsided smile.

Every evening after work he returned to a generously portioned if indifferently cooked tea, consisting frequently of potatoes. Despite a great number of hints he was not invited to draw his chair to the range fire afterwards, but she did see the sense in saving coal in the parlour by allowing him to work at the kitchen table once the dishes were cleared away. He came to enjoy those quiet hours at the end of the day, measuring, cutting, sewing and whatever other job could be accomplished outside the workshop, while his landlady dawdled in her own armchair by the range, usually with a stocking and a darning needle limp in her lap, doing for the most part nothing at all, except when she stirred herself to poke the fire or add a meticulously rationed coal. She had washerwoman hands all right: raw and sore-looking.

His attempts to engage her in conversation were generally rebuffed, but there was nothing to stop him observing her as he worked. Glancing over at her listless hands and the expressionless gaze she presented to the fire, he began to recognise the ebbing of the day's strains in the changing lines of her profile. He watched her jaw relax, as if her teeth were only now unclenching, the tension subside in her shoulders, the truculence unknit itself from those remarkable eyebrows.

With familiarity the dislocation of bone in one cheek, robbing her face of symmetry, became less remarkable. Indeed, as the weeks passed, what occupied his surreptitious attention was no longer the deformity of the widow's features but the way her skin glowed in the firelight, the glinting lights of silver and copper in her lightly pinned hair, the slender neck, the shadowed eyes, behind which lay emotions he could only guess at. He looked at her and tried to connect the woman before him, composed to a laconic fault, with the howling in the night. Listening for sounds from the other side of his bed closet had become a nocturnal habit of which he felt a little ashamed, but what was he to do? The architecture of this apartment was not his fault, nor the havoc it played with his sleep to be tensed for sounds of distress from a pillow only inches through the wall from his own.

Some nights he heard nothing. On other nights the muffled animal cry reached him again through the cool stone, and he did not know what to do.

New customers began finding their way to his workshop on Stonelaw Road. It was a fair-sized premises on the airier side of town, near to golden woods and extensive meadows which were in the process of being colonised by prosperous villas built by the kind of people who could afford good shoes. This was exactly as John Wilson had said.

'Promising little Scottish town right next to Glasgow, dear boy,' his mentor had assured him on the steamer from New York. 'Chemical industries and the like are spreading over the river at a thundering rate, but south of the main thoroughfare there is still a good deal of countryside. I hear that better-off Glasgow people can hardly wait to escape across the river for the healthier airs, not to mention cheaper land to build on and lower rates than they will get anywhere in the city's west end. They, my dear boy, will be your customers.'

Mr Wilson himself had moved in with his eldest daughter's family in one of these splendid new houses, and seemed to be taking advantage of every social occasion to inform his fellow citizens that they could do with handmade shoes. He wondered if the older man was feeling guilty.

On his way home from work he formed the habit of calling in at the public library to read the day's news and inform himself about the country he had fetched up in. His attention was quickly drawn to events in the north of Scotland.

There were rent strikes going on in the Highlands, he read. Tenants were also protesting by sending their cattle to graze in areas that the landowners had allocated for sheep farming and deer hunting. Policemen had been sent in to enforce the law, which gave him an odd feeling. A Royal Commission under Lord Napier had been going round the country to enquire into the conditions these Highlanders were living under. Crofters, they seemed to be called nowadays: people who had been removed from their livings in some of the old townships and assigned individual plots elsewhere with a tenure as fragile as ever. He learned that evidence had lately been given to the Napier Commission by a Reverend Gustavus Aird, Free Church Minister in Bonar Bridge.

'Is it wise policy for the rulers of this nation to allow such a class of people to be treated as if they were serfs?' the minister had demanded of the commission.

Seeing that name before him, hearing that big voice thundering again through the newspaper print, shook him to the core.

He remembered reading an article once, years ago when he had left the employ of Mr Wilson and was working in the American South, about the characteristics that each of the trades supposedly develops in its artisans. The butcher was said to be serious and full of his own importance, the house painter rakish, the tailor sensual, the grocer stupid, the porter prattling, and so on. The shoemaker was said to be distinguished by a restless spirit and a talkative temperament, which had in turn contributed to his historical tendency to make speeches to crowds and lead riots. It was a tendency encouraged, so the argument ran, by a less physically demanding job, which gave the shoemaker the opportunity to read, think and reflect, and by the privilege of working for himself, which left him free to express opinions without fear of what an employer might think.

At the time the article had prompted an amused inspection of his own case. While he might admit to a restless spirit, nobody had ever accused this shoemaker of talking too much. Nor had leading a riot presented the smallest temptation: he had never been inclined to put himself to the trouble of challenging how society organises itself in any way at all. It was only now, working his way back through old newspapers in Rutherglen's cramped reading room and marvelling at the polemic of the elderly Gustavus Aird, that he began to consider why this should be. Why had he not engaged more with radical ideas?

Close behind that one, a bigger question began uneasily to stir. Why had he not allowed himself to think deeply about anything much at all in his forty-two years? He knew himself to be capable of it. He read when he could. He had every chance to reflect. A decent enough early education lay behind him, even if it had ended abruptly. He could claim personal experience of social oppression in two continents. Why had he never applied his mind to anything beyond sculpting leathers, hammering nails and endlessly moving on?

At home he continued to wonder about his landlady. As the days passed, he began to notice a habit of repeating an instruction she had delivered before – sometimes, indeed, rather shortly before. There are ways of repeating a point for emphasis, or out of natural bossiness or a predisposition to nag, all of which would fit what he had experienced thus far of the Widow Bain. By the same token he took no offence at being ordered thrice to be in for the coalman, since, as she intimated imperiously, she had a living to make too and he might as well make himself useful. Rather it was her use of the same words each time, the same inflection, an air of the thought having occurred to her that moment for the first time, that began to alert his attention. While acquiescing cheerfully enough in whatever was demanded of him for the third time, the absence of awareness that she was doing it occasioned in him a faint sensation of unease.

Sometimes the preparation of the evening meal was barely started when he arrived home at the time he had been expressly ordered to be there to eat it. Once he let himself into the house to find her already clearing her plate from the table, with no second place set. On that occasion a look of fleeting puzzlement met his enquiry about whether he would find his own dish in the oven, before belligerence came to her rescue with a demand to know why he was late and what made him think he could waltz in here at any time of the day and expect his tea on the table. But he knew to the minute that he was not later than usual. Lord knows, he had clocked in and out of the button factory often enough to embed a habit of punctuality that would have returned him on time to Anne Street if self-preservation alone had not.

Nor did it escape his attention that they could easily go a week without a sausage. Or that while potatoes continued to be plentiful, they were sometimes boiled to powder and at other times not far removed from crunchy, which in both cases seemed to surprise the cook herself when she put fork to mouth, although she recovered quickly and any dismay on her part could not be said to equal his.

He began closing up the workshop early and bringing more of his work home, ensuring that he was back in time to keep an eye on the cooking. Occasionally he would dare to sidle over and sprinkle in some salt when her back was turned, or contrive a means of diverting her attention if he judged the water in danger of being drained too soon. His early training on an antiquated Newark stove came to his aid in many useful ways.

He even offered to shop for her if she ever wished, a suggestion received with outrage. Did he want her to become a laughing stock, sending out a man for the messages? The outrage seemed genuine enough, and understandable: it is not every man who has done his own shopping for most of his life and thinks so little of it. For a man who carries his pride somewhat lightly (a truth about himself he is sufficiently aware of to relish, which may be pride of a different kind), there could be worse hardships than lining up at MacPhail's counter with a bunch of scandalised housewives, especially if it secured a couple of mutton chops now and then. But there was something excessive in the heat of his landlady's disdain, an element of performance to the angry tilt of her chin and straightening of her shoulders, that made him sense he had infringed more than the social proprieties with his offer.

Here was a woman whose pride was not worn lightly. More than once she had mentioned, in that unsettlingly repetitive way of hers, that she knew to the minute how late in the afternoon to call in at the butcher's to be sure of haggling down the price of the best cuts of meat before closing time. He discerned that buying well on little was important to her sense of her own dignity. Perhaps it even counted as a measurable achievement in a life that might not, from the look of it, be able to count many others. It had not escaped his notice, either, that during his tenure at Anne Street thus far these supposedly fine cuts had not found their way to the table very often at all.

II

December was raw and inclined to showers of wet snow. The afternoons darkened early and the streets were filthy with slush, although thankfully there was no horse fair to add to the challenge of picking his way home in beautiful shoes. During the November fair the mud and ordure churned up by horses the length and breadth of Main Street had made the route between workshop and house more than usually testing. These fairs happen seven times a year, God help him, and they cause enough mess for the town to have been nicknamed Driddledirt, which is not a word, whatever it means, to endear itself to a man fastidious about footwear.

As he walked, he was remembering New Jersey in the snow and ice, the Passaic river dusted white in winter, broad and beautiful in his mind's eye, great boulders stranded in it like whales. He remembered the weight of borrowed wooden skates dangling from each arm and the clutch of icy air at his chest as he sped upriver.

The Algonquian people had once inhabited the lands around that river. Peaceful Valley, they called it, and his memories have retained that quality of spacious and dreamy calm, however far from peaceful the banks of the Passaic can really have been by the middle of the 1850s, when he arrived with his mother and brother.

In the summer evenings he used to go diving. Work over for the day, he ran with the other boys on the waterfront, diving down through clear water not yet spoiled by effluent; down, down till his lungs were bursting, then scrabbling for a handful of mud at the bottom and shooting up again to show off his prize. There was always the hope, too, that you might bring up more than soil from the river floor. Mussels grew at the bottom of some of the streams up Paterson way and there was a time late on in the fifties when a big pink pearl was found in one. Chap by the name of John Quackenbush discovered it. He had it valued by Mr Tiffany in New York and it ended up, so everyone said, in the possession of the Empress Eugenie, who was married to one or other of the French Napoleons. There was a mad craze after that, which had every boy scouring every stretch of water for miles around for mussel pearls. He never did find any.

He caught shrimp and crabs in the Passaic, though, and there were little striped bass everywhere for the taking and an occasional white perch. He was good at frying them up with some corn when he got home.

The river was his refuge, an oasis for swimming and fishing and watching the steamships and the sailboats cleave the water and later on, during the war, the big blockade runners drop anchor above Centre Street bridge while their cases were settled in the courts. The river was where he put the button factory out of mind. For an hour or two it also let him forget the vacant woman in an airless room nearby, who sat waiting for a boy barely out of childhood to cook the supper and put her to bed.

Looking forward to a warm meal, eager to be inside, he bounded up the stairs two at a time. Unusually the door into the kitchen had been left open, a transgression for which he himself had been rebuked with a lecture about keeping the warmth in. Cold air met him on the threshold.

He took in the moist chill of the room, the empty grate in the range, the bare hob. At the table, head in hands, sat the slumped figure of Mrs Bain. Her hair hung about her shoulders in messy hanks. It covered the fingers at her temples and plastered the puckered hollow below the hairline that gave her forehead its cratered appearance. A couple of redundant pins stood out from her head at a rakish angle.

There was a shocking intimacy about her dishevelment. Shocking, because no matter how early he came through from his parlour bedroom in the morning, he was used to finding his landlady composed for the day. There she would be, stirring the porridge with her back straight, her dress smoothed of creases, a clean apron tied behind in two neat loops, the mass of her hair swept up from that rather fine neck in an esoteric arrangement of knots and folds that she had managed, by some feminine magic, to effect in private without one solitary mirror in the whole damn house.

He hesitated at the door, uncertain of his reception. Or rather, wholly certain of his reception. Then he made up his mind. He lived here, he paid his rent, he was cold and hungry. He hung up his coat on top of hers, brown over black, took a step into the room and pushed the door behind him with his foot.

He was dismayed by the sight of her.

God forgive him, he was excited by the sight of her.

When she looked up, he could see she had been weeping. Her eyes, red-rimmed but clear as stars, furiously defied him to notice. It was the ferocity of that gaze that moved him: the vulnerability both exposed in it and resisted at the same time. His heart responded with an unexpected lurch. He felt a disconcerting urge to reach for her, this aggressive matron who would have him back on the street in a trice if he put a foot wrong, never mind two well-meaning arms.

His legs had the sense to disobey. They took him only as far as the other side of the table, where he seated himself opposite and studiously avoided her eyes.

Burrowing in his pocket for inspiration, he drew out a folded piece of calfskin he had in mind for a child's shoe. Waxed calf, supple and plump. He examined it for a moment, sensing her attention, then tugged it this way and that between his hands.

'Nice and firm,' he murmured, not looking up, 'but just enough give if I pull it like so.' He gave a stronger tug. 'I'd have liked a better grain, to be honest, but the flesh side here is soft and silky, which is the main thing.'

He raised the skin to his face and rubbed it against the smoothest part of his cheek, the patch between the spreading edge of side-whisker and the presently slightly disappointing extremity of moustache.

'Yup, that's fine. And when I fold and press it like this, see, and then unfold it, we shouldn't see a crease mark. There we are now, fine and dandy. Would you like to feel it?'

Only now did he look up. She shook her head.

'Then I might get my size-stick out now and make a start, if you've no objection, Mrs Bain. I have it in my work bag. You might like to watch how I measure for a child. It's really very—'

'You haven't eaten,' she said in a flat voice.

'Oh, I'm not hungry,' he lied heroically. 'I could use some heat, though. Why don't I lay a few coals and get us a fire going, to save you the bother of getting up.'

'I got lost,' she said.

'Lost?'

Still the flat voice. 'Lost in my own town. Lost in my own street. I didn't know where I was.'

'I see.' He nodded slowly. 'Has it happened before?'

'Not so . . . completely.'

'Then how about I make a start on this fire and you tell me about it.'

Without waiting to be refused, he stood up from the table, took off his jacket and hung it on the back of the chair. Calmly he rolled up his shirtsleeves. He thought about whistling a tune into the dead air and decided against. He knelt down in front of the range, reached into the scuttle and drew out a neat oblong parcel, which he knew to be the coal dust she had already dampened and wrapped in newspaper.

'How many of these?' he asked over his shoulder.

'Three. And mind you put them right in the middle before you build the coal round.'

He smiled to himself. 'Yes, ma'am, that's exactly what I'll do. Now how about you tell me what happened, while I just work away here.'

There was another long pause, during which he laid out his

implements in methodical fashion along the floor – shovel, poker, tongs, brush – and wished she would get on with it. He was hoping she would find it easier to talk to the back of his head, but the danger of her attention being drawn instead to the deficiencies of his fire-making could not be discounted.

Then she began to talk.

She had delivered the last of the laundry, she said, and was walking home. She went into Brodie's in Main Street on the way. She had timed it exactly right and came away with a couple of fillets of something she could not recall for the moment. She stepped out of the shop and thought, which way do I turn? Which, as she said, was the first thing to alarm her, because when do you ever have to ask yourself which way Anne Street is when you're on that side of Main Street?

'I didn't know where I was,' she said, the bleak voice back. 'I didn't recognise the road, the shops, the houses, anything. It was an awful feeling. As if I'd never been there in my life before.'

He shovelled some nuggets of coal around the newspaper parcels, careful not to add too many, although he did ache for big flames and extravagant heat and money wasted just once.

She had chosen a left turn and stumbled along one street, down the next, slipping and sliding in the slush with no idea which way to go next. She began to run aimlessly, the panic rising. As she crossed one road she was staring up so hard at a building on the other side, grazing the windows for a clue, that she was almost mown down by two horses drawing an omnibus. The driver yelled at her. She sat down at the edge of the road for a long time, shaking and bewildered, trying to think her way through this predicament. Every tenement looked the same; the entrance to every close could have been hers.

She stood up and must have left her basket behind her on that nameless street, because it was not with her when she found her own close at last, staggered up the stairs, put the key to the lock and discovered that it did not fit.

'Can you imagine the terror of your own key not fitting your own lock? The terror of not being able to open your own front door and not understanding why?'

Without turning round he inclined his head.

It was not her own door, though. She grasped that at last. Down the stairs she ran, back into the streets, darkness chasing her now. The streetlamps were being lit, throwing more shapes and shadows over the buildings.

On she talked, telling the story in her soft accent with a lucidity quite at odds with the derangement she was describing. Her voice was becoming stronger all the time. At last he laid down the poker and turned on his haunches to look at her. This was the most she had said to him in weeks, the most, by a long stretch, she had exposed of herself. He could not listen any longer with his back to her.

Already she was looking less wild. At some point in the narrative she had pushed the hair off her face and reassembled some pins.

She had come upon the gas-lighter, who was just pulling down his ladder. But, horror, his face was a grimacing Halloween turnip, huge and sickly in the lamplight. She shrank against the wall of the building behind. 'Go away!' she shouted at him.

But on he came, advancing towards her with a long stick. She thought she might have screamed.

'Are you all right, hen?' said the man. The monstrous features rearranged themselves into a large nose and toothy mouth. He tucked the lighting rod into his bag.

She paused here in the telling, breathed slowly and tried to find the words to explain.

It had felt, she said, as if everything ordinary and familiar in the world had become something other. As if she had wandered into a fairground of grotesques, where whatever she looked at was a nightmare vision of itself. But now she was sitting here realising that she was the one who had been distorted; that her own mind was the nightmare; that she was the other.

He could tell from the clarity of her eyes that the nightmare had passed, but he also saw the effort it was costing her to create order out of an experience that had so recently bewildered her. He was aware too of a level of eloquence, a sophistication of expression, for which nothing in their terse dealings so far had prepared him. He dwelled further on this later, when he had leisure to review the evening in his unappealing room.

How unreal it all felt to him. How unlike the curt and contained Widow Bain to be confessing her emotions like this. The intimacy of the situation continued to unnerve him.

'I'm lost,' she had told the gas-lighter. 'Well, tell me where you're off to,' the man said, 'and I'll put you right.' She opened her mouth and out came the words, 'Anne Street. I live at 13, Anne Street.' The detail that had vanished so completely from her mind flew back in an instant from nowhere.

The gas-lighter gave her a yellow grin. 'Och, is it no' your lucky day, then? You're in Anne Street right now, hen.' He shouldered his bag and looked around. 'Number 13 now. That'll be across the road and down. See where I'm pointing? And you'll see your way fine down there, because I've just been along.'

Across the road, down the road. Which building, though? The first one she tried smelled wrong. But this is better, she thought. If there's a wrong smell, there will be a right one. She was working things out again.

'Not to be able to think,' she said suddenly, with a burst of aggrieved passion. 'The horror of not being able to think. Can you imagine?'

'I'll try to,' he said.

He eased himself upright and joined her at the table again. His hands were stained with coal, but he was not going to disrupt the moment by diverting to the sink. He would have to watch himself with that calfskin, though.

'I stopped at the next close and looked in,' she said. 'The light outside was showing up some markings on the floor, wee squiggles all the way along to the stair. And I recognised them right away. They were my flowers. I knew them and I knew I had drawn them and I knew I was home.'

They drew him home, too, these designs. He could tell when it was her day to clean the close by the same line of powdery patterns along the edge of the wall and up the stairs that he had noticed the evening he arrived: bluebells nodding at hyacinths, rows of tiny violets, dozens of toothy alder leaves.

'I followed the alders up the stair,' she said, 'and the key fitted and I was back. And I've been sitting here since trying to make sense of it.'

'How do you feel now?'

'Empty,' she said. 'Like the cupboard is right now.' She gave him a wan smile.

Why that smile should have made him feel that this was the moment to reach across the table and touch his landlady's face is not a question easily answered.

He did it, though. He stretched his hand out and was making, to be on the safe side, for her good cheek when she looked down and lowered her head a fraction, so that his hand landed on her forehead instead. Oh hell, her crater of a forehead. He pressed his thumb to it.

In for a penny.

She flinched. She glowered at him from below those brows that kept reminding him of somebody. The surprise, though, was that her head remained at exactly the right height and angle for him to continue pressing. Which is no doubt what encouraged his thumb, pretty much of its own volition, to start rubbing.

Her eyes shone with tears, which she tried angrily to blink back. At the sight of them his preposterous heart started playing up again.

'You could fit a cannon ball in there,' she said.

'What are you talking about? It's nowhere near as big as that.'

'Well, that's how it feels.' A more familiar note of disgruntlement was creeping in, but she made no move to draw her head away.

He held his nerve. 'See'– the rub became a circular stroke,

round and round the rim of the cavity – 'see, it's hardly bigger than my thumb.'

She stared at him a moment longer with an expression he could not read. And then, to his relief, to the inexpressible delight of his insubordinate heart, her eyes drooped shut. Her mouth relaxed. The battle line of her lips loosened.

For a long time neither spoke. The clock above the range ticked into the quiet. A child on the floor above screamed, 'Mammy!' A coal collapsed. On went his right thumb.

With growing confidence it progressed to the other contours of her forehead. It explored the ridges and the wrinkles, the soft places and the bunched frown lines. It smoothed out her eyelids, first one and then the other, registering each tiny tremor under the folded skin. Bravely it felt its way along the angle of ill-mended cheekbone.

In for a pound.

It was just setting off for the newly loosened lips when they spoke.

'What's wrong with your thumb?' she said, in a tone just short of irritable. Her eyes were open.

He dropped his hand. 'Pardon?'

'There's something very funny about your thumb. Let me see it.'

His is not a nature much given to turbulent emotions. His mother used to say he was the one who gave her least worry about how he would fare in the world, because from earliest childhood the world always presented itself to him in such an obliging light. True, the world made no great effort to oblige him after the age of twelve, but if his temperament has a bent it is towards an equanimity not easily disturbed. After his mother succumbed to her injuries in their slimy-walled room near Newark's waterfront, he never invited another responsibility that might discompose him, nor permitted a grip on his affections complex enough to unsettle him. North America presented a paintbox from which a smart and personable young immigrant could in any case choose his own colours. From the beginning he had selected those that were light on the eye and swift to scrub out. Which is not to say that he was wholly deficient in feelings; merely that they were not tenacious. Later on he was conscious of not exerting himself in relationships with women that might with effort have yielded a deeper satisfaction: children perhaps, family, solid ties to one place. But it provided no more than a buzz of regret. He reached middle age without his equanimity having been submitted to serious challenge. Arriving at Anne Street in October, his emotions had been flowing along as silky a channel as they ever had.

Which may be why, on the day his acerbic landlady lost her way home, he was so unprepared for the way her discomposure and her vulnerability affected him. The welling up of some strong feeling that was more than sympathy, the powerful longing to reach across the table and touch her face that was more than idle lust – it all so unsettled him that when she opened her eyes and asked what was wrong with his thumb, he wondered what on earth she was talking about.

For a moment he stared stupidly at the coal dust on his fingers. In a panic he stole another glance at her face. No, it looked clean. Then he understood what she meant, pulled himself together and began to tell her about J. D. Percy's.

Imagine, he said, a city called Newark, the booming manufacturing centre of New Jersey to the south of New York. Imagine factories belching smoke and fumes right along the east side of town and all the way to the waterfront. Imagine cotton works and tanneries, breweries, chemical works, silk mills, sugar mills, carriage and harness makers, smelting and refining works, bone fertilisers, leather works, makers of belts, corks, barrels, hats, hat blocks, corsets, cutlery, bolts, agricultural tools, jewellery, paper boxes, cigars, trunks, carpets, lamps. Imagine, he said, in danger of losing himself again in the wonder that Newark had inspired in a boy from the place he had come, imagine, he said, buttons. Imagine the sheen, the shimmer, the fragile daintiness of a pearl button.

She was listening. She might even have been imagining.

'Have you ever wondered how you make one?'

She had never, it transpired, wondered how you make a button.

Perhaps she would care to imagine for him, then, the sea creature called a mussel. A shell streaked with midnight blue, silvery white on the inside, its two sides miraculously hinged. Imagine hundreds of such creatures, thousands, millions of them clamped to wave-lashed rocks and scattered along the floor of the Pacific Ocean around islands soaked in sun, islands further from here than even he ever thought of venturing. Imagine boys with sleek dark bodies diving for these mussels, boats loaded with mountains of them, ships steaming the seas to deliver the dark-blue shells to a warehouse on the Passaic river.

Now imagine barrels of fresh water inside the factory and the shells poured into them to soak. Imagine the leftover scraps of meat still clinging to the insides. Imagine the greasy skin of decay forming on the surface of the water. Imagine yourself gagging at the putrid smell of it when you put your arms in days later to pull those shells out again.

The rank water seeped into the wounds in your hands and arms; it poisoned your blood; it brought death to the unlucky and repeated bouts of fever to everyone else. Every one of you had raw wounds vulnerable to this fate, because the business of making buttons from the shells slit your hands open all the time: first when you cut the shell to different sizes of blank with sawing machines; then when you steadied each blank with a finger against a revolving wheel to remove the skin and make the surface even; then when you made holes for the thread with a stamping machine that penetrated your fingers as often as the button. A moment's inattention at any stage and a finger could be off altogether.

It was a vile place, he told her. The workrooms were damp and evil-smelling, and shell dust lay so thick in the air that everyone became hoarse. Sometimes they would sing at the workbench to keep their spirits up, or attempt to. His Irish friend Michael Reilly wept his way through every song and then roared for more. But there were men there who could never sing because their throats had seized up. Those who had been there too long struggled to speak.

'We called it the slaughter-house,' he said, 'for the butchery of human beings that went on there.'

He was lucky, though. His fevers cooled after a day or two, the repeated lacerations of his skin healed, his youthful lungs never packed in completely, and he escaped in the end with ten whole fingers, even if they did remain needled for ever with the tiny holes from the stamping machine that his landlady had felt on her skin as his thumb explored her face.

In the silence that followed his explanation, he looked down again at the patterned pads of his fingers. He had half a hope that she would seize them and press them to her lips, exclaiming tearfully at the old pain he had borne so manfully. But the Widow Bain was in command of herself again.

'What a time you had of it,' she said coolly, putting up a hand to check that her pins were back in place. After a moment's pause she added more warmly, 'I'm sorry to hear it.'

That was the extent of her attempt to rescue them from the awkwardness that had settled like soot over the kitchen table. Now he could hardly wait to be out of there.

'Well, Mrs Bain, I guess I should retire now,' he said heartily.

He thrust back his chair and made an ungainly beeline for the door, after which he spent a hungry night listening to the stentorian singing of Anne Street's homecoming drunks and wondering if the erratic beating of his heart meant he was ill.

In the morning no reference was made to the evening before, beyond what could be deduced from the appearance of an extra wad of fried bread on his plate, which he took to be an acknowledgement of the meal he had gone without. He was as impressed that she had remembered as at her unwonted thoughtfulness in acting on it.

Concluding a tidy scrape of his plate, he said, 'Thank you, Mrs Bain. This will see me nicely through the day.'

She clattered the dishes into the sink under the back window as impatiently as usual, keeping her back to him as he left the kitchen. Yet there hung about their brisk going through of the motions a self-consciousness that could not be disguised. The room's greasy breakfast air was charged with knowledge.

12

Over the weeks that followed their awkward intimacy across the kitchen table, he continued to observe quietly. He noticed how fastidiously she crowned the mountain of hair with her black hat before she went out, and how irritably she tore it off in a shower of pins when she returned, as if raging that the day should have defeated her again. He pondered the relationship between thwarted intelligence and ill temper. He glimpsed the hand ferreting in her apron pocket for the gin bottle of an evening, the covert sips when she thought he was absorbed in his leatherwork, and he wondered.

They were conversing more now, and he gathered information about her previous life like a collector swooping on a rare stamp. He learned that she had moved to the tenement in Rutherglen after her husband had been obliging enough, as she put it, to die. There had been children, who had not lived either. The longest to survive, a boy of fifteen called Archie, had been taken with consumption in the past year, thereby enabling her to rent out the spare bed and reduce the amount of laundry she had to take in. She related these facts with a closed demeanour that did not invite questioning – indeed she swatted it away – although she did vouchsafe on one occasion that the late berries, winter leaves and dry thistles with which she kept the room decorated came from hedgerows and ditches around the churchyard where the son was buried. It was curtly told, but he was becoming more adept at reading her eyes and noting the omissions in these sparing confidences.

She asked about his own life. When had he emigrated to America and from where? Who were his family and what had become of them? The answers elicited a thoughtful nod and the occasional stare.

She refused to be drawn about her own family and where she had spent her earliest years. Her accent declared the geography of her birth, but when he rummaged in his own memory for the native tongue of the Highlands, she made no reply. It was hard to tell whether she had understood him or not.

'I only asked if you missed the mountains,' he said. 'I was assuming you came from a place where Gaelic is spoken.'

'Were you, though?' she said drily, looking about her for more yarn.

The language came back to him with such little effort that he felt a pang of disappointment when she discouraged his efforts. He told Dr Epstein about this. By then he had started telling his most faithful customer about a great number of matters, usually without meaning to, which was a knack the old gentleman had.

Dr Joseph Epstein had strolled into the workshop shortly after it opened. A Jewish physician from Prague, he had practised for some time in Glasgow before seeking out more salubrious air for a retirement which, as he confided with a throaty laugh, was no such thing, since his patients had merely followed him across the Clyde.

Professionally busy he might be, but his private life was clearly less so, for the doctor kept coming back. He first arrived with a pair of Oxfords for resoling. Collecting the Oxfords, he dropped off a pair of high, two-toned leather boots which looked as if they had last seen service at Waterloo. He picked up the boots but returned a week or two later with an embroidered house-slipper missing three beads. The shoemaker half suspected Dr Epstein of having nipped the beads off himself, so eagerly did he settle himself into a chair by the window to continue their conversation. He was soon ordering a pair of Wellington boots.

'This Scottish rain. I have been meaning to buy such a pair for years,' Dr Epstein explained cheerfully if not entirely plausibly, stretching out his thin legs and observing with small, lively eyes the mysteries of the craft unfolding at the workbench, in which he professed the keenest interest.

And what was there to object to in having him there, a lonely old man with a shrewd gaze and a large, hoary head? He was easy company, content at first merely to watch the work, silent but for an occasional murmur about the wonderful ease with which the human tendon connected muscle to bone or the pleasure he had once taken in studying the action of the humble ligament, although having practised for so long as a physician of the less tractable mind, he did admit to being out of practice with feet.

When he began staying on in the workshop long enough for the kettle to be heated over the fire and the fact that he would be staying for a refreshment cordially understood between them, there followed tales of his travels in Europe as a young man to undertake his medical training, of evading pogroms, refuge in Scotland, a devoted marriage without offspring, and the interest in afflictions of the brain that had led him into his present field of practice. Therein, he believed, resided many of the mental ailments which were either dismissed by doctors today without investigation or subjected to treatments bearing little prospect of success. Here was the point at which he was wont to become animated. He had much to be grateful for to the country that had made him welcome, but the complacency of the medical profession here, its ignorant resistance to some of the more radical ideas beginning to stir on the Continent, was much to be regretted.

Occasionally the doctor would ask a question. What are the names of your tools? Why did you become a shoemaker? Where do you think of as home? Even in the earliest days of their acquaintance there were hints that the softest and most innocuous questions from a man whose delight was to study the human mind were the ones to beware of.

The shoemaker himself was at his most comfortable talking about his craft. This is a last, this is an awl, this is for measuring the medio-tarsal joint of the foot, this leather is called cordovan, these nails are sparables and not to be confused, doctor, since you ask, with the brad or the cutbill. Itemising his tools like this reminded him of John Wilson in the early days, whose first lesson in Newark had been to insist that naming is important: master the names of your tools, my boy, the names of your working bones, your leathers, your nails, your measures, your threads and your stitches and you are on the first step towards mastering the complexity of the noble craft of shoemaking itself.

It was the July of 1869 when he met John Wilson, the day the Newark and New York Railroad opened with tremendous fanfare and free rides for all to the Manhattan ferry and back.

He liked trains. Newark had long been full of locomotives steaming across the Passaic with supplies for the army or freight to the rest of the Union, and since the end of the civil war new railroads had been arriving nearly as fast as the factories. A free ride was not to be passed up.

Outside the window the summer heat was shimmering, and it was crowded and sweaty inside the car. But he enjoyed the sensation of swaying with the sun on his face, luxuriating in the beat of the car on the rails and in a feeling that was growing on him, stronger with every mile, of possibility. He has associated this swelling optimism with train journeys ever since.

Earlier that month he had buried his mother. His brother was long gone and he had nobody else to think of. Somewhere along that brief train journey he said to himself, you will never make a button again.

On the return journey to Newark a fellow passenger eased himself into the seat beside him and began to converse in an easy manner. He was a stout, bluff, balding fellow of fifty or so, with small round spectacles that his handkerchief never succeeded in polishing entirely to his satisfaction, thereby requiring the repetition of the operation at frequent intervals. Mid-polish he asked what the young man did for a living. He replied that he was working at Percy's in Newark, but, as he confessed shyly, on this very day, on this very train, he had decided to leave and seek another line of work.

'Let me see your hands,' said the man, who for all his stoutness had elegant fingers himself, long and shapely. He took up the young man's hands in his own and turned them over.

'What happened?' he asked, inspecting the minute holes in the pads. On hearing about the stamping machine he shook his head with much sympathy. 'Do you still have feeling in your fingertips?'

Sure, he still had feeling in them. Too much feeling, he could have said.

'Enough to feel an imperfection in a piece of lambskin without looking?'

Well, how was he supposed to know that?

'Sure,' he said.

The man smiled. 'Good. You talk well and you have a personable manner, which is important in my trade.' He restored his handkerchief to his breast pocket with a flourish. 'Can you read and write?'

'I can, sir. I was taught both at a parish school in Scotland.' In a rush he added, 'And I learned more than reading and writing.'

Suddenly it seemed important to show this stranger that he was more than a pair of hands for butchering, more than expendable flesh in the cause of pearl buttons.

'We also studied Gaelic, Latin, English grammar, geography, book-keeping, arithmetic and the Bible. I read when I can, but there have not been many opportunities at J. D. Percy's.'

'I dare say,' the man said, observing him thoughtfully.

'Why do you ask, sir?'

'I'm a shoemaker, not long arrived from Manchester, England. I have been looking out for a smart young man to train up.' He reached out a shapely hand. 'John Wilson. Pleased to make your acquaintance.'

Mr Wilson had come to America to learn mass production, and there was nowhere better than Newark, famous for its shoes. There were still shoemaking premises across the city in the same family homes they had been in for generations, but now that machines were being invented for the most laborious tasks, the industry was changing. He would be hiring machinists, of course, but the quality of the footwear produced by the new methods could be regrettably shoddy. He needed assistants skilled in the art of handcrafted quality as well.

Under John Wilson's tutelage he soaked up the demanding intricacies of the new craft. The great amount of processes to be studied and the infinite number of problems to be solved in the making of a boot or a shoe inspired rather than daunted him. He devoured so many books on the anatomy of the foot that he could have passed a surgical exam. Yet it was not the knowledge and the achievement alone that he relished. He was surprised to discover the deep contentment of observing a finished shoe operating in harmony with a multitude of human bones: it fulfilled a desire for order and beauty he had not known he possessed.

John Wilson was an exacting teacher. There were times when he suspected the master of deriving more pleasure from correcting the angle of his apprentice's awl than from taking delivery of the latest machine to grow his profits while delivering the next blow to his beloved craft. In time, J. C. Wilson Boots and Shoes opened in Broad Street, and the apprentice began to feel like a cog himself. The machines were becoming so sophisticated that all you had to do was start and stop them. Soles and lifts and uppers could be cut to shape at a single stroke. Pegging, nailing, paring and finishing proceeded by magic. No need for beautiful hand-closing when you had a sewing machine to produce your stitch with a single thread and a double-pointed needle.

That was when he knew it was time to leave.

Dr Epstein looked up from his teacup. They both knew he preferred coffee. He had already offered to bring in his own pot and make it himself.

'Where did you go?'

'South,' he said. 'I went south.'

South from the northern cities in thrall to mechanism, south to states where life was slower and industrialising still had a way to go. Wherever he went, he set up premises, searched out materials and found himself custom. 'You have an elegant ankle, sir. May I ask who makes your boots?' He charged well for bespoke design and made do with cobbling when orders were thin.

'A life of moving on, then,' the doctor said lightly. 'You did not marry?'

He did not marry. He fell for women from time to time, although falling suggests a loss of control, a surrender to appetite or feeling, which rarely occurred within relationships in which he neither gave nor received enough to hold him. Comfortable within the skin that protected his emotions from assault, he poured his energies into other people's feet.

13

All this time his landlady knew exactly who he was, as he would one day discover. Gallingly, she continued to offer no hint of her own identity. He puzzled afterwards over how he could have been so slow to recognise her. Should he not have felt the connection in his bones or sensed it beneath his skin? Experienced it as a prickling of his thumb, perhaps, the first time he touched her? What kind of dullard was he not to have been struck by a single visual clue, unless you count the slight premonition of familiarity about the eyebrow? Granted, he had been a child when they knew each other, and she so much older: nine or ten years is a generation at that age. Further to excuse himself, the face he encountered in Anne Street rendered the adjustments one might have naturally made to thirty years of wear and tear more complicated. Then, of course, she was Bain now, which gave him no clue, while she had only to fit his name to a forty-two-year-old face and an American accent.

Perhaps his acuity in penetrating the mystery his landlady was determined to sustain was affected by the way his mind had closed itself to the early part of his life. It would not have occurred to him to wonder about this if Dr Epstein, less and less inclined to keep his profession out of the workshop, had not encouraged it.

'When you were in America, did you never think about the home you had gone from?' the doctor asked. 'About the circumstances that led to it? The people left behind?'

He made to say no, never, because that was more or less the truth of it. Dr Epstein waited.

Then he put down his scissors and rested his elbows on the workbench. 'I guess there was one time,' he said.

And he began to describe the day that President Lincoln's hearse was carried through the streets of Newark. It was April 1865, almost nineteen years ago, the day a guard in his mind came down that he had never suspected was up, and memory made it through.

The manufacturers of Newark were opposed to the civil war when it started in sixty-one, and no wonder. They had been clothing and shoeing and saddling and harnessing the planters of the South for so long that they were loath to lose their market. But it was his impression, working at the button factory, haunting the waterfront, that most of the citizens supported the Union with fervour. The February before the war began you could hardly find a space on Broad Street to watch Mr Lincoln being driven to the railroad station at Chestnut Street, on the way to his inauguration in Washington; and just as well Broad Street was as wide as its name, because there were thousands and thousands of people bunched together in the snow that day as the coach went by, far too many for him to see over.

They were out lining those same streets four years later,

shocked and silent, when the president returned from Washington in a hearse. He was carried through Newark from train to ferry and sent on his way to New York, just days after everyone had been jangling bells and firing cannons and embracing strangers all over town because General Lee had surrendered. Some of these mourners would have been the very same people who had cheered the streams of marching men as they set out for the South, and then crowded around the office of the *Daily Advertiser* in sixty-two as news of the Jersey Blue's fortunes in Virginia came in over the telegraph, nearly trampling each other in the stampede to get at the lists of killed, wounded and missing that some bright spark thought it a sensible idea to fling from a window.

He reflected on this while he and Michael Reilly were waiting for the cortège to come by, their factory closed for the day, like every other.

It was Reilly who had brought them to Newark in the first place, the boy and his mother and brother, a fragment of family in a new continent with nowhere to go. His brother had no interest in staking out land over there, as generations of Highland immigrants had done on reaching North America. Big-town life was what Donald craved, not years of heavy labour with no guarantee of reward. Caring for their biddable and incurious mother as well as they could, they were working their way down the east coast when a diminutive man of indeterminate years sprang across the latest roadside tavern and demanded to know what language they were speaking. 'Gaelic,' his brother answered in English. 'I thought so,' said the little man in a tongue both like and unlike their own. 'But it's not the true Gaelic of the Emerald Isle now, is it?'

Like them, Michael Reilly was newly arrived in America, and declared himself delighted to be among companions he could converse with in a mongrel Scots and Irish Gaelic that suited them all better than English in the early days. But unlike the brothers, this immigrant knew where he was going. He had cousins in Newark, New Jersey. That was the place to find work. There were so many factories in Newark, you would not believe it.

Reilly might have been as old as forty or as young as twenty. He had wild hair the colour of wet sand, old eyes in a pocked face and such a persuasive tongue that it was the work of moments for the Scottish boys to settle their mother back in the barrow and set their feet in the same direction.

Ah, but they would never regret it, Reilly assured them, and not least because Newark had more saloons than Cork had potatoes. It had nearly as many Irish families as Cork, too, he reported on the authority of yet another cousin, and a fair number of Scots, and plenty of Germans as well. The Germans were despised for their customs and considered the most inferior of all. 'Takes the heat off the Scots and the Irish,' he said with a wink.

The family rented a damp room near the riverfront, far from the gracious and shady sidewalks of Broad Street, where ever vaster emporiums were selling the immense number of products being manufactured in Newark's industrial boom. There their mother sat placidly all day long, greeting her sons cheerfully when they returned from work and causing no trouble to anyone beyond her inability to complete a single useful task on her own.

Donald was quick to find himself a job behind the counter

of a dusty saloon and spent the rest of his time, and an increasing proportion of his wage, bestowing his custom on the others. Michael Reilly secured the younger brother a job alongside himself and his Cork relatives in a faceless square brick building with black windows. They had been at J. D. Percy's ten years when the president was shot.

As they waited for the procession, Reilly kept up a low grumbling about feckin' top hats spoiling the view. But all he was thinking about himself that April day was how much pent-up longing was spilling on to the streets, how many old agonies were finding expression in the communal grief over this one shocking death, how unexpected and unfamiliar was the welling of emotion in his own breast.

It took nearly an hour for the procession to pass, from the mounted guardsmen at the front to the gentry bringing up the rear in their carriages. In between was a throng of dignitaries and clergy and every kind of soldier in and out of service, the invalids rattling along in wagons, with never a sound made but that and the rolling wheels and the steady tramp of men. In the middle of it were the six horses in heavy black palls pulling the hearse, which was swathed in red, white and blue with black and white plumes. He has never forgotten it.

Nor has he forgotten what he wished for, standing there with Michael Reilly, who was often maudlin but rarely serious. He wanted his brother. He wanted Donald, who had never been able to disguise the troubled temperament behind the languor he presented to the world, nor bear it without a drink; Donald, who, even if a word was never spoken between them, might have understood what he was feeling today.

But Donald was not there. Forgetting which side of the counter you are supposed to be on is a habit that gets you fired from serving liquor pretty quick. It had happened to his brother three times in three different saloons, before he abandoned that line of work and took up with a wholesale scrap dealer. Soon after that he announced he was off to New York. He knew a man who knew a man who was setting up in scrap metals with a sideline in used rope and leather. Anyone could see Newark was no more than an overgrown factory town anyway, for all its pretensions to be a great commercial city. It was time to try his luck across the Hudson.

Donald had kissed their mother's forehead, closing his eyes briefly as he buried his face in her lank hair. Then he slid out of their lives with an assurance that he would write to them as soon as he found a place in New York.

Ann Munro, shocked out of her vacancy by some inexpressible instinct of loss, wept for a long time when he left.

'Just like his father,' she said, tears coursing down the folds of empty skin. Perhaps she understood that she would never see her middle son again.

In April 1865, as Abraham Lincoln's cortège passed under Newark's overcast skies and miserably flapping flags, a great gust of loss engulfed him. The ache that stormed him was not only for Donald, not only for the bulging curves and floury palms of the mother Ann Munro used to be, but for the far-off glen he had forgotten all about and for the people at home – home, he called it to himself for the first time, home – whom he had thought he did not miss.

'I dare say I recall the moment now only because it was remarkable to feel as I did that day,' he concluded with a shrug, picking up the scissors again. The afternoon light was draining already. Shadows had begun to hollow his visitor's face.

'Interesting,' said Dr Epstein, and the shine in his eyes suggested that he did indeed find it so. 'The effect of an experience like yours in childhood is really very interesting.'

14

Recognition arrived with startling suddenness.

On Sunday afternoons it was the Widow Bain's habit to go to the burial ground. Usually she returned with a wintry armful of stiff brown grasses or budded twigs to replenish the jug on the dresser, berries, she had explained, being hard to find at this time of year. On a day in February she came in from the cold with her cheeks bright and a bundle of snowdrops in her hands, carried reverently into the kitchen like a votive offering.

He watched as she took the sugar bowl from the shelf and began to place the flowers inside it, arranging each head on its emerald stem with a tenderness he had not observed before. Tiny lumps of dark earth still clung to the trailing roots, and she added more from her apron pocket. She patted and pressed the soil around the stalks, drawing out another handful and sprinkling more in as needed. Then she took a cup to the sink for water. Her widow's skirts flapped as she passed.

He looked down quickly. He had lately been promoted to sit by the hearth, and the way to guard this privilege was to keep your nose in a book and on no account, until the moment that she alone decided a conversation was merited, let Mrs Bain know you were paying her any attention at all.

The corner of his eye reported the drizzling of water around the roots and the wiping of crumbs of earth in dark streaks down the hips of her apron. She stood back to contemplate, teased a stalk here, a blossom there. Personally he was less interested in the snowdrops than in what she had done with the sugar, and whether it still lay buried inside that bowl, and if so whether it could be rescued. He was in the process of calculating, were exhumation to prove impossible, how many cups of tea he would have to consume before any more sugar appeared in the house, when his attention was drawn to a small background noise.

Well now, here was a sound not heard before. The Widow Bain was humming.

With an ostentatious rustle he turned a page and restored his gaze to 'Chapter Two, Leggings and Gaiters'. Furtively and intently, he listened.

It was astonishing how fast his brain made the connection. A few notes of music vibrating in the air while he and his landlady were both engaged in something else – and yet within a second of hearing the tune, less than a second, a fraction of a second, he had matched present with past. Even more astounding, he became from that precise moment unable to figure out why he had not made the connection in the first place. His brain then went on to make a further, lightning calculation which, pending confirmation and a fuller investigation of the facts at a more opportune moment, effected an equally swift accommodation of the deformed cheekbone and damaged forehead.

It was like adjusting a fairy-tale mirror. Angle it this way and here is your landlady of middle to late years, a woman you are wary of, puzzled by and unnervingly attracted to. Angle it another way and these very same eyes, the formidable eyebrows, the slender neck, the good cheekbone and the threads of gold in the motley hair have transferred themselves to a girl you used to pad behind as a kid.

He stared at her, the book limp in his hands.

It has been raining. The world is dripping wet. Trees, grass, earth, stones, everything is wet. He is wet. He hovers indecisively, squelching mud between his toes and trying to decide whether to retreat at once or hang around to see what Jamesina Ross is up to.

Jamesina Ross. The older girl from Lizzie's house, mad songstress of Greenyards. She is standing motionless among the alders, upright as a tree herself, soaked through and not seeming to mind in the slightest.

Her hair is all over the place. Sodden strands lie about her shoulders and her cap is sliding down one ear. With a finger to her lips she frowns at him to be quiet.

He cottons on that she is listening to a bird nearby and gives serious thought to escape, because who can tell how long Jamesina is going to stay there being entranced by a bird. He stays, though. He always does stay.

After a while the bird hops out of the undergrowth and begins to peck about in the ground, which means he has to stay and watch that too. Then it flies off. This time he really is about to fly off gratefully himself when Jamesina smiles over to him and starts trying out words and feeling her way along a tune, the way he has heard her do so often before.

There is a fluttery thing she does with her left hand when she is singing, to make sure she has the beat right. It fascinates him, the twist of her wrist, the patterns her fingers make in the air.

The meaning of the song is not easy for a boy of twelve to make out first time. He deduces that she is sad, but that something about the blackbird or its mate is making her happy. It will take him longer to understand that the song is about the future, her future, and that she is the blackbird.

This is the song the Widow Bain was humming as she wiped the earth of the graveyard from her hands that afternoon. She carried on with the tune while they stared at each other, moving her head slightly from side to side with the slow pulse of the music. Falling silent at last, she came over to sit on the other side of the range. She gave no sign of intending to speak.

'Mrs Bain,' he said at last, leaning forward and clasping his hands between his knees, 'was your name once Jamesina Ross?'

'That is a very personal question, Mr Munro,' she replied, her expression haughtily amused. 'Mrs Bain will do nicely, thank you.'

He waited for her to say more. Patently she thought any obligation to say more was his, which, since she had decided to be disagreeable about it, he determined not to do. He lowered his eyes, forced aside the revelation for private inspection later, and was trying to find his place again between 'Modes of Fastening' and 'Strengthening Seams', when she gave in and said in a matter-of-fact tone, 'You were an irritating little boy.'

He closed the book slowly. 'Well, I guess I might have been. I remember the day you composed that song. Would you consider singing it through for me, Mrs Bain?'

'I do not sing,' she replied with such stiff affront you would think he had issued an invitation to pull her chair close and rest her head on his manly chest.

'Ah,' he said, wondering how she classified humming. 'I'm sorry to hear it. I seem to remember you singing all the time at Greenyards.'

'Well, I don't now.'

'And you composed some fine songs. I know a few of them still.'

She lifted the poker and lunged at the fire.

'And did you not have thoughts of writing?'

'You know of many Highland women in poverty who write, do you?' More vigorous thrusts at the fire, at which three pins flew from her hair. 'I'll just compose a pamphlet between washes and perhaps you would be kind enough to run along and publish it.'

'I can see I've offended you,' he said carefully. 'I hope you understand how far it was from my intention. I guess I'm just excited at finding you.'

'And I *guess*' – he winced at the caricature – 'that you are mocking me,' she replied, drawing her brows together in a way he now perfectly remembered.

Part VIII

The Kitchen Bed

After midnight
Thursday, 24 July 1884

15

Funny to be sharing a bed with your lodger. Lodger as was. You pull yourself out of the places your mind keeps landing in tonight and you look at him lying on his side there, sleeping as neatly as he lives his life, not a hair out of place, his breathing slow and steady and quiet (never much in the way of snoring, thank the Lord, not that she's completely sure she doesn't succumb on occasion herself), you look at him and you think how strange this is, how strange he is, how astonishing it all is that the knock on the door last Halloween should have led to him being here.

The flummox she was in that evening when she had nothing to give the guisers. She had been starting to forget to do the things she meant to. Not all the time, mind, but it did frighten her a bit that night: to be sitting there pretending that Archie was still in the bed behind her, and hear the chapping at the door, and look across to the dresser for the bag of apples, and see it wasn't there, and wonder how it could have happened that an intention that was in her head when she put her coat on to go out and get them could have left it again just like that. She stared and stared at the place the apples should have been as if they had taken themselves off somewhere on their own, flown over to the sink maybe or hung themselves from the pulley, and such a fear and a frustration came over her it's a wonder she ever did get to her feet to answer that door.

And there he was. No time to go scooping up lost intentions and smoothing her mind out. There he was, one of Big Ann Munro's boys from Greenyards, doffing his cap on her doorstep and asking if he could rent her room.

Big Ann Munro. Now there was a woman. Anna *Mhòr*, they called her then (and see how these Gaelic words have come back since they were up there again). Stout woman, tall. Can see her now. Square as a barn and near enough as sturdy. She ruled her sons like an army sergeant, which was what her man had gone off to become and never come back yet. Such an arm on her she had for beating her sons, and anyone else's sons who got in her way. Folk said she never once needed a stick.

She and her sons lived up the hill from the battered cottage that became home to the two Glencalvie refugees (*re*, 'back', *fugere*, 'to flee'), when they arrived from Croick kirkyard with their belongings on the back of a pony. The cottage belonged to their Greenyards relative, Lizzie Ross, and a poor place it was all right, sagging unhappily from above and pinched in the middle where the turf had taken too heavy a blow from wind or neglect. The two houses, Lizzie's and the Munros', looked down on the Carron river from the brae that rose above its southern bank on the eastern march of the township. The river ran through the middle of the township, and she can remember how its caprices fascinated her at first, the way it could be lapping for docile stretches over slippery beaches fringed by oak and rowan, willow and alder, but was always only a bend or two from turning white and dangerous. One minute it would be hurling itself through glistening gorges; the next it ran so broad and shallow that a bairn could be trusted to ford it in the summer to borrow an egg.

A burn, fair chaotic with rocks, plunged past Lizzie's house on its way to the river. The alder trees overhanging it were something to remind her of Glencalvie, although not even they made up for the squashed cottage.

'The pair of you will be welcome in Greenyards if you work your share,' Mr Aird had announced heartily as he delivered them. 'Lizzie has need of the help and Mistress Munro up the hill there could do with a hand from you as well, Jamesina. There now, Mistress Ross, don't you go weeping when God has provided. I've had your pallets from Glencalvie put in already and you'll be at home in no time.'

The minister patted their shoulders. She was as tall as her mother by then. A shift of responsibility had also occurred when she was not looking.

'There'll be others don't do as well,' the minister said, 'but I promised John Gillespie I would see his family right and here you are. You'll have some air into the house and straw on the floor in no time.'

Old Lizzie Ross is hard to bring to mind. Maybe today she would pay more attention to the pile of clothing with thin hair and dead hearing in the box bed along the back wall; maybe spare some sympathy for the infirmities that made Lizzie demanding in old age, and ungrateful, and everything else her younger self never thought to try and understand, not knowing, what lassie ever does, that she would lie in a bed in Anne Street one day wondering when it was that she became demanding and ungrateful herself, with a tongue that could scour as hard as her mother's.

145

The Munros' house was close enough to Lizzie's to hear the shouts as the boys baited one another and catch a glimpse of flailing fists in the grass. Ann had been looking out for Lizzie herself till then, stomping down the hill every day to spoon her some porridge and empty her pan and see to her chores and her animals. Ann had been a Ross by birth too, before taking up with the most disreputable, faithless, no-good Munro in the whole of the Highlands, as she was pleased to characterise her absent husband. Five sons had survived, although it could feel like twenty when they were all in the house together. They went by age from Niall *Beag* at the bottom, up through Douglas, Donald and James, with Iain *Mòr* at the top, big as his name. Iain will have been sixteen, a couple of years older than her, when she and her mother arrived in the May of 1845. James was around her own age. But truly she felt older than the lot of them. As the chosen confidante of special commissioners and kirk ministers, she considered herself wise in the ways of the world. She was a Woman of Education, a Person with Plans.

A pain in the neck, she is thinking now, not without tenderness. She has the same soft feeling for the vain girl who was once herself as came stealing over her the other day when she was examining a cocky young starling that lay dazed and wounded on Anne Street, shaking her head at the vaulting ambition that had whacked it straight into a tenement window and broken its glossy wings.

The older Munro boys had the reddish colouring that was inclined to produce a fiery beard in the Ross men and bestow on the Ross women a glint of gold if they were lucky. For a time her immersion in romantic English poetry led to an ardent yearning for what she would describe to her friend Grace across the river as golden tresses, these to fall about her shoulders like, like a fountain in sunshine or some such nonsense, although to be fair to that artless lassie, she had never seen a fountain. Her actual tresses – messes, confesses – were more indebted to the dull dun of the Gillespie inheritance, for which she peevishly blamed her mother and which Grace assured her were bronze.

The youngest two boys had got themselves raven hair from somewhere. The women of Greenyards never wearied of reviewing the fatherhood of Douglas and Niall Munro, although their mother used to point out good-humouredly that the heroic clansman of old on her husband's side, Domhnall *Dubh*, had not been called the Black Munro for nothing.

She touches a finger to the head beside her. Even in the midnight pall of the kitchen its sleek darkness is stark against the pale pillow. That he should be here. To think that the boy should be here. That there should be nothing to connect her to the girl she was at Greenyards, the life she led, the enthusiasms she brimmed with, the talents she sensed in herself, even the face she once had on her, but this man alone, who was never a man when she knew him, who found his way to her again by chance and recognised her from – of all things – a hum, and somehow, how did he do it, has wheedled himself into an inviolate part of herself that she would be pushed to name. To think that there is nothing left of Jamesina Ross of Greenyards but him. Nothing left of the place itself. Nothing left of the things she used to do – what were the things she used to do? –

stacking peat,
making songs,
lugging buckets from the river,
making songs,
milking cows,
grinding oats,
peeling potatoes,
making songs,
walking cattle to the high grass,
collecting lichens for the dyeing,
making songs,
stamping cloth in tubs of piss to get the sheep's grease out,
washing it after in the river with Grace,
oh, lots of things and—

Grace.

Grace beside her at the river's edge. Dipping the cloth together as the water rushed over. Spreading it on the flat rock to dry.

Grace Graham with her calm smile and her ethereal gracefulness.

God's grace, Grace's grace, the Graces, *gratia*, grateful, grateful for Grace.

Grace, with wrists transparent as paper and the lustrous hair she would have liked herself. Grace, who lived on the other bank and crossed at the ford so they could blether without shouting. Didn't Grace want to marry a shoemaker? To think. It was because her feet were always cold, she said, and she used to lie in bed at night and dream of boots. True enough, her feet were thin and gauzy as her arms.

Her own confidences shared, too. In the fulness of time she

expected to be marrying *The Times*'s own special commissioner and spend her days composing poems and articles about the government's immoral treatment of the Highlanders. They would live in an elegant town house in London, which it was not at all unlikely would afford a view of Westminster Bridge, along with a goodly number of ships, towers, domes, theatres and temples (few of which could be rendered into Gaelic very easily, but Grace looked impressed anyway). Grace would be very welcome to visit and would likely find herself tripping over shoemakers there.

Grace receiving the invitation as gravely as it was offered. 'I wish I had ambitions like you,' she said.

What else?

Sitting around the waulking table with the other women, singing out their refrains in time to the beat of cloth on wood, the wind at their backs. Margaret Mackenzie arguing with Annie Mackenzie over whatever that pair had found to argue about this time, always something. Hughina Chisholm telling them both to get on with some work. Big Ann Munro or Christy Ross, usually one or the other, silencing the lot of them by making a start on the singing with a question sung out for everyone to chant back the answer as they found their beating rhythm. Stories in music of lovers gone and hearts stolen and how fine it would be to sky the fly, no, fly the sky, as a seagull.

Joining in herself, improvising a line, the thrill of hearing it taken up by the others. The cloth heavy at her wrists. Arms straining to thump it up and down on the table. Up down, up down. Sore next day.

Making songs.

The broken moon in a puddle. The shimmer on a salmon's

back. Watching a stone of hail on her shawl change to a miracle of water and finding a phrase for the wonder of it.

Donnie Chisholm on his pipes by the river's edge. Thinking of words to fit the pibroch he played, something wild and forlorn in the melody, formal and grave. The mountains in those notes, and the sounding winds and waters, and the restless skies, and the mists that soften the edges of all things.

What else?

Reading with Mr Aird in his study at Migdale. There was no more school after she flitted to Greenyards. Although one or two of the Munro boys walked to the parish school when work allowed, her mother said she could not be spared. But in the long summer evenings she was welcome at the new manse high above the port of Bonar. Sunshine memories she has of running through the strath, across the Bonar bridge and up the steep hill behind, gulping down the sight of the loch and its hem of waving grasses, such a different beauty from Strathcarron's stony braes and jostling rivers. Loch Migdale was fringed with foxgloves and frothing meadowsweet and yellow meadow pea, and on a fine day it shimmered. Her rivers – the Carron, the Black Water, the Calvie – never stayed at peace long enough to shimmer. For her the Migdale air will always be humming with bees. The heathers are out in her memory tonight, softening and colouring the hills around. Far below lies the shining skein of water they call the Kyle of Sutherland, on its way to collect up the Carron and lose itself in the sea.

Delving into stories at the minister's desk. Bible stories. Tales of crafty Odysseus on his astonishing journey home. Dispossessed Aeneas sailing away from Troy.

'You see from the story how this has happened the world

over and I dare say since the dawning of time,' Mr Aird said as they were reading the *Aeneid*. 'People have always had to leave the places they love because of the folly of others. They get by in the end, most of them, and some may even flourish, but no one should imagine on that account that dispossession is right.'

Why then was it allowed? She can recall the exact moment she asked this and how much she wanted to understand the answer.

'In this country,' he said, 'it is about race.'

'What kind of race? I didn't know I was part of a race.'

'You are first and foremost part of the human race, born, as you know, in the very image of God. But you also belong to the race of Celts, one which it is become habitual to consider inferior to the Anglo-Saxon race in these isles. I am of Celtic stock myself, but it is not Highland clergymen who are the target here.'

He shoved a newspaper at her and stabbed a finger at one of the columns. 'See you this proposal for a "national effort" to effect the mass emigration of between thirty and forty thousand people?'

When he got himself worked up, the minister spoke as he wrote, with flurries of emphasis and eye rolls instead of capital letters.

'The idea is to rid the Highlands of what some fellow at the Treasury is pleased to call "the surviving Irish and Scotch Celts".'

She found the place. '"This exodus might allow for settlement of racially superior people of Teutonic stock in districts from which Gaels had been removed,"' she read aloud. 'What is Teutonic stock?'

'German people.'

'Like Prince Albert?'

The minister looked uncomfortable. There was no need to be bringing the royal family into this.

Mr Aird had a soft spot for the upper classes, although his general fondness did little to temper his disdain for the particular actions of particular members of the upper classes, notably the ones who exploited bad laws to ruin people. The two attitudes coexisted in him in much the same harmonious way as St Paul eyed Homer across his bookshelves.

'But what makes German people better than us, sir?'

The minister sighed. 'The argument seems to be that they work hard and don't cost so much in poor relief. So it is better to get the Highlanders off the land and let the *industrious Germans* try their hand.'

'Will that happen?'

'If you read further you will find the Treasury man explaining his views. Let me have the paper back. Aye, here we are. Sir Charles Trevelyan welcomes, let me see, "the prospects of *flights of Germans* settling here in increasing number – an orderly, moral, industrious and frugal people, less foreign to us than the Irish or Scotch Celt, a *congenial element* which will readily assimilate with our body politic."'

He began to pace the room. 'Since you ask, I see no evidence of the Highlands being overrun by people of Teutonic stock, even during the shooting season, but there is no doubt of its having become intellectually respectable to view the Gaels as the foreigners in this land. Lazy ones, at that. You might ask me for the *proof* of their *native indolence?*'

More eye rolling and sarcasm.

'The proof is the failure of the Highland economy to recover in recent years. You and I, Jamesina, might regard the aid that alleviated so much suffering in the potato famine as a success. But no, we are to worry that *dependence on charity* might become such an agreeable mode of living that no Highlander will lift a finger again.'

She could feel her face becoming hot. 'Foreign to us' is what hurt. This man in the government, the newspaperman reporting his views, the people reading these views – they were 'us' and her folk were the 'other'. That this northern other might have skills suited to the circumstances they were raised in and the economy they operated, might have schools that taught three languages and a list of other subjects besides, which made it possible for one of them to be reading this very newspaper now, had seemingly not occurred to anyone.

'There is no need to flare up like that,' said Mr Aird, speaking over her thoughts, his own face positively aflame with flarings. 'Those who espouse such views are so *profoundly ignorant* of the seasonal rhythms of labour in a Highland glen that I have longed to lead them by the forelock to Strathcarron in the winter months and invite them to engage as productively as they insist its inhabitants should be engaging every day of the year – as if the hibernating ground could be pulled through a cotton machine or smelted into iron or hammered into the hull of a ship. And then let them write their splenetic diatribes about the sloth of the peasantry, once they know what they're talking about.'

He stopped pacing and raised his already prodigious voice further. 'I tell you, Jamesina Ross, that this *pernicious racial theory* is all that many a landowner will need to be finally convinced of the rectitude of removing a population so offensive to the leaders of thought in this country, not only from their ancestral foothold but from these very shores.'

Mr Aird sat down heavily after this considerable diatribe of his own. He waved towards the books laid out before her and made an effort to calm himself. 'Derivation of *superior* and *inferior*?'

'Comparative of *superus*, "above". Comparative of *inferus*, "lower".'

'Correct. These are the only facts worth remembering from this conversation, in which I fear I have allowed myself to become carried away.'

He pulled a bundle of papers towards him, opened a weighty Bible at the page already marked for his attention, and picked up his quill to resume the composition of Sunday's sermon.

And that's why I wanted to make songs, she is thinking as she twists about in bed, wishing she had not insisted on the drawn curtains that make it hotter still, trying not to disturb the sleeper at her side but maybe not trying all that hard because it's beginning to annoy her that she can't sleep for thinking tonight and there he is, slumbering away quite the thing, when he is the one who got her into this tonight with his singing, not to mention the traipsing about they've been doing up there these last few days, which was all his idea as well.

She will need to get past him in a minute for the chamber pot, and if that wakes him it's his own fault, too, because he was all for having that side of the bed from the word go. He could have had the wall if he had wanted his repose undisturbed (*turba*, 'a tumult') and free of clambering wives in the night.

Making songs, though. She had seen it as the way to fight for her race. Yes, she could make them in Gaelic, minutely evoking the land and the loved places, but if she was to bear witness some must also be in English and spiked with protest. Could dispossession not be lamented in verse? Could elegy not be angry?

> *Glencalvie, oh Glencalvie, where the waters meet,*
> *Glencalvie, my Glencalvie, that the people left.*
> > *See the walls upon the grass,*
> > *See each roof embrace the floor,*
> > *See how rain and nettle finish*
> > *What men began.*

It was difficult to get across a truth that also contained a feeling in a language not her own. She had meant to spend the rest of her life becoming better at it.

16

The day they got back from Strathcarron they were talking, the pair of them, about Iain *Mòr*, eldest of the Munro boys, who had no more feeling for a poem than how to brown a bannock. Would that have been yesterday, now, or the day before? Anyway they were not long off the train and mulling things over while they waited on the kettle.

She told him she had tried Wordsworth on Iain in Greenyards one time, and how he had just looked at her with his mouth open.

'The thing about your brother,' she said, taking the cups down, 'was that he had no imagination.'

'Poor Iain,' said he. 'Wordsworth is hard if you're not much in the way of English, whatever you say. And I'm not so sure Lucy at the springs of Dove is my own cup of tea either, if I'm honest.'

'I thought you liked poetry as a boy. You seemed to like mine all right.'

He stopped filling his pipe a minute. 'I did,' he said, 'although it might be as near the mark to say I liked you.'

'Well, I can see my poetic sensibility is wasted on the Munro family,' she retorted, mostly to cover the way it moved her to hear this, although she thought he was likely making things up backwards, as is very easy to do. She has an idea she used to think herself that the mixture of gravity and floppy-haired cheek the Munro boy had was going to beguile some woman one day, but it would be like her to imagine a memory like that, seeing as there is no harm in tidying up here and there if it gives your life a shape.

'You're a snob, Jamesina,' he said cheerfully.

Well, maybe she is. Everyone needs something to feel superior about – *superus*, 'above', *inferus*, 'below' – and it's better to be a snob about poetry than race. But her poetry was wasted anyway and there was not a soul else to blame for that. Not even Willie Bain.

She did have a strong sense of being superior to Iain *Mòr* Munro, though. Which was becoming a problem, since Iain *Mòr* Munro was out to marry her.

He was a decent soul, Iain, big and broad like his mother and fair to look at. As the years went on, he was open about his feelings for the girl down the brae in Lizzie's house. Lying here in the dark beside his brother (just thinking of that is such a very, very strange thing), as far from sleep as it is possible to take yourself in the middle of the night, it occurs to her that it would not have been hard to predict that the inchoate feelings aroused by Thomas Langton (*inchoatus*, from *incohare*, 'to begin', a favourite of Mr Aird's; why was that, something to do with the *h*?), feelings that were not fully formed and a bit incoherent (which will likely be from *incohare* too) – where is she going here? Somewhere incoherent. (What was it about that *b*?) Begin again. Iain is where she was going. The juvenile feelings she had for Thomas Langton (*juvenis*, 'young'), and how predictable it was that they would be reanimated by a keen young man who had the advantage of being there in front of her most days and not a dubious figment of memory. It was exciting to exchange meaningful glances with Iain across hearthstone or haystack, although she was always a bit hazy about what meaning exactly hers were supposed to convey.

Iain's own intentions became clear enough in time. He was ready for a wife to bed and a home of his own, although where in Greenyards he thought that was going to be she could not say. All those brothers. So little land to keep being shared, generation after generation. Mr Aird said it was one of the reasons the township system could not go on the way it was. The wife was the easier problem for Iain Munro, or so it must have seemed when the lass from Glencalvie bounded into their lives, singing her songs and spinning her tales of a life in some unlikely future that not a single person took seriously.

Big Ann Munro would have knocked the pair of them flat if she had caught them at anything more than stolen glances – and in that the matriarch had the full support of Greenyards. The women of the township policed every other woman's body with the utmost relish. Ann Munro and Christy Ross were in their forties then, with tongues as vigorous as their arms. They ruled the rest of them by gossip and shame, expertly aided by the midwife, skinny wee Hughina Chisholm, who had an infallible eye for breasts and bellies that showed signs of rounding in advance of a wedding. The community knew what was best for you and the threat of disgrace was how they kept order.

Grace discovered that. Dear graceful Grace, too graceful by half. Got herself in the family way early on with who was it again? He went off to be a soldier. Donald John McKay. But she refused to admit it, even to her best friend, because she was ashamed of what was growing in her belly, and it had that effect on you, the fear of the pointing fingers and the whispers, that you thought if you didn't talk about it and you didn't think about it except to do a lot of praying in the dark, it would maybe just go away.

Grace said nothing and kept saying nothing and the women started to talk anyway because they knew the signs. She defended her friend with fiery denunciations of the gossip, and Grace smoothed down her dress as flat as it would go with her bone-thin arms and smiled her merry smile and said she did not need anyone to defend her. What agonies she must have gone through, praying for a miracle while the narrowed eyes of the township inspected her waist, until one day she was hoicking up the hay and was suddenly bent double, clutching at her sides and moaning. No time to get her back over the river, so she was helped into the nearest house. Five or six women rushed round to have their suspicions confirmed.

It was hours later that Ann returned to the Munro house with the weary news that the mite had come too early to live. She waddled in and plumped herself down on the chair and said not a word else for a long time. Women like her were not bad folk. They were the first to protect the place from any outside threat that came up the road in a uniform and the first to bear down on anyone who upset the way life was to be lived on the inside. But now, with Grace lying there so pale and frightened, it was sympathy that held sway and the women closed in together. They were mothers themselves, the most of them, and they knew what it was to suffer.

'What happened?' she asked Ann, cold with the horror of it.

'She called out to see the baby.' Ann sounded awful tired.

Wee girl it was. Grace had given birth – such a monumental, elemental, adult thing to do – to a daughter.

The midwife had wrapped it in a napkin and was for putting it outside straight away. But when Grace asked for it, Hughina Chisholm had looked at Ann Munro to see what she thought and Ann had nodded, and the teeny scrap of a bundle was laid on the mother's chest. Ann said Grace grasped at that tiny dead bairn like a ravenous bird. Just like. She kissed it and kissed it and stroked its hairless head that you could see right through, and embraced it and wept over it as if she would never let it go. It was Ann who dislodged her fingers in the end, uncurling them one by one, gentle as she could, and then the midwife whisked the wee thing outside.

Afterwards she thought and thought about the way Grace had held that bairn. Kept wondering at the mysterious transformation of a slight lassie who dreamed of warm feet, barely more than a bairn herself, into a ravenous mother.

She thought about it later on, too: how you are never ready and you are never the same again.

Grace took a long time to recover and, while some folk were kind enough in their way, she was ever after a lesson to the township in what happened when a woman strayed. That is what she became: a lesson. The errant lover who, according to Grace, was no lover at all and had tricked his way into her drawers before she even understood what he was doing, had gone off with the recruiting sergeant and her family was shamed. No decent man would marry her now.

Grace knew this. She knew this. Everyone in Greenyards knew that this was the way it was.

'And that's what will come to you, Jamesina Ross,' Big Ann was never done telling her, 'if you dare let my Iain lay so much as a finger on your knee before you're wed.'

Iain's fingers did rest in the general area of her knee many an evening in the shadows of the Munro firelight. With his sniggering brothers on hand and the women on full alert, that was to be accounted an achievement. But for all the embraces behind Lizzie's saggy house in the moonless nights, she was never once tempted to risk Grace's fate for Iain *Mòr* Munro.

'Iain and I do not have a spiritual bond,' she confided.

'Spiritual bond? What book did you find that in?' Grace said, and her eyes filled.

Grace no longer had much sympathy for the airy ambitions that had impressed her when they were younger. She was too sweet-natured to say so – not once did she say so – but it was obvious that she thought it an indulgence to be hankering after intimate poetry sessions with some character in London last seen eight years ago, when a man like Iain Munro was offering himself in the here and now. Grace liked Iain *Mòr*; she approved of his steadiness and his honesty. Whatever happened to Greenyards he would look after a wife and Jamesina should be careful what she threw away.

'You don't think it counts for something,' Grace said, 'to be wanted so dearly and waited for so long?'

She had nothing to say to this. She was ashamed of herself then, although not nearly ashamed enough.

*

By October 1853 there were rumours that Greenyards' time for eviction was approaching. Everyone was on edge and Iain was agitating for an answer. She was past twenty by then, too old not to be married unless you were Grace Graham.

'Let's go and look in Bessie's mirror,' Grace said when Halloween came round. 'Let's find out if Iain is your own true love.'

Grace had retained a wistful respect for supernatural intervention in matters of the heart, for all that the spirits of All Hallows' Eve had signally failed to warn her away from Donald John McKay a few autumns past, when she could have done with a reliable sign.

The cloud was low that October night and there was no sign of moon or stars. Now, eyes closed in the kitchen bed, it is easy to imagine the moisture needling their faces as the girls walked to Bessie MacKinnon's house, to savour again the tang of smoke and mulch on the damp air and the slide of mushy leaves beneath their toes.

The MacKinnon mirror was always in high demand at Halloween. Its prodigious powers of revelation had sanctified many a riotous betrothal in its day, although nobody was ever in much doubt about the forms that whisky breath can conjure on glass. It evoked just that wee tingle of expectation and dread all the same. Whatever you told yourself, whatever you heard in the kirk, the ancient Halloween traditions made you uneasy.

She and Grace could hear guisers roaming the hill in sheep's heads and hare-skin shawls and anything else the younger ones could get their hands on to keep the chancy shades on side in the winter that was coming. Truth be told, no self-respecting spirit was ever going to be fooled by Douglas and Niall Munro clattering around in matching bucket-heads, but in the really dark dark you could feel the presence of something old on All Hallows' Eve: boundaries about to breach, the skin of reality stretched so thin you might go seeing through it any minute, to your benefit or your harm.

If you really wanted an answer, you would get it on a night like this. So Grace insisted. Just listen to the alder leaves stirring without a breath of wind. Hear the river falling over itself to get away.

At the MacKinnon house there were folk blethering around the fire. Bessie's father nodded at them to take the lamp and go on through to the back room. Grace grasped her hand and tugged her in. The lamp threw sickly shadows around the room, which made them feel a bit sick themselves, although they were nudging each other and giggling as if it was all a huge joke. Which it was not. Iain *Mòr* Munro wanted an answer and the mirror was going to tell her what to do.

It was propped on a chest of drawers against the house's end wall, a big ornate piece that had belonged to Bessie's mother and her grandmother before that, a present from some lady she had worked for. Not that it looked much now, all blighted around the frame and across the bottom with black spots and stains.

'Now you'll find out for sure,' Grace whispered.

For a while all they could see in the mirror was their own heads. Then she saw something else. She really honestly saw something else. She tries to conjure it again. A blur of shadow. An outline in smoke. A wispy fume of silver as blurred and miraculous as one of those photographs she would not have known existed then. It was unmistakeably a man's head.

She and Grace fell silent, and the silver man looked back at her.

'Do you see anyone?' Grace said.

'I think so.'

'Can you tell who it is?'

The face was not bulky enough to be Iain's, no doubt about that. Nor, ah dear, could it conceivably be the man from *The Times*. This was a long face, thinner about the cheeks.

'No,' she whispers back. 'I can't tell.'

'Move closer.'

She begins to inch forward. The silver man swims before her eyes. She takes a step back again, trying to hold focus.

There are shouts from outside, a clatter at the other end of the house and the sound of charging feet. A blast of October air whirls through with some leaves. From the next room Bessie's father is growling, 'Shut that door, would you!' And suddenly the place is full of boys.

Grace groans. 'The Munros. I might have known.'

And there they were, here they are again tonight, the brothers. James the worse for wear, or is that Donald? No, it's James with the funny eye that always went the wrong way. Donald, slim and sleekit, is skimming his way through them to the front. Young Douglas has a glassy look, which means he will have been at the whisky as well. And Niall *Beag* still has the bucket over his head and is getting in everyone's way.

'Have you got Iain in there, then, Jamesina?' Donald says, first to make it to the mirror.

The others surge after him, trying to shoulder each other away so they can peer in behind her. James's skelly eye dislodges Donald's nose behind her left shoulder. Douglas's flushed face pokes into view below her right arm. Young Niall must have hauled the chair over, because at the back of them the bucket rises majestically for about two seconds. He manages to haul it off his head for long enough to issue a whoop of triumph before crashing forward on to Donald, who swings around with a wild fist and hits James. The brothers transfer themselves to the floor and tear into each other. When she turns back to look, the mirror is empty.

Donald pokes his head up from the fray. 'Who was it then, Jamesina? Who did you see in the mirror?'

'She doesn't know who it was,' Grace says primly. 'And it's none of your business anyway, Donald Munro.'

'All I saw was us,' she fibs, trying to sound nonchalant. 'Looks like I'm going to be marrying half the Munro family and Grace for good measure.'

'That would be everybody except Iain *Mòr* then,' says Donald, who could be sly.

The brothers are all listening now. It used to amaze her how quickly a scrap could start from nothing and how instantaneously, like dogs picking up a signal from afar, those boys could stop fighting, all together at once, in a blink.

When Iain came in, stamping his feet, his broad, pleasant face ruddy with whisky and good cheer, wanting to know what everyone was up to, nobody spoke. She waited for his brothers to embarrass him, for Douglas to shout out gleefully, 'You're not the one she saw in the mirror!', for Donald to slap him on the shoulder and commiserate with a facetious, 'Sorry, old man.'

But the boys were unusually muted. Maybe they felt oppressed by Halloween as well, the night when truths are sometimes learned.

'There was nobody there, Iain,' she said, going to him and taking his hand. 'It's all nonsense.'

17

She clambers over him and back to her side of the bed. She can go a whole night if she gets to sleep at a decent hour, but not when she has been awake like this for hours on end. A wee mouthful of something would have put her over nicely. 'Medicinal purposes only,' he had the cheek to tut-tut at her after they were wed. 'I am here now to help you get to sleep.' Nobody as glib as a man who has never lost what he loved.

She should have let him know it had helped with more than the sleeping. But she has never brought herself to go there, never told him that without it she might have screamed the night away, because Archie is in her mind every minute of every day and there were nights when she lay in this bed by herself and thought of the shape her boy used to make in it, small for the age he was, tousle-headed on the pillow, that she gave vent to her pain and her loneliness where nobody could hear.

'Would you tell me about your son,' he said to her once, 'the one who used to sleep in the kitchen bed?'

'There is nothing to say,' she said. How do you describe to a man with a neat life behind him the thing that lies unspoken beneath the hard faces of all the women he will ever meet who have watched their children die?

When your bairn dies, the air leaves you. Is that what she was supposed to tell him? You forget what you have to do to get the air in. You have to tell yourself, Breathe. Which is not the same as telling yourself to place this foot in front of that foot and you will move, or direct this square of bread to your mouth if you want to eat, which are also things you have to will yourself to do. Breathing is different. Your own seems to go with the bairn's breath, flying out the window hand in hand with the bairn's soul. You would die yourself, gladly, gladly. But you can't die because your breath does come at last, enough of it anyway to keep your heart going. Only, the air keeps getting stuck. It's getting stuck now just thinking about it. And everything inside you goes dry.

The first two bairns she had with Willie Bain went within weeks of each other, aged one and nearly three. Consumption went round the Calton tenements so fast there was nothing you could do. There were too many buildings built too close, too many folk squashed into them to escape the diseases. And it was not just consumption, though that's what took her own children, but scarlet fever, measles, cholera and plenty more illnesses she never knew the names for. When she first arrived in the Calton, she thought she would die herself if she had to stay there. She was sure she would not be able to live one more day without Highland light and crystal water, that her leaves would curl till they dropped for want of the white wind. Turned out she was one of those hardy plants that carries on whatever the abuse. She kept on living. It was only her infants could not do it.

Dear God, the horror of consumption. The dread of hearing the first cough or seeing the first chills of a fever. The stories you told yourself: who's to say it's fatal; who's to say this child can't be nursed, rocked, crooned, fed, willed back to health; who's to say, who's to say? Impossible to protect them, nowhere to go.

The next bairn was lost during birth, fat when he came out with the cord wrapped round his neck, chubby folds at his wrists and a light blue face. She thought then about Grace, falling on her bairnie like a hungry bird.

Constance died at five, the only girl, her blue eyes shining like polished metal in her flaming cheeks. Too shiny, too blue.

Constance, Constance, Constance.

Constance learning her letters and practising them in the wash house, concentrating fiercely, her grave face framed by Gillespie eyebrows. A is for *ant*, B is for *beetle*. She had seen plenty of those.

Another baby gone at two months, so weak from the first she should have known he would leave her. But hope is such a monstrously clever deceiver that you can believe literally anything you tell yourself, even while you are not believing it. She never even knew what took that son, he was in such a hurry to be off.

But Archie did not die. Archie, with the roguish blue eyes and the golden Ross hair she had once craved herself. Archie, who could make anything with a piece of wood. Archie, who would never walk anywhere but ran with his back straight and his head back and little trotting steps that made her laugh. Archie, who loved stories and dreamed dreams as daft as hers had been, and was set on discovering Troy when he grew up, which was about as normal in the Calton as having a mother who cried over the fate of Hector.

Hector, running round and round the walls of the city, unable to shake off Achilles. Homer said it was like a dream where you can't be caught and you can't get away.

Zeus raising his golden scales, a portion of death in each.

'I'm Zeus,' Archie said, banging his fist down on the fly that was making a meal of his jam piece.

Archie the survivor.

How was she supposed to say all that? How is she supposed to do it now? Where would she ever, ever start?

He stirs and moves to enclose her again, squashing her left ear with an elbow as his arm lands. Blindly his hand finds her forehead and starts rubbing the hollow with a drowsy thumb, round and round, once, twice, until his fingers relax and trail down her cheek.

Her lips brush his hair and she inhales the scent of him. Tobacco, leather, that stuff he puts on his moustache. She stretches her leg along the length of him, where it fits so very well.

Funny now to think that for weeks and months after he came to be her lodger, he had no idea who she was. When he bent his head over a heaped plate, it amused her to see silver at his temples and remember a boy with urchin hair; to know what he so plainly did not. She was not above relishing the petty power that comes with exclusive access to knowledge, but it was more than that. The Widow Bain had too much pride to let him see what Jamesina Ross had become.

He was on to her in other ways, though. He noticed things she was doing or not doing. He tried to help. Put salt in the potatoes when he thought she wasn't looking. Took to mentioning what day it was so often that she yelled once, 'For God's sake, I know it's a bloody Tuesday!', shocking them both. She understood that he meant well. He was not to know how insidiously (*insidere*, 'to lie in wait') it flattens your sense of yourself to have someone else beating you to the answers and drawing attention to your mistakes and thinking he would be better doing the shopping.

Resist, she thought. You have to resist.

She resisted his questions about Archie. She resisted his attempts to help. She resisted his stroking thumb on the day she lost her way home, the deep and spreading comfort of it so surprising, the desire for it to continue too shaming to let him see. She resisted the way his presence in the house was beginning to unruffle and unmuffle her. Ruffle, muffle, scuffle, truffle. She resisted becoming self-conscious about her face again, just because a man felt at liberty to study it while pretending to examine the sole of a shoe.

Resist and resist and resist is what she had to do, because she was not going to let herself depend on any man again. Not in this life or the next. And certainly not in her very own house.

And when he did realise who she was at last, she resisted that too.

18

The day he recognised her she had just come back from Archie's garden. It's not far to walk and she is there every Sunday, rain or shine. They had found it together, she and her last son, when they arrived in Rutherglen, how many years ago? There is a kirk with a quiet graveyard to one side and a bower of hawthorns lining the long grass by the wall. She can remember how satisfying it felt to place five stones under the trees in a row, all different shapes and sizes, and to call them hers, as good as any gravestone. The grey ball streaked with creamy lines was for Constance, because her daughter had liked pretty things. When Archie was young, he used to decorate the stones with leaves and berries, and hang daisies about them in the summer. He blew dandelion clocks over his siblings' memorials and tried to catch the fluff again before the wind carried it away.

Good, clean air, she thought. This will make him better.

They had still been living in Glasgow when Archie began to decline. *Decline*. The word folk use when they mean die slowly from consumption. Willie Bain was gone by then, like all but one of his bairns. Archie would have been coming up for seven. She noticed his rosy face becoming sallow, the eager trot slowing, his appetite going. She was taking in washing by then. It was a fair long walk from the Calton to anyone who could afford to send laundry out, but she saved enough for a doctor. What can I do, doctor? What can I do? This child would not be allowed to die.

The doctor looked uncomfortable. She recalls that very well. He had a bald head and too much beard in his collar, which had soup stains on it. She would have liked a dab at those. In the apologetic tone of someone advocating a health-giving trip to the nearest star, he finally said that fresh air might help.

'And where am I expected to find that?' she flung back at him, as if, poor man, he was responsible for the slums folk had to live in, as if he personally had stolen the sky.

He meditated a moment, maybe weighing up what a widow of her class would have a chance of earning.

'There are places not far from Glasgow where the housing is less congested and the air easier on the lungs,' he said at last. 'Perhaps you might be in a position to see if a move south of the river would aid the recovery of young Archie, or at least hinder the progress of the disease.'

She decided then and there that Troy could wait and her son was going to be a doctor when he grew up.

When the horse-bus took off across the cow-back bridge to Rutherglen, the mare given her head and the passengers holding their breaths in case they met a carter coming the other way, she wondered how much difference a few miles could make. The foundries and printmakers on the Glasgow bank were matched on this one by a chemical factory, a paper mill and what looked like a boatyard. It had been silly to imagine that the smoke choking the city would magically disperse the moment the bus careered away from the southern bank of the Clyde. Yet the air lifting Archie's hair as he hung over the top rail did seem fresher as they rode. On the way into town they passed green fields and thatched farm cottages. And further away, through the town and out the other side, she could see a swell of slopes that would be close enough to walk to. She would take her son there and he would be well.

Anne Street was another world from the Calton. The tenements down her side were older and dirtier than some, but the street was broad and light. Mrs Anderson up the stair could not believe there were just the two of them in one room and kitchen, when there were so many in her own family to fit the same space on the floor above. 'And you without a man either,' she sighed admiringly.

A wood full of living trees beckoned them along the Stonelaw Road. Hawthorn blossom creamed the hedgerows on the way to Cathkin Braes. Shockingly blue hyacinths peeped from the roadside verges. In the hills beyond the town Archie's lungs filled with air as sharp as a blade, air blessed by angels, and his legs learned to scamper again. The rain on the braes tasted sweet as burn water and the wind made mother and son laugh as they whirled in it, twirled and birled in it. They took in views over dipping valleys and the silvery threads of far-off rivers, winding north to a Scotland she once knew.

After the narrow wynds and alleys around the Calton, the broad Main Street through the centre of Rutherglen was a luxury. It had been made wide for the horse fairs, in the days when the town won its reputation as the best place in the country to buy the great Clydesdales that will pull anything. When Archie was well enough, he was off down Main Street with the other lads to earn some pennies for holding a horse's head while the farmer went off for a dram. A fine sight it was the first time she saw the street filled with this shuffling, jangling mass of horseflesh, hundreds of beasts in untidy rows right the way down to the far end, nose to hind, the ones at the sides snuffling curiously into shop doorways. The traffic still has an awful job to get between them today when the fair is on, never mind folk like her who have to inch past heaving hindquarters and steaming mountains of manure just to secure a quarter-pound of mince from MacPhails. You come back smelling like a horse yourself.

She liked it here from the start. Borrowed a hammer from Mrs Anderson's man and put the name BAIN on the door. Then she worked out how much washing she would need to collect, wash, dry and deliver in a week to pay the rent. She pinned up her hair, donned her black widow's hat, her black widow's coat and her most respectable widow's smile, and went knocking on doors in the posher parts of town until she had custom enough. It was easy in those days, when she never had to think twice about where she was going; never took the wrong basket of folded laundry to the wrong house; never forgot what she had done with the wash house key.

Rutherglen gave her and Archie years together. Years and years. Years of school for him, football in the back courts, Sunday walks to Cathkin. A full, good life. Right enough, he was never completely well for longer than a few months at a time, and there were fewer and fewer spells of energy and appetite, but he rallied so often that she thought they could go on like this for ever. She really did.

That Sunday afternoon in the graveyard she spotted snowdrops in the wet soil beneath the wall. She dug them up with her fingers, liking the feel of clean, moist dirt on them, the smear of earth on her skin, earth that is earth wherever you are.

Rolled round in earth's diurnal course.

She thrust some extra soil into the apron inside her coat. She had forgotten to take it off before she went out and hoped Mrs Anderson hadn't noticed and was not even now spreading another story about the daftie down the stair. But it was just the thing to carry her booty home.

She had no trouble finding Number 13 because by then she had a mental chart to guide her if her mind happened to go white. In point of fact, her lodger was the one who suggested it. A truce in the resistance was forced on her there, right enough, because he did come up with some good ideas. He mentioned a few landmarks, like the cracked window at the far end of the street and a kink in the stonework two closes down and the lamp post right outside. And these do help. What you have to do is think hard about where you're going and not expect the direction to be there every time for the asking. You have to will yourself to ignore the clamour of sounds and the press of people along the way, which are louder and more alarming than they ever used to be. You have to try not to let the roll of wheels or the screech of the costermonger startle you from the map inside your head. And it all means you are exhausted – dear heavens, it's exhausting – by the time you climb the stairs and fumble for the key.

Fumble, mumble. It's what old women do.

But you're not old yet.

Yes you are.

No you're not.

It's only him telling you, the way he does. My beautiful girl, he says. Plenty of time to start living again, my beautiful girl.

Never done with his smiling fictions.

She put the snowdrops in the bowl. It was restful to be making something pretty – nothing to remember, nothing to forget – although she should maybe have thought about taking the sugar out first, as he did mention later, very casually.

Never mind. The snowdrops made her happy, and maybe even him being there at the fireside reading his book while she was putting them in the bowl, not saying anything, just being there, made her happy too. The tune was on her lips before she knew it.

The moment she turned from the dresser she could see on his face that he had recognised it. The wide-eyed look he gave her. It took her straight to Greenyards. The sun just out after a pounding of rain. The branches glittering with moisture. Somewhere among the trees, or below them, or behind them, a blackbird singing. The boy watching her, as she began to sing too.

'Give us a song, Jamesina,' Douglas Munro used to say. He was the second youngest, a year or two older than his brother. Always spoke first. Always the leader.

She would start on a song, never needing to be asked twice, but within two verses Douglas would be up and off with a roll of his knowing eyes. Trailing behind would be little Niall *Beag*.

At the beginning he never stayed still for long either, but when he was older he would peer up at her through the curtain of straight black hair with that shy smile that took up half his face, looking as if he would quite like to stay. He never said much that she can recall. He used to tap at his lip, first one side then the other, as if he was trying to wipe away a crumb of oatmeal with his finger, and jiggle silently from foot to foot. She would say, '*Thig a seo*, Niall, and sit you down.' And he would perch somewhere to listen, cheeks pressed into his hands.

Sometimes he sang along with her. He picked the tunes up quickly and piped away with a reedy earnestness that makes her want to laugh now to think of it. Likely it made her laugh then too, although she rarely paid him enough attention to make the kind of memories that keep. Can't even remember whether he was irritating or not, whatever she has told him. In a house that was full of them he was just another boy, with the watchfulness and the judicious self-effacement (*judicium*, 'judgement') that came of being the family's youngest. In and out of her memories of Greenyards' final months he flits, plaiting his horsehair rope, tinkering with a rusty old pistol he had for shooting crows, singing one of her melodies up some tree as she passed beneath, making owl noises with his brother.

They heard an owl when they were in Strathcarron the other day and right away it put her in mind of sitting in the twilight outside old Lizzie's house, the sky dimming around her and an owl starting on its unearthly call right at her shoulder. Then another one began from another tree and before she knew it there was such a hullabaloo of hooting that it could have been a concert just for her. Which it was, of course. As she listened, quite enthralled, to be honest, the performance ended and the youngest Munro boys burst into view, doubled up with merriment at their own cleverness. The taller one hooted derisively right in her face; the smaller one grinned. They were off before she had a chance to catch them.

She and Niall were sitting in the gloaming outside the inn in Ardgay when they heard the real one.

'Do me your owl,' she said to him.

'You want my owl impression? It's been a long time.'

There really isn't a thing on earth that surprises this man or puts him out. Without another word he cupped his hands to his mouth and made a hooting noise. Developed the performance from a general whooping to a back and forth conversation with calls and answering calls and, once he had her laughing, a few unowlish flourishes to end with.

'Will that do,' he said, 'or would you like my alligator impression next?'

19

It was the early spring of 1854 when she heard the blackbird.

It had taken the laird of Kindeace nearly nine years after Glencalvie was cleared to turn his attention to Greenyards. Maybe he had not enjoyed seeing his name in the papers that time; maybe his factor was too busy removing other folk from other glens to get round to them. There were plenty of removals going on beyond Strathcarron in estates near and far, though, and every one of them reminded the Greenyards folk of how vulnerable they were. But the years went on and nothing happened.

From this distance she can see that Glencalvie and Greenyards were both no more than details in a story of township clearance that had been going on a hundred years. From here it seems as inevitable that Greenyards would fall one day as that Archie Bain was always going to die. Maybe they knew it then too, deep down. Folk went on working and sleeping, christening their bairns and burying their dead. They prayed they would see out their own mortal days where they could watch the red kite gliding over the grassland – but likely most of them suspected they would not.

So when rumours started that the flit and remove notices

were to be delivered at last, there was nobody she can remember being that surprised. When the rumours were flatly denied by those who should know, it was hard to be sure what to believe. By the time spring came round, an undertow of anxiety was tugging at every conversation.

Her spirits were as low as anyone's. On the day she heard the blackbird she had fled the speculating and the arguing and her mother's what-are-we-to-do-now lamenting to wander outside and be miserable in the wet. Which she was for a while, standing among the dripping alders, licking rain from her lips.

But then the rain stopped, and the sun came out, and a bird began to sing. And as she listened to those liquid notes, her spirits revived. Hopefulness – a wonderful, joyous tide of hopefulness – washed right over her.

She was Jamesina Ross. She remembers saying it to herself: I am Jamesina Ross. She could write. She could count. She could think. She could parse a Latin sentence and decline a Latin noun. She could hear melodies in the white wind and the restive waters and the pulse of rain on leaf, and make songs of them in Gaelic and English. She could read a newspaper. She knew who Virgil was and how Aeneas founded Rome. She knew that people condoned inhumane practices and that words could persuade them to recognise it. There was a world outside the strath and she would possess it yet.

The blackbird's song was likely a warning to love rivals to keep away, but no harm in that. Stay your ground, bird: it's all you can do. Out he came at last, hopping into the watery light and stabbing his beak into the sodden earth. No sign of his brown mate, nor sound of her, though she was surely there too. The female blackbird's song is harder to hear. Like any woman she might have had plenty to say in there, and nobody to listen.

That was when the words came to her, and the makings of a tune. She stood under the drip of the trees, watched by Niall Munro, this skelf of a boy with his earnest, pointy face, and allowed the cadences to form.

> *An lòn-dubh a'ceilear as dèidh na froise,*
> *Teine mu sùil*
> *S an gob buidhe,*
> *A' seinn airson leannan*
> *Agus beatha as ùr.*

> *After the rain the blackbird sings.*
> *Eye ringed in fire*
> *and yellow beak,*
> *he sings for a mate*
> *and a life to come.*

> *The lass he courts is brindled brown*
> *with naked eye.*
> *Not black at all.*

> *The brownbird bides in the undergrowth,*
> *wombing her voice,*
> *she who will one day sing*
> *of life and promise*
> *at the end of the rains.*

The boy's eyes grew bigger as he listened. Skinny arms hanging at his sides, head cocked, he stopped fidgeting and became very still. He was trying to understand it, she thought, funny wee thing.

Those same eyes on her when she was humming the tune at the dresser. Those same eyes widening as he looked at her from the chair by the range and started to understand.

He began asking questions. He said he was excited to find her.

Excited.

Willie Bain raking her ruined face with mocking eyes while his fingers were busy elsewhere. He had been excited to find her too. 'Not many men would give a woman a second glance looking like that,' he said, 'but I'm not the sort to care about appearances.'

Resist. *Re* plus *sistere*, 'to make a stand'.

'Regard the prefix *re*, Jamesina. Note the number of cases in which it is employed in English to indicate repetition.'

To make a stand again and again and again.

Part IX

The Silver Man

Spring 1884

20

Their shared past was now in the open, but his landlady continued unyielding. The difficulties she was encountering with everyday tasks also made her short-tempered. When Mrs Anderson came hammering at the door before breakfast to ask for the key to the wash house, she shut the door in her face. He found the key in the cutlery drawer and slipped it to their neighbour on his way to work.

In the evenings she spoke little. Always there were shutters he could not pull up, places she declined to let him enter, hurts she would not speak of, frustrations beyond his power to avert. At night, being on the alert for sounds of distress on the other side of the wall was still costing him a good night's sleep.

He pondered their situation while he fitted up a last in the workshop or fiddled over a pattern. Intruding himself with too many questions – Have you remembered this? Where are you delivering today? Would you like me to finish off the darning since I'm handy with a needle? – only provoked her, but gestures he did not advertise could ease tensions. Sometimes he sensed that his being there was a comfort to her. Sometimes he had a feeling she actually liked him. Sometimes in the evening quiet, nothing between them but the hiss of the gas lamp and a coal sighing into the grate, he felt her eyes resting on him across the room. Understanding the terrain better, he made sure to keep his own on his work.

The great surprise was how much he relished the challenge of deeply understanding one other person. Unusually, exceptionally indeed, for someone who had required so little excuse to keep moving, he was never tempted to extract himself from a situation that was not beyond straining the seams of his own temper. The neat folds of his life were becoming daily more rumpled by feelings he could not explain for a woman with beautiful eyes and a bitter tongue and a proud black hat of inferior felt and a mind he longed to know better. In her company he had the sensation of being stripped of skin. It made him feel more vulnerable than ever he could remember being, but at the same time oddly confident, jubilant in fact, that here at last, skinless, was where he belonged.

Truthfully, he would have liked to be able to define for himself what was being created here. He was used to processes that, once identified and followed, would produce a polished product. But the relationship with his testy landlady could be neither assembled from any pattern nor, he very much doubted, ever submitted to polish. Whatever it turned out to be must be allowed to be itself, however jagged the edges, however erratic the stitching that held it together.

All he could have said for sure about the thing being made between them was its name.

*

Dr Epstein smiled at the spring flowers in a jar on the window sill. As if Wellington boots were not enough to repel all the rain in the kingdom, he was in today with an order for galoshes.

'I did not take you for a horticultural man, Mr Munro,' he murmured, lowering himself into his usual seat.

'They're for my landlady.' Good lord, was he blushing?

He had noticed primroses sprouting from dusty crevices on the floor of Stonelaw Woods, where he sometimes ate his midday sandwich now that the days were warming. The shy yellow blooms had made him think about the jug on the Anne Street dresser, the snowdrops in the sugar bowl, the pipe-clay drawings along the edge of the close. On a whim he had plucked a handful.

'Mrs Bain has a liking for flowers,' he muttered.

He was sketching a design to show how the galosh would look: oil-grained calfskin, laces to go about the leg like so, bellows tongues and hooks, wide welts, two rows of nails in the soles.

'Did you possess shoes as a boy, Mr Munro?' the doctor asked.

He answered without looking up. 'I ran the waterfront of Newark without them to start with, and to be honest I can't even remember noticing.'

'And before that? When you were growing up in . . . where was it again?'

'Greenyards.' He smiled. 'I had clogs of alder wood in the winter, as long as there was a pair passed down that year. Bare feet the rest of the time, though.'

Wet grass and mud. Sharp pebbles along the river's edge that were no trouble for a boy's weathered feet. The sting of cold water on bare ankles. His toes curving a nimble path, stone by slippery stone, across the ford. The river. The great rushing river, loud in his head now although he's not there, not at the river but somewhere else. Where is he? Up a tree, veiled by catkins. Seeing it all. Hearing it. A symphony of cracks and crunchings of wood on bone. Jamesina's friend being handed across the river along a chain of outstretched arms. She didn't make it to the ford. Why did she not make it to the ford? Run, Grace! Run!

His pencil slipped to the floor.

'Mr Munro?' The old man leaned down and picked it up for him. A soft exhalation of air as he straightened his back. 'What have you remembered? Would you care to tell me about it?'

No, he would not.

'Forgive me, sir, but perhaps another time,' he said and took back the pencil.

The flowers were not a success. He should have known she was a woman unlikely to be impressed by romantic gestures.

'I thought they might remind you of home,' he said lamely.

'Then perhaps you would be so kind as not to presume.' She turned back to the hob, leaving him to do what he wanted with the primroses drooping from his hand. 'I would rather not be reminded of anything, except maybe the day of the week and on a bad day where on God's earth I am.'

Jamesina has an exceedingly tart tongue.

But what had he been thinking of? Strathcarron was no more her home than his.

'Just you get on with being a lodger, will you, Mr Munro,'

she added for good measure, 'and stop pretending to yourself that I can give you anything more than you pay your rent for.'

Well, that was him told, as Jamesina would say. He laid the flowers on the dresser and took down the sugar bowl.

'And see and take the sugar out first if you're going to do that,' she called over.

He laughed. Couldn't help it. He laughed and laughed as he poured the sugar from the bowl into a cup. He waved it at her to show what he had done, chortling away like a madman.

She stood watching him with her arms folded and, thank heavens, an amused lift of her eyebrows.

'Would you like a cup of tea?' he said. 'I am pleased to report we have plenty of sugar.'

She was laughing herself now. 'That smile of yours,' she said. 'It always could charm the birds out of the trees.'

Thus encouraged, he proceeded with his next idea, which was going to take some nerve. Flowers would not be involved.

It was the kind of April day in Scotland that has your umbrella confused: rain tipping out of the heavens one minute, sunshine the next as if it has never been away. The latest shower cleared as he was turning into Anne Street. The sun on his face made him feel he could dare anything.

He hung up his cap and went into the kitchen. She was standing at the range, clattering pans about and not best pleased about something. She had got into the way of venting the frustrations of the day when he returned from work. By and large, he viewed this as progress.

He asked her to come and join him at the table, to which

she consented without protest. Once seated, she regarded him suspiciously. They were in the same position as on the evening he had leaned over to touch her face. This he had not planned, but it struck him as a helpful omen.

He took a breath.

'Mrs Bain, I am now going to call you Jamesina. And' – he swept on as she opened her mouth – 'I mean to tell you something important.'

'I wait with bated breath.'

'Do you remember the mirror in Bessie MacKinnon's house?'

'The Halloween mirror?'

'That's it. Exactly. Something happened there the Halloween before we left Greenyards.'

The dishcloth she had been using to lift a hot pan was still in her hands. She began to fold it. 'Were you there that night, then?'

'I was. I recall that I was wearing a bucket.'

'A bucket?' She frowned.

'It might come back to you later, but you can take it from me. It was my Halloween disguise and I was mighty proud of it, although I think my head must have been bigger than Douglas's, or it was a smaller pail, because it wouldn't come off.'

'I do remember that mirror,' she said slowly. 'What a lot of nonsense we believed in those days. And I remember the pail.'

She was starting to smile. The look she sent him could almost be described as affectionate. No, it *was* affectionate.

He reached his arms towards her, palms open on the table. She ignored them. He pressed on.

'You and Grace were peering into the mirror, do you

remember? We all crowded round. But I was at the back and I couldn't see a thing. So I climbed on a chair, and somehow or other I yanked that pail off my head and caught your eye in the mirror. Oh yes I did. You saw me.'

She was not having it. 'I think I saw every one of you in that mirror, not to mention Grace. My lovely Grace. Did you ever hear what happened to Grace?' She flapped out the dishcloth and started folding it again. He was losing her.

'Never mind Grace. I want you to focus on this one point. That Halloween night in Greenyards you looked at me.'

It could have gone either way. At least she stopped folding the damn cloth.

'I did see someone in the mirror,' she conceded at last.

'Correct. It was me.'

She shook her head so decisively that a pin flew out. 'No, it wasn't you jumping about I saw. It was something in the mirror itself. Someone. An outline of a face. Silvery. Quite eerie. All I could think was that it didn't look like Iain or the— like anyone else I knew.'

'Was it like me, then?'

The urgency of his own question took him by surprise. Planning this scene on the way home, he had imagined a light exchange about a half-remembered Halloween ritual. He had meant the story to ease his path into the trickier territory ahead. He had not foreseen the discovery that this part mattered to him. He did not believe in spirits.

'Jamesina,' he said again, 'could the figure in the mirror have been me?'

She held his eyes. Whatever she saw in them caused her own to moisten.

'It was a longish face. Slim. That's all I remember.'

He ran a hand in a V down his reasonably long cheeks. His fingers stroked his definitely narrow chin. His heart, most ridiculous of all, set about dissolving. Passionately he declared that his features were surely long enough and slim enough to satisfy the long-departed shades of a Greenyards Halloween.

At that she threw her head back and laughed. It was an open-faced, open-mouthed, open-hearted Jamesina Ross laugh, bigger than any he had heard in all the months he had been there.

'Well, Niall Munro,' she said at last, 'you really do want to be my silver man, don't you?'

He was recovering. 'My feeling on the matter is this,' he said. 'Even if you imagined the face in the mirror, and regardless of whether it is my adult form to a T (which we can agree it is), I would ask you to consider this. There was a real boy in that room making enormous efforts to leap into the frame. And you held his eye, and he remembers it. One way or another, the real love of your life was in Bessie MacKinnon's mirror. And if that is not a message from the other world, I don't know what is.'

She was not laughing now. 'If you say so,' she said, looking at the table and sounding suddenly weary.

'I do say so. And it's why' – just come out with it, man – 'it's why I am paying court to you now.'

'Oh, that.' Well, she sure did know how to build a fellow up. 'It's hardly proper when we're living in the same house.'

'Well, nobody can tell what goes on inside these walls,' he said lightly.

'Aye, and the stair has not stopped gossiping since the day you got here. Mrs Anderson has had a field day.'

'Then marry me right away, Jamesina Ross. Marry me now.' Again he put his two palms out to her on the table. 'I am asking for your hand.'

21

She looked very fine in the church with her straight back and her proud cheekbones and her silver-copper hair set off by a sea-green bonnet. Very fine indeed. He told her she could pass for a duchess any day. She said she had no interest in duchesses. Jamesina is extremely bad at taking a compliment.

He had been up three nights in a row finishing her shoes. Kidskin, straps across the front, tiny satin bow in the toe to match her hat. She came over rather misty-eyed, and said she had never in her life had feet she could not take her eyes off. He could not take his eyes from her.

At Jamesina's insistence there were no guests, although he would have liked Joseph Epstein to have been there. ('My dear Mr Munro, give the matter no thought. I'm sure I shall meet your wife in good time.') John Wilson would also have come gladly. Indeed, if there had been only one wedding guest to wish the couple well, just one, he would have wished it to be him, the man responsible for enticing him here. They would have caught one another's eye across the rows of polished pews. Mr Wilson, in the act of whipping off his spectacles, would have winked. And he would have grinned back, knowing they were both remembering the letter.

It had reached him on a sweltering afternoon in Atlanta, Georgia. In it John Wilson regretted to inform his dear boy, whom he knew to have been fond of Mrs Wilson, that he was now a widower. In the latter half of 1883, once he had sold the factory and the store in Newark and concluded all his other affairs, he planned to return to Britain to live with his eldest daughter and her husband in a pleasant town on the outskirts of Glasgow. He had made arrangements to take over a small shoemaking business there, from which the owner was shortly to retire. His former apprentice would not be surprised to learn that the prospect of returning to his roots in hand production excited Mr Wilson a great deal. However – and here, doubtless pausing to hold his glasses to the light, Mr Wilson came to the point – he was no longer young himself.

'Come with me, my dear Niall,' he urged, 'and let us share the business. We shall work together and see off the rubbish that people like me have been seducing the populace with for too long.'

Niall stood at the door of the shack he used for a workshop, enjoying the afternoon sun and reading the letter through for perhaps the fifth time. He wondered about accepting the invitation. Then he reminded himself that he was doing just fine ensuring that the better-heeled residents of Atlanta remained exactly that. Then he wondered again. Then he told himself to quit wondering. As he mused and pondered and changed his mind back and forth, he realised he was whistling a tune.

Glencalvie, oh Glencalvie, where the waters meet.

Where did that come from? And what did empty Glencalvie have to do with industrial Glasgow? Mournful melodies were for sentimental emigrants like Michael Reilly, not Niall Munro with his face to the future. And yet some impulse from the song did reach him in that balmy southern street. It was a connection sensed rather than understood, the intimation of some undefined possibility that had nothing to do with business. Impossible to grasp as any silver image in a mirror, it made up his mind for him.

Mr Wilson chose a point safely into the Atlantic crossing to tell him that he had been having second thoughts about starting again at his age. Amid a spectacularly energetic bout of spectacle polishing, he said he would receive it as the kindest of favours if his dear boy would, not to put too fine a point on it, undertake to run the little Scottish business on his own. Bespoke shoemakers were of course hard pressed by the competition from mass production – here Mr Wilson did have the grace to look sheepish – but he was confident of a respectable clientele in Rutherglen and would do his best to encourage it in Niall's direction.

He has a suspicion yet that John Wilson, who stops by the workshop every now and then to lend a hand with some finishing, planned it this way all along.

When the couple returned to Anne Street after the wedding, the situation was exceedingly awkward. They both found it so. Between leaving the house and returning, their old roles had vanished and the new ones pledged in the dim church were hard to act out with conviction. Jamesina put her apron on and barged around with the kettle, and he seated himself self-consciously by the range, wondering how he should go about installing his shaving pieces near the kitchen sink and trying to predict which side of the recess he might end up sleeping on that night without making it look as if he was eyeing the bed for something else. It was strange to be marrying your landlady, or your lodger, and neither of them knew how to be with the other.

In the afternoon he decided the moment had come. The table had been cleared and the dishes washed. The clock was ticking down more lengthy minutes of embarrassment until teatime.

'Close your eyes,' he said, and made for the parlour. Miraculously she did as he asked. She was still waiting in the middle of the room with her hands folded and eyes tight shut when he returned with his package. She looked about ten.

'Right,' he said, 'you can open your eyes.'

When she looked to him for direction, he cocked his head towards the table. There, beside a sheaf of the most dazzlingly white paper that Main Street's stationer had managed to lay hands upon, lay a goose quill pen and a bottle of ink. Jamesina looked back at him, eyes brimming.

Well done, Munro. You have made your bride cry on her wedding day.

But he knew what kind of tears these were.

She sat down at the table and picked up the slim grey feather. She ran it along her lips. She dipped the nib into the pool of dark ink. She pressed down on the top sheet of paper. The feather was not too stiff and not too pliant, and he should know: he had tested a dozen in the shop. Still, she was finding it hard to master after all this time. There were blotches and scrapes, a lot of tutting and sighing as she practised the letters.

Best not to watch. He took out his measuring tools and began fiddling with a scrap of leather. He had no idea what he was doing. He was in an agony of worry in case this went wrong.

He looked up. She had shoved the paper away. She was putting down the pen.

'All right?'

'I have nothing to write,' she said. 'The words are gone.'

'The words will be back,' he said, thinking, God, I hope so; what have I done? 'Try again. Just start writing and see what comes.'

She bowed her head and pulled the paper back towards her. He watched as the ink began to flow.

'What have you written?' he said when she was finished.

She began to read:

> *I wandered lonely as a cloud*
> *That floats on high o'er vales and hills,*
> *When all at once I saw a crowd,*
> *A host, of golden daffodils;*
> *Beside the lake, beneath the trees,*
> *Fluttering and dancing in the breeze.*

'Very nice,' he hazarded. Did clouds float? Were they ever lonely, as such? 'That's not one of yours, is it?'

She shot him her superior look. 'It's by William Wordsworth. I'm glad to have remembered it.'

'Very nice,' he said again. 'But I think I prefer yours, Mrs Munro.'

She laughed then, quite fondly. Doubtless even Jamesina had no objection to being told her poems were better than Wordsworth's. He laughed too. Then she said she had better be getting the tea on and how would he like his egg done? He said he might have a read of the newspaper.

And that is how they spent their wedding day. Which is to say, very happily in the end.

Part X

The Kitchen Bed

First light

Thursday, 24 July 1884

22

A suspicion of light in the room already and not a wink of sleep yet. You would think it would be easier to nod off when the person beside you is deep in slumber, but it never is. The breathing starts to annoy you, for all that it's quiet, and there is a part of you starts thinking it's not fair anyway, and what did he do to deserve such a good night's sleep, and why is it never his lot to get hot for no reason and then lie awake with thoughts and memories and griefs tumbling on top of each other, cupboards opening left, right and centre. Would it not be the decent thing for him to wake up and share some of them with you, never mind you were in such a hurry to be left in peace to get on with them in the first place? And why are you so contrary anyway? Is there not a single nice thought you can keep in your head for more than five minutes?

One nice thought.

He reached her through the mirror.

It made her laugh, his desperation to be her silver man. It surprised her. His eagerness moved her – and his guile, too. But when she realised where the Halloween mirror was leading him next, oh, such a weariness came over her.

It's not that she minded the way she had caught him looking

at her sometimes. It was not a look she had been expecting to see in a man's eyes again, or had been missing in the smallest degree, dear Lord no. But nobody is averse – *aversus*, past participle, 'turned away', he's *aversus*, she's *aversa*, what would *aversum* go with? 'table' maybe? no that's, what is it? that's *mensa*, but *mensa* is feminine, why would a table be—

Nobody is averse. To something or other. To whatever she saw in his eyes. But, Lord, the thought of having to start all that again. Heaven help her if a man was what she needed now.

A ruined face is one thing. Easy to forget when you never pass a mirror, and there is nobody less visible than a washer-woman anyway. Ruined below, though – that's different. You are aware of it the whole time.

Six children shoved themselves out that way, and there would have been more if Willie Bain had not done the decent thing and shuffled off this mortal coil, as Mr Aird would say, before she ended up with as many bairns as Agnes Anderson, and heaven knows what she's like down there, not that she would dream of asking her, though it's daft, when you think about it, that women never do go mentioning anything important to each other. The Queen had nine bairns herself, so she'll be the same. Can't see how it's going to be otherwise, no matter how royal you are. Funny to think of that, though maybe not so funny for Her Majesty. Bound to be the same for every woman, everything getting looser and looser as the babies come and the years go by until you are practically falling out of yourself. Think of all the thousands and millions of women having to finger their bulging insides out of the way every time they sit on a pot till the day they die and never saying a word about it to anyone, so there's nobody to warn their daughters that their body is going to start collapsing like an old jelly before their husbands lose their taste for a tight passage to bliss. The only consolation is that the breeding stops one day, and if your husband is considerate enough to drink himself to an early grave you get to lie on your own at last and sleep away your woes in peace. Bed to yourself. Covers kicked aside when the heat-storms arrive. A tot under the pillow.

All this came rushing through her head as he was coming out with his proposal. What he had in mind was not even going to involve marriage at first, if she understood aright. Cheek of him. And she so tired of a sudden and thinking, can I really be bothered?

And then something else.

He opened his hands to her on the table, and she looked at him sitting there: Niall Munro, the boy she had known and the man he had become, full of the optimism she had laid to rest herself long ago. His face had lines on it, etched into skin so leathery he could have used it for a pair of shoes and saved on stock, but eager yet. If you could see your way past the monstrosity on his lip, it had not changed that much at all.

He was baring himself, and it touched her.

She put out a hand to join his. It was a gesture of fondness, no more. She was not accepting his hand in the other sense. She is fairly sure about that, although none of it is very clear any longer because of what happened at the touch of their fingers. As skin met skin a shock went right through her. It was the most astonishing thing, this ripple of desire that set off, there and then, for a run around the ruins.

The first time he had touched her, the time he pressed his thumb to her forehead and caressed the bones and crevices of her face, she had felt comforted and safe. This was different. She could have been a girl at Glencalvie the way it took her, throat closing over, wild battering of heart, something liquidy going on with her insides.

With her other hand she reached across to his face, which she realised just then that she badly wanted to touch.

Their wedding followed with what the stair decreed was indecent haste. It took place as soon as the banns were read in the kirk next to Archie's garden. No guests, although Mrs Anderson was on and on at her to come and Niall had a couple of elderly men he thought of inviting. No, she told him. She wanted no fuss, no folk in the pews to go whispering to each other, well, that's a funny one for him to choose, handsome man like that; older than him, too, as anyone can see.

She bought herself a green hat and he made her the best-fitting shoes she had ever had on her feet. Grace would have loved this man, she thought.

'With my body I thee worship,' he said to her in the kirk.

Well, she took that with a pinch of salt.

She had made up her mind she was not going to apologise for what he would find in her bed. If she could wear her hair as high as a duchess, walk tall in shops she could not afford and carry other women's sanitary rags as if they were the crown jewels, she could surely be proud of herself in her own bed.

Only it was not pride she was feeling as he reached for her on their wedding night. How can he want this wrecked body? she was thinking. How can he love this dry heart? It was more like fear than pride, the kind of fear that so tangles itself in hope that you don't know which is which. And at the same time she was telling herself that she was as she was, that she had not asked for this and he could go straight back to the bed in the parlour or a lodging somewhere else if he did not like it.

Which did help. Especially when she realised he was nervous himself. Hard to remember how she knew and it's difficult to tell with him anyway. He is inclined to smooth himself out like drifting snow when she would rather be keeping an eye on the shape of his footprints. (That's quite poetic.) But there was something he said about hoping his moustache didn't bother her, knowing it was not his best feature as far as she was concerned, which made her realise she was not the only anxious one that night. And that calmed her right down.

And that is when she thought, well, never mind me – let's just see what he's got going for himself down there. And it was fine after that. Fine.

With my body I thee worship.

Who would have thought it?

That night she gazed on him with a kind of awe as he slept. After all the misgivings and insecurities, what she had not accounted for, not for one minute prepared herself for, was what it felt like to have him close: the particular pleasure of hearing the breath of another living being who was not Willie Bain competing with her own, now slower, now faster, and feeling the vibrations of another chest rising and falling, rising and falling, as if – and here was the revelation – as if life could be borne, the piling griefs of it, the disappointments and confusions of it, as long as this chest continued to rise and fall at her side.

Add this, then, to the scales. Not Paul's scales, or was it Saul? Not Zeus's scales, weighing out godly portions of death. Just the ones Mr Pinkerton has for weighing out tea.

Marriage scales.

A brass weight on one side for having to put up with the heaving about on nights you are not in the mood for worship. This to include the general nuisance of not being able to claim some peace in your own bed whenever you feel like it or help sleep on its way with a mouthful of something that is no business of his.

Another weight for the times you are so hot and bothered you can hardly bear another body within two yards of you under any circumstance whatsoever.

A weight on top of that for having to put up with a man you still think of as a boy sometimes, really you can't help it, waltzing in and taking charge in your own house, complaining about not having a mirror, dragging you to see a head-doctor without a by-your-leave, maddening you with his implacable placidity, or placid implacability, which is it? same Latin root, *plac-* something, don't know, should know, *placere*, maybe? to do with pleasing. He pleases me, yes he does, he pleases me a lot of the time, most of the time, but it's aggravating to have him going on and on with his, have you remembered to do this and do that? although he tries not to, she can see that, and him always thinking quicker, working out bills faster, likely able to turn his hand to darning a sock better if he is ever let loose on it, which he never will be, not in a million years.

Down go the scales. Clunk.

Then you start on the other side, and there are times you can't think of a single thing to put there. Not a thing. Peace and quiet is all you want. Peace to scream out your grief in the night if you feel like it. Let me alone, you want to say. You do say it sometimes. Give me back my surly widowhood, my solitude, my routines, my regrets, my defences.

But then there are other times you look at him lying the way he is now, so tidy and quiet and solid, and you start pouring the tea or whatever it is, sugar maybe, into the grocer's bowl on the other side of the scales and you can't stop. You're pouring to the brim, the bowl is overflowing, you've got tea leaves and sugar all over the place and still you are pouring.

The weight of your head in the crook of an arm.

The touch of a punctured thumb on your forehead.

A steady voice when agitations come in the night.

Salt in the potatoes.

Primroses in the sugar bowl.

A song in the dark.

A feather dipped in ink the colour of the night sky.

The glimmer of an understanding that it might be safe to visit the person you used to be, the person you stopped being when a policeman's baton swung at your head and Willie Bain took his vicious pity on you and your children left you and your songs died and the sort of life you never dreamed could happen happened because that's how life takes the dreamers sometimes – the beginnings of a sense, put this in your scales, that it might be safe to go there all the same, one step at a time, because when you come back you know he will still be here.

Part XI

The Sheriff

March 1854

23

Sheriff-substitute Dougal Rankin, Ardgay Inn, near Tain,
Ross-shire
To Sheriff Kenneth Miller, Castle Hill, Inverness

31 March 1854
9 a.m.

Sir,

*I am pleased to report that the expedition, conducted early this
morning in accordance with your instructions to enforce lawful
delivery of summonses of removal to the tenantry of Greenyard in
Strathcarron, has proved successful.*

*Twenty constables from Ross-shire and fifteen from Inverness
marched during the night from Dingwall by way of Alness to
Midfearn, where they joined my own party on arrival from Tain
before daybreak. We proceeded by carriages to within two miles of
Greenyard, after which we marched with all speed to surprise the
people. However, it became quickly apparent that they were
prepared for us. We soon heard whistles from different quarters,
which we knew were signals of our approach. On the arrival of the*

Police party, we found the people already assembled and ready to resist.

Your instruction was to act 'with vigour' against the lawlessness for which this County has now an unenviable notoriety, not least because it has been suggested that the forces of the law have not used their batons with proper spirit and energy when under previous attack. I trust you will conclude, when furnished in due course with the full details, that vigour was not wanting.

May I emphasise, however, that the Police acted with great restraint. Although I deeply regret the injuries which occurred, I am satisfied that if the Police had not forced a passage into Greenyard in the manner they did, our party would have been deforced and maltreated, as has happened on numerous previous occasions, not least in the Strathcarron glen itself in recent weeks. In short, they would have been stripped naked by the women; and, without decisive action, it would have confirmed the idea that women have an immunity from attack (for which reason they are always put in the front of the mob), thus encouraging the refractory spirit among them. I am glad to report that the constables themselves sustained no injuries during the encounter.

Due in no small part to the forethought which went into this expedition, the trial of strength (if it does not unduly elevate acts of repeated insurrection to describe them thus) between the peasantry of Ross-shire and Her Majesty's Police Force has come to a satisfactory conclusion. It will be applauded by all who have deplored the almost systematic opposition to the law in this County, whereby the inhabitants of an Estate believe themselves at liberty to prevent a landlord from exercising his legal rights to serve notices of removal upon his own tenantry inhabiting his own land.

After taking some little rest here after the rigours of a long night,

I shall return to Tain, where the ringleaders of the riot will appear at the Tolbooth in due course. A private intercession regarding bail has already been made to me by the minister of the Free Church at Bonar, Reverend Gustavus Aird, who pressed his concerns with some importunity as the Fiscal and I alighted at the inn. You may rest assured that due process will be followed when the prisoners arrive in Tain, whither they are being escorted as I write. Further arrests may be expected to follow.

 I remain yours faithfully,
 Dougal Rankin, Sheriff-substitute

Part XII

The Kitchen Bed

Dawn

Thursday, 24 July 1884

24

Gathering with the other women that day, Friday, the 31st of March 1854. There's a date she will never forget, or maybe she will the way things are going, but she is remembering it now all right.

It's nearly light in the room. She's not going to be able to sleep at all, is she? Not a hope of it now.

The Greenyards sky is also just beginning to lighten, as she is seeing it now. There is a faint whiff of wild garlic in the air. It came to her again one spring on the way to Cathkin Braes, when she and Archie were dawdling past a verge of greenery capped with snowy flowers. The scent placed her back in Feàrnaich field so fast she had no time to run, and the boy had to tug her away.

The field lies just above the river, at the point where a cart track emerges from the trees and into the open. Up the brae is Lizzie's house, and a curl of smoke beyond that marks the Munros'. The land down here is pocked with furrows and ditches, some of them filled with overnight puddles you can hardly see, difficult to walk across with a skirt at your ankles. All the women stumbled a bit as they were lining up. A mallard has just skittered into the river, honking his outrage into the silence and making everyone smile.

There are clusters of trees right along the riverside and all the way up the burn. When she saw them again the other day, they looked much the same. They are alders mostly, the trees that gave the field its Gaelic name: *Feàrnaich*, alders in abundance. The roots of the alder enjoy sucking up the wet, so they have a high time of it in Strathcarron. Abundant alders. *Abundare*, from *unda*, 'a wave'. Waves of alders, dripping with catkins in March and waiting for their leaves to come.

When you cut an alder, its pale flesh turns an angry blood-orange. There were stories about that, how a bleeding alder meant bad luck. There were even one or two folk who shunned the tree for that reason, which was difficult when alders were everywhere, but those were usually the same ones who said the fairies wore clothes dyed in its flowers. It faded in time, the bleeding of the cut wood, and then it became brown and useful for all sorts of things.

It was the kind of morning on the threshold of dawn when you sense everything holding its breath: the ground soft and expectant, the air eager for the sun, the stillness pregnant with vitality but not quite there yet. Any day now the trees would explode and flowers shoot from the earth and toads make their bid for freedom and scents assail you and the rowdy geese roister home. But for the moment the land was waiting.

She was waiting too. They were all waiting, maybe sixty folk in lines four or five deep, very still, very quiet, very alert, waiting for the light, waiting for the policemen to tramp the last couple of miles down the cart track to the Greenyards boundary with the eviction notices: those dreaded papers, written in a legal English that most of the folk whose lives were so hurt by them would have struggled to understand. They required the main tenants to flit and remove themselves, their bairns, family, servants, subtenants, cottars and dependants, their cattle, goods and gear, and to leave the said subjects void and redd, that the pursuer may then enter thereto, possess and enjoy the same in time coming. Something like that. She had it off by heart once.

Possess and enjoy. Hard to imagine the laird of Kindeace enjoying old Lizzie's house.

Most of their own men had stayed away from Feàrnaich field, same as they did at Glencalvie all those years before, when the women stopped the sheriff at the bridge. Women were always to the fore when the notices arrived at Highland townships. There must have been a first time somewhere, some time, when one woman had looked at another woman and said, 'It's up to us to stop them.' And maybe they had set light to a notice and jeered some nervous message-boy of a sheriff's officer back the way he had come. And maybe nobody got put in jail for it. And maybe the word had spread to other places that this was the way to do it. However it started, by the time the Strathcarron townships were being cleared it was accepted that resistance would be led by the folk least likely to be arrested.

In the eyes of some men, holding off the summonses from being delivered was as much women's work as stirring the oats – and maybe that suited them. Maybe it suited a few of them to disappear when trouble came. They had trouble enough in their lives, these folk, and they were weary of it.

But the women never hesitated. Not that she ever saw anyway. If they could stop the notices getting into the hands of the tenants named on them, they might win the community another season, another crop cycle, a few more months or even years before the authorities came back to try again. And that was always worth it. It had been worth it at Glencalvie, even if they did find themselves trudging to Croick's graveyard in the end, on a bleary May morning with their homes on their backs.

Still, it was not all women there that morning on the eastern march of Greenyards. Some men stood at the back. She remembers waving to an old soldier, jaunty in his blue bonnet, who was watching from the side.

She was at the front. Big Ann Munro and Christy Ross were next to her, one on either side. The sisters Margaret and Annie Mackenzie were behind, along with wee Hughina Chisholm the midwife. Grace had slipped across the ford to join them. Bessie MacKinnon, pale, limp sort of lassie, had wandered along to watch as well.

She enjoyed the smooth chill of the stone in each fist. The boys and girls who had been out watching on the hills all night said they had never seen so many police before. It felt good to have something to grip.

Rumours of removal had been worming their way around Greenyards for most of the year past. Reports also arrived from other townships in the same position, and spirits rose or fell with the fate of them. Grave tidings came from Knoydart, way over in the west, but folk were heartened by accounts of successful resistance in Coigach by Loch Broom. The sheriff's officers had gone there five times to deliver the summonses and five times they were thwarted. In the end the Coigach women took the notices off one of the officers, stripped every stitch of clothing from his back and packed him off in his boat as naked as the day he was born. And that was that: the law never came back.

They talked of little else at Greenyards that year. She can hear those women debating tactics yet, their voices, their faces, the ebb and flow of their arguments.

Ann Munro thought humiliating the men into staying away was always the way to do it. Shaming was a useful weapon when you had no others, and Big Ann knew all about that, as Grace would have been the first to tell you.

Young Margaret Mackenzie – quiet lassie, thoughtful blue eyes in a forest of freckles – was more likely to point out that men did not like being humiliated, and especially not, she would have thought, lairds and sheriffs. Would Coigach's success not make the law all the more determined elsewhere?

Her sister Annie – freckly woman too, a bit older – always had to think the opposite of whatever Margaret thought. The women used to laugh about it. Annie said Margaret should hold her tongue until she had something sensible to say: the Coigach folk were in their homes yet, and if it could work in one place it could work in another.

Pointy-faced Hughina Chisholm said the thing was to wear the authorities down, never mind how long it took, because people were writing about Coigach and Knoydart in the news-papers and it was making a lot of folk in Glasgow and Edinburgh uneasy. London too.

Christy Ross was never one for reasoned argument. This time that she's remembering, Christy just folded her arms, big as hams, and said no sheriff was going to take her house off her that had just been thatched last summer and a beautiful job her man had made of it.

'But what about Knoydart?' says Margaret Mackenzie.

Knoydart. A peninsula, they call it, which is a lovely word that Mr Aird taught her, just lovely. Latin *paene*, 'almost', and *insula*, 'island'. An almost-island poking into the sea across from the isle of Skye. When people wrote about Strathcarron being remote, they had likely never tried getting to the townships along the sea fringe of Knoydart, which were being cleared that year to settle the debts of some laird, whichever one that was. A ship was arranged to carry the whole population off to Australia.

Likely some of the Knoydart folk were glad to get away. They had had a terrible time of it in the potato famines and were poor as poor. But not everyone wanted to go. There were all sorts of people who didn't think much of their chances of surviving the journey – sick folk, old folk, women expecting bairnies, nursing mothers – and others who were just plain obstinate about not going to a place they knew nothing about when nobody had asked them in the first place. When the ship anchored off Skye, plenty of them did as they were told and got into the boats to be ferried across, but others refused and took to the hills. The factor's men went and destroyed every house after that, whether it belonged to those who had sailed or those who stayed, and they were left with nothing.

There was a man alerting folk to what was going on in Knoydart. He was a Glasgow lawyer by the name of Donald Ross, who was born on the Skibo estate not that far from Strathcarron, if she remembers correctly. Mr Aird told her about him. He had been writing angry letters to the *Northern Ensign* about what happened after the emigrant ship sailed. Even after all this time she can recall the shock of reading about folk living in mounds of earth like molehills. The hole where one old woman cooked and slept had put the writer in mind of where he kept his pet rabbits as a boy. A man and four bairns lived in the space between a collapsed roof and a wall. Another family was trying to shelter under an old sail, while the freezing winter winds birled in from the sea.

She was the one who helped Ann Munro and Christy Ross to get Greenyards organised. Her task was to send the older lads and lassies out to keep watch on the approaches to the strath. She dispatched some up Ardgay hill, others to watch the road along the firth from Tain, a few to keep an eye on the drove-path down from Alness.

She has a memory of black-haired Niall Munro earnestly practising his whistle: two fingers of each hand in his mouth and a screaming blast. Would this do? Was it loud enough? How many times should he make the signal if he spied strangers? What should he do after?

One long whistle was fine, she told him. That should be loud enough for the next person to hear and pass it on. 'And no false alarms, Niall *Beag*.' Then he was to run down the hill and fast as he could along the river, shouting a warning to everyone he passed. He pushed his hair out of his eyes with that thin hand of his and looked at her in the assessing way he had. Aye, he said, she could rely on him.

*

Twice that March they had a visit from the authorities and twice the system worked well. The whistling started, the women ran out and the notices were never delivered.

First time it was just the one sheriff's officer came, with a witness in tow. Christy Ross strode forward and wanted to see the evidence that the summonses had been authorised by the tacksman, who lived in a good house on the north bank and held the lease for the tenants. He had kept on denying that any removal was planned. When the sheriff's officer could produce no such evidence, Christy and Ann, who had more beef on them than either of the men, grabbed the officer, searched his pockets and set light to the notices from a fire they had ready in the usual fashion.

You would not be calling those women gentle, but there was no harm done to anything that day save some male pride. Afterwards a couple of the Greenyards men went to the Ardgay Inn with them and bought them their supper and a dram to prevent any hard feelings, although that would not be what the sheriff's officer told his superiors likely. He definitely left with all his clothes on, whatever was said after.

Two weeks later the whistling started up again. This time the message came that three official-looking men were on their way. Seemed they had already been drinking at the inn and were weaving about the road. By the time they got to where the women were blocking their way, they could hardly put a sentence together and were finding it all a great joke. There was a fair bit of banter backwards and forwards, and some laughs at their expense because these men hardly knew the time of day – until the moment came that Ann Munro demanded sight of the authorisation for the removals, when it turned ugly.

The leader of them, glaikit character with a lot of whiskers, can see him now, put a hand in his pocket and took out a pistol. He jerked it towards Big Ann.

Everyone just stood there taking a breath in and thinking what to do next, when out between the women bursts Niall *Beag*, half the size of this man. And what is he holding in both his hands but the old gun he kept for crows. And he's pointing it at the whiskery man and shouting at him in his squeaky voice that if he dares to meddle with his mother, he will face the consequences.

There was a horrible pause. Ann Munro looked as if she didn't know whether to kiss her son or skelp him. But thank the Lord, the man took one look at the boy, made some sort of tipsy calculation and shoved his pistol in his pocket. Then the three of them turned on their heels and lumbered off back down the road.

The women let their breaths out. Big Ann must have decided on the skelping, because she roared for Niall *Beag* to come here this minute. At which he dropped the gun and made off faster than the men had.

There were celebrations in Greenyards that night all right. Looking back, it's hard to believe they could have imagined this was the end of it. She does remember freckly wee Margaret Mackenzie shaking her head and saying could they not imagine the tales being told of them right now in Tain, and did they really think those men would admit to being chased away by a bunch of women and a boy with a crow gun? It would be an armed riot by the time they told their stories.

'Don't be so daft,' said Annie Mackenzie. 'You know fine we never touched a hair of their heads.'

'That's not what they'll say, though,' Margaret said. She also muttered something about not being surprised if Niall Munro came to regret that gun. Big Ann said she would be seeing to it that he regretted it the moment she caught him, but likely that won't be what Margaret meant.

The light was growing rosier over Feàrnaich field. It was the third time they had gathered to resist the summonses, but the atmosphere this morning was tenser, with none of the usual banter and bravado. The whistling that summoned them had been clamorous. Not just one or two sheriff's men but dozens of police constables had been seen spilling drunkenly out of their carriages at the point where the road from Ardgay gave out and anyone pressing forward must do it on foot. Now the lookouts were streaming back and had been told to keep out of the way.

Sounds from the trees. Brushed leaves. The crack of twigs. Careless feet approaching.

She is back there again.

A horde of black uniforms looming out of the grey wood and lining up in untidy rows before them. Shock at how many they were up close.

A man at the front shouting that he was the sheriff and they had to clear the way so that his officer could serve lawful summonses of removal on the tenants.

Christy Ross bustling forward to show the sheriff some letter she had that proved, so she was shouting, that the removal had not been authorised.

Batons raining on Christy's head. Her own breath buckling

at the sight of it. Christy's cap shredded. Blood all over. Women screaming as she goes down.

Big Ann bellowing. Big Ann on the ground.

Policemen hitting out. Women scattering.

She is running too, Grace in front of her.

Screams everywhere, roars everywhere, policemen everywhere, flailing arms in uniforms, Grace falling.

Don't touch her. Don't you dare touch my Grace.

She is pummelling a policeman with her fists. She is trying to get Grace to wake up. She is shaking her shoulders.

Wake up, Grace, wake up. *Fosgail do shùilean.* Please open your eyes.

25

He is startled out of a troubled sleep in which an enraged Miss Elspeth Taylor has been brandishing a giant shoe at him, screaming that it's all wrong, a monstrosity, look at the size of it, how could he do this to her, she will refuse to wear it. 'It's horrible!' she is yelling, launching the shoe at him, which is now as big as a boat. He puts up an arm to protect his face, only to find hands there already, dozens and dozens of hands. They are pawing and clutching at his face. They are suffocating him.

'Woah,' he says, prising them off. He grips the fingers tight in his own. 'Woah, woah, woah, what's this?'

His eyes adjust to the shape of his assailant. Jamesina is kneeling over him, pleading with him to wake up.

'It's all right, *mo chridhe*. I'm awake now. It's all right.'

He brings her hands to his lips, first one, then the other.

'Where's Grace?' she is saying.

Still holding tight to her hands he wriggles into a sitting position and draws her beside him, until they are both resting against the back wall of the recess.

'Look at me, Jamesina. Can you see me? It's over now.'

'Where is Grace? I want to know where Grace is.'

'You know where Grace is, Jamesina.'

'She's hurt. She's terribly hurt.'

He eases her head to his shoulder. 'That's better, *mo chridhe*. That's better.'

With his free hand he strokes her forehead and begins to hum a tune.

On no account, his mother said, was he to come anywhere near Feàrnaich field that morning. He was to get on with his watch duties, pass on the warning if strangers were seen and then be gone. If she got so much as a sniff of him within a mile of the Greenyards march, he would not be sitting down for a week.

It had taken diligent planning to sprint back through the twilight dawn in time to drape himself along the bough of one of the alder trees over the burn before the first of the women arrived. He managed it, wedging himself behind a veil of catkins at a height which would command an unobtrusive view of the people gathering, his mother in particular.

No mistaking his mother. Bulging arms crossed, back dangerously erect, eyes shrunk to grim dots, Anna *Mhòr* settled into an intimidating pose at the front that boded ill for the other party in any dealings to come, as well he knew from experience. Jamesina Ross stood next to her, a much slighter figure than his mother but also radiating danger. Her eyebrows were folded into the determined expression he knows all too well today. Her arms hung at her sides, weighted by stones.

A woman on Ann's other side had a piece of paper in her hand, which she began holding aloft like a flag long before there was anyone there to show it to. Christy Ross. She and his mother were of similar age and physique, with a great many children between them. He remembers them being close, always in and out of each other's houses. 'As Christy says' added every kind of weight to Ann's stories.

Anyone who encountered these three women, the boy in the tree was thinking, must surely quail.

Around and behind them were neighbours he recognised from both sides of the river and from further along in Amatnatua as well, although most of their names he has long forgotten. Were they carrying weapons? He has a feeling that a few had stones, but if so they never had a chance to throw them; if any had sticks, they were useless. The charge when it came was as swift and savage as a pack of dogs let loose among Jamesina's hens.

Not a sound came from the women as thirty or forty men straggled out of the trees and into full view. It was a dreadful shock to see the numbers, the clenched wooden batons, the air of menacing intent. Here were no reluctant messengers to be thwarted by humiliation, no beardless youths to be tricked out of their clothes and their summonses, no clueless bunch of Tain gentry who could be fobbed off for now and soothed later by a dram in the inn. Here was an unshaven force of Her Majesty's constabulary, fired up by whisky, a night without sleep and, by the look of it, some very specific orders.

They halted in front of the women. Christy Ross stomped forward to show her paper to the man in command, still waving it high and trying to explain something as she approached. At the same time his mother marched over to one of the policemen and demanded in her most stentorian voice to see the authority for the removals, because it was her understanding that it had not been received. 'Go you and ask the sheriff for me,' Ann said loudly.

He remembers a second, two seconds, of feeling proud of his mother: of her size and magnificence; of her gay blue dress; of the big shawl about her chest that he was not so many years past burrowing into to sob out the grievances of a persecuted youngest brother; of the courage it took to speak out with all those men in their scruffy uniforms arrayed in front of her, fingering their truncheons. The gush of pride was still surging through him when he saw the policeman glance from his mother to the sheriff, who was undergoing a similar tirade from Christy Ross, and the sheriff return the glance. And then there was mayhem.

Three men made for Christy Ross and she crumpled. One of them followed up his baton with a kick to her head. Niall stared with such horror that he missed the blow that felled his mother. But he did hear her voice. She was sitting on the ground, knees drawn awkwardly to her face, head held in both hands. 'Murder!' she cried. Which had plainly not occurred, or at least not yet, because enough air remained in her lungs to yell it again very loud indeed. She was silenced with such a volley of blows that he made an involuntary yelping noise. He shoved the knuckles of his left hand into his mouth to stop himself doing it again.

In the years and tens of years after the battle of Feàrnaich field, Niall Munro rarely looked back. Following the sun, he never willingly glanced over his shoulder at childhood shadows. But there were times he could not help it. Whenever he came upon an alder tree over water in an early New Jersey spring, he would be spirited back to Feàrnaich field, regardless of will or desire. As soon as he caught a whiff of that faint, spicy sweetness he was back in this tree: the boy on the branch, curtained by catkins, with a gnawn fist in his mouth.

Now his mother was motionless on the ground and two men were standing over her. After considering a moment they squatted down on either side and heaved her on to her back. That it should take two men to move his mother sent another billow of pride through him. He could see her face again now. It was matted with earth and blood and coils of stuck hair, and her eyes were closed. One of the men sat down on her stomach, seized her wrists and thrust her hands into a pair of iron cuffs. At least she could not be dead if they were arresting her: nobody went to the trouble of arresting a dead woman. He could see blood on her cap.

The rest of the field swam into focus. While the first two women were being dealt with, the main force had leaped forward and policemen were striking at any flesh within reach of their batons. Women were fleeing in all directions. There were two sisters, he remembers, who were always bickering with each other. He and Douglas used to imitate them. 'I assure you, my dear, that white is black,' Douglas would mince. 'You are quite wrong, sister, as you always are,' he would reply in a shrill whine. 'How can you be so foolish as not to see that black is always and in every conceivable circumstance white.'

Now the younger of them lay sprawled on the ground, a crumpled bird, and the other came rushing over with a wail of anguish. She knelt down and wiped the earth from her sister's mouth and eyes. How well he remembers the tenderness with which her hands moved over that bloodied face. She tore a strip from her apron and was busy tying it around the younger sister's head when an officer approached from behind. Niall saw him coming. He might have shouted a warning, perhaps, if it had not happened so fast, although what defence would an alert have afforded her? He thinks he heard her skull crack. Perhaps he did.

Once, when he was nursing his mother in Newark, wiping tears from her eyes, snot from her nose, drool from that generous mouth, the clubbing of those two sisters on Feàrnaich field returned to him with shocking force. He put both hands over his ears, as if that would put an end to the racket of fracturing bone inside his own head. Then he ran outside, stood with his face to the wall of the house and shook. He has never spoken of this to Dr Epstein. There are some things he will not put into words for anyone.

The older woman toppled across her sister's chest under the impact of the blow and they remained like that, piled on top of each other like discarded dolls.

The wounded lay all over the field. Women with their blue gowns shredded across their backs. Women bleeding from head and face. Women kicked in the groin. Women with elbows broken, shoulders cracked, skulls smashed. Women knelt on as handcuffs were locked. Women chased through ditches and in and out of trees. Women screaming as bone shattered. Women groaning. Women prostrate on the gory earth making no noise at all.

He watched and he listened to it all.

Careering between jumbled boulders and listing trees on its way down, the burn spilled into the Carron a short distance below his tree. Further along the river, drawn by the commotion perhaps, more women were crossing at the ford. Tiny blue-skirted figures they looked from where he was. They came running one by one along the beach of pale stones and began clambering up the grassy ledge and on to the field. Perhaps it was only then that they understood they had arrived in the middle of a battle, that here was a rout, that there would be no escape. But it may be that those who came late realised exactly what they were entering and faced it with the same courage his mother had shown. Dropping to their knees to tend the wounded, they were attacked with such ferocious speed that some could not have known whence the blow came.

You never forget what terror looks like when you have once seen a mouth gape and lips draw back; seen eyes dilate; caught the exact instant when an entire body is paralysed and the next when it understands it must fly. There was one woman who had only just arrived from the other side – not Grace, older than Grace – and was stooping to assist someone on the ground, when two policemen spotted her. They were already bearing down by the time she looked up, and it was then that he caught the look of terror. She leaped up, bunched a handful of skirt in one hand to liberate her legs and raced away towards one of the copses at the field's fringe. Leaping over every ditch in her path she was almost at the wood, almost beyond his sight and the reach of her pursuers, when she came on a third officer. The man was crouching in the grass, waiting for her like a cat.

She saw him in time, veered to the right and headed back towards the river. The pursuers stayed close behind, gaining on her enough to land an outstretched baton on one shoulder but not to stall her. On she ran above the riverbank, dodging in and out of thickets, catching more glancing cracks as she went. He could tell what was in her mind. She was trying to reach a point where the river was shallow enough to wade across. But it was deep here and fast, foaming in its rush, and the men were nearly upon her.

Jump! he thought. Do it now.

On the other side of the river people were also watching. He remembers the clamour as the woman, policemen at her heels, took a great leap from the edge of the field into the water.

A shout arose from the opposite bank. It was the woman's husband, so he heard later, who had not even been aware that she had crossed the river until he recognised the flying hair as she leaped, and the patterning of her shawl.

For a moment her dress billowed out like a blue sail on the deep. Then it darkened. Then it began to sink.

Her husband jumped in from the other side. He tried to grab her, but the current was so strong that she was already past him. Her head appeared and was lost, appeared and was lost. The man lunged for her in a frantic struggle to overtake the current. The onlookers on the far bank were running alongside, calling their encouragement as the tiring husband kept trying to throw himself after the bobbing head, until at last the river carried both of them past the gaze of the boy in the tree and he could see no more.

By the time he restored his attention to the field, Bessie MacKinnon was about to fall. Her mouth opened in an O of pure astonishment at the raised baton, and she went down like a hewn branch, felled by such a heavy blow to the ear that he closed his eyes. The little Greenyards midwife, a tiny woman whose name he can't recall, was already on the ground a little distant. She started crawling over. 'Bessie,' she was calling, 'oh, Bessie.'

Bessie's attacker turned. The midwife saw him coming. Up she stood, found her balance, waited for the baton to descend and then – is this why he has never since been tempted to confuse brawn with mettle? – she grabbed the end of it. A woman no taller than he was himself, she twisted a deft wrist and hurled the baton into the trees by the burn, a little too close for the solidity of his own bowels. Then she made off up the brae as fleet as a roe.

And all this while, which can't have been very long because the whole attack was over in minutes, his mother was still on the ground in handcuffs and he was wondering not very coherently what he could do to help her. A handful of their own men were tackling the policemen now, creating a noisy melee in the middle of the field.

Off to the left, the old fellow who used to tell him and his brothers stories about Waterloo (a swerve always advisable if you had a task to finish) was on the ground too. A few feet beyond him a young woman was urging another young woman to open her eyes.

'Wake up!' Jamesina Ross was shouting, shaking Grace's wispy body. 'Wake up!'

Whirling round, she aimed a punch at the nearest policeman. He whacked her across the head with his baton, and she collapsed at once. But the officer, huge fellow, was not finished. He set about kicking Jamesina with his big, black boots. He kicked her shoulder first, and then he kicked her face.

*

238

The thumb of his stroking hand finds the dent in her forehead. He circles, presses, rubs. Round and round.

Mo chridhe, mo chridhe.

He kisses the broken cheekbone, feeling with his lips for the place where it has never knitted from that day to this.

The policeman moved on. Jamesina lay without moving, but Grace was now swaying to her feet. She began to weave towards the river with a motion between a crawl and a crouch. Another constable, detaching himself from the grunting male skirmish in the middle of the field, noticed her.

'Run, Grace,' he breathed from his tree.

The man caught up with her as she reached the water. The flat stones where the river could be safely forded were still too far off, but the pursuer was close behind so she waded in anyway. The water rose to her waist.

For many long moments Grace stood swaying in the middle of the river. From the vantage point of his tree, he could see her dilemma. She was reluctant to hazard another step in case the river went suddenly too deep, as it did thereabouts. Her pursuer hung about on the shore watching her, until at last he stumbled back up the polished beach and on to the field. As soon as he was gone, Grace waded back the way she had come and collapsed on a bank of sand.

Now the onlookers on the northern bank acted. One after another they slipped into the water, each linking hands with the next until they had strung themselves across the broad stream in an untidy line, some up to their chests in water. Each man had to find a foothold on the stones beneath before the next link could be made. He knew those stones, knew their treachery, knew the force of the river if your feet slid off.

At last one man reached the sandbank. He scooped the limp bundle into his arms and passed it to the next man. The last the boy saw of Grace Graham was her hair dipping in and out of the water as her thin figure lolled along the line of hands to the far bank.

The last he saw of Jamesina Ross was her crumpled body, her face pressed away from him into the ploughed earth of Feàrnaich field.

'Better now?' he says.

She snuffles a nod into his shoulder.

'Would a cup of tea help?'

Another nod.

'How about I go and make us both a cup, then,' he says.

26

Now that he has drawn the window curtains open, the shapes in the room are coming back. This weakly dawn light is different from the retreating light at the other end of the night. She is not exactly sure how it's different and is too tired to work it out. All she knows is she has not had a wink of sleep between the one and the other.

They are sitting up in bed together, shoulders touching, each steadying a cup and saucer on the bedclothes. Getting the fire going again to heat the kettle was a bit of a palaver and she was itching to tell him not to bother, but it was worth the wait in the end.

Congratulating herself on a heroic degree of self-control, she has not commented on the strength of the tea or the two leaves swimming prominently on its surface. He must be tired too.

'I'm sorry,' she says, taking a careful sip. 'I didn't mean to turn the night into a party.'

'Not to worry. This is cosy, isn't it?' Really the man is a saint. 'And it's always good to get some practice in with fixing tea the way you like it.'

'Fixing?' These expressions he has picked up on his travels. 'How in the world do you fix tea?'

He ignores her, which is a thing he is good at when it suits him. Instead he warms his hands around his cup and starts musing.

'Do you know, I have been remembering a good deal about Feàrnaich field tonight. I suppose seeing it again has brought it to the surface. But I was thinking there when I was making the tea – *making* the tea, you note – how little I ever knew, or asked, or even wondered, about what happened to the women who were hurt that day. All I knew about was my mother. I had no idea what happened to you afterwards. I never heard what became of Christy Ross, or Bessie MacKinnon, or those two sisters who used to argue with each other, or the woman whose husband tried to rescue her from the river, or any of them. There must have been such—'

'Damage,' she finishes for him. 'I've been thinking it too. There must have been such awful damage.'

Ancient damage.

She takes another sip. 'If it had not been for Donald Ross, nobody but the folk of Greenyards would have known about any of it. Not the way it really happened anyway.'

'Who is Donald Ross?'

'A man we should be grateful to,' she says.

It had taken a long time to understand that she was in a strange bed, that this was Migdale light playing on the wallpaper, that it was Mr Aird's housekeeper bringing in trays of food she could not eat, that it was a doctor whose touch on her cheek made her scream in agony, that her mother was the person who kept footering with her pillow and whose brisk bedpan manoeuvres shot bolts of pain around her body. Her mother had come to nurse her as soon as she was brought to the manse from Feàrnaich field on Mr Aird's orders, fretting that she should have been on the field herself instead of sitting inside with old Lizzie, listening head in hands to the cries from down the brae. Every time she looked at her daughter, she wept.

It was days before she could focus on a face herself, or take in what anyone was saying, or say anything back. Words cavorted in her head but refused to line up in the right order before her lips. Folk drifted in and out of her room, took a seat by the bed and stood up again, spoke and fell silent, prayed (in Mr Aird's case) so energetically that her head sounded with the noise of it, cried so often (in her mother's) that she would have ordered her to stop if she could have worked out how to do it. All of it passed in a haze of pain and nausea.

She has an idea that Iain Munro visited before she was able to take his presence in properly. She would open her eyes and find him in the room, his face white as a mistletoe berry, and then she would decide it was easier to shut them again, and that's what she did.

When she was well enough to receive a stranger, her mother helped her to sit up, fussed over pillows and insisted on pinching her good cheek to put some colour in, as if there was not plenty to be going on with in the other one.

The visitor was a dapper gentleman with very intense eyes. Mr Aird introduced him as Mr Donald Ross, the lawyer whose letters to the *Northern Ensign* had exposed the dreadful effects of the clearances in Knoydart. He had come all the way from Glasgow to investigate what had happened at Greenyards.

'Pray do not concern yourself with trying to speak too much,'

Mr Ross said, seating himself by her bed at the minister's invitation. He explained that he had interviewed Dr Gordon of Tain at great length and so already had a good medical note of what had happened to her and to a good twenty other of the most severely injured women, but that he believed it important to see for himself. In the township itself he had spoken to as many of the women carried from the field on blankets and litters as were still capable of comprehension and speech, and received accounts of the behaviour of the police from many sources.

Her head was still bandaged, but he asked if he might be permitted to examine the bruises that, according to his note from the doctor, had been inflicted on her shoulder by a policeman's boot. Mr Aird coughed in that ministery way of his and said, 'That is hardly necessary, sir', but she just tore open the neck of her nightgown and showed him.

Mr Aird was a bit wary of Donald Ross, because he put a lot of emotion into his writing and had been accused of exaggerating before now. And sure enough, he went and named the pamphlet he published soon after 'Massacre of the Rosses', which you might be calling an exaggeration because nobody actually died there and then on the field. Mr Aird turned up in the pamphlet himself, speaking out at its end for the good name of the Greenyards and Amatnatua women, naming this person and that and saying how well he knew them and how peaceable and law-abiding they were. He had to read his contribution out to her, because the words shifted on the page when she looked at them. But she remembers yet how Gustavus Aird had ended his message with a hope that the day was not far distant when even in the Highlands of

Scotland people would be looked upon as of more value than beasts.

Maybe she has remembered it today because the word *even* made her cry, and the tears stung her sore face.

Iain *Mòr* came again when she was a bit more herself. He sat down in the bedside chair, which was too small for him. She remembers the way he planted his feet on the floor and held his blue bonnet in his hands between his knees, and twisted and squeezed it as he spoke. His open face was ruddy from the walk. It had a look on it she was slow to interpret at the time. Pity, she thought then. Now she is thinking it might have been embarrassment.

He had come to tell her he was making arrangements for his family to leave Greenyards. He and Douglas were to go looking beyond the strath for work or a piece of land to till, whatever could be found. He could not predict how far they would have to go or how long it would take, but when he was settled he would return for her. He wanted her to know that he would not go back on his word.

He said this without looking at her, mumbling it in the direction of the twisting cap. And maybe that is what gave his words a lack of conviction which, now she's reviewing it, he might not have felt. He will have been shocked, must have been, to see her bandaged head, the pulped face greening and purpling as the bruising spread, and watch her struggling to gather her muddled wits. Coming straight to Migdale from a whole township of injured women with disordered brains, including his own mother, must have cast him low. He was having to send half his family to the other side of the world, too. That will have been hard for Iain.

None of that entered her dull head as he raised his eyes to her twisted face and blurted out that when she was well enough he would of course make her his wife.

'No need for a sacrifice like that, Iain,' she said. She was pleased, may the Lord forgive her, to discover she still had the command for malice. 'You never had my own word on the matter, so just you go as far as you please and stay away. I wish you would.'

He did not say another word. His face crimson, Iain Munro stood up, nodded to her and walked with his heavy tread to the door. And there, out of the manse, down the road by the loch and over the shining Bonar bridge, went the path her life might have taken as the wife of a good man.

'You're a fool,' her mother said. 'Do you think anyone else will want you now?'

Her mother was wrong about that, of course. Although not about the fool.

Mr Aird arranged a job for her in Glasgow. She was still having headaches by the time she set off, and finding it so hard to wrap her mind around a thought that the minister worried she would get herself fired in the first week. He sent her off in the coach anyway.

'There are folk from all over the Highlands making their way in Glasgow,' he said. 'If you can get a good start in service, it may prove no bad place to be when it comes to your future plans in the . . . writing line.' She heard the hesitation. Remembers the damp realisation that not even her one champion on earth believed she could do it. 'There is nothing for you here, my dear.'

Neither he nor she, delighted to be off, paused to ask themselves how familiarity with the works of Virgil in the original would fit Jamesina Ross to excel (*ex* plus *celsus*, 'beyond lofty') in domestic service in the west end mansion of Mr Robert Mathieson, Glasgow shipbuilder and devout supporter of the Free Kirk. But thinking back, she managed all right. She came with plenty of practice lugging water and needed no training in how to clean out a fire. She could empty chamber pots as well as anyone and steam herself faint with heat in the scullery without having to think at all. It was not even all that hard to learn the ways to clean finer clothing than she had known existed, the tricks to get stains out, the importance of a good squeeze through with the mangle. It soothed her sore brain to discover how lavender made the laundry smell of summer, to pin up a well-boiled sheet in the back garden and watch it lift in the wind.

She made sure to avoid the house's many mirrors. Her mother's stricken features were all the looking glass she would ever need. But to judge from the reaction of the other servants, she was grotesque. She traced the sharp angle of the fractured cheekbone with a finger, felt its distance from her left eye and prodded the tender places between. It took an effort of will not to explore the hollow in her forehead with a knuckle every time she pinned up her hair. Every person who encountered her stared. Shiftily or sympathetically, they all stared.

Everyone, that is, but Willie Bain. When he arrived at the shipbuilder's house to take on some outdoor joinery, he followed her with his eyes all right, but in a different way. He had pale, watchful eyes. He declared, the first time he caught her alone, that her own were scrumptious. This was a word she felt sure Mr Aird would not admire, and for that reason savoured, feeling herself to be modern and daring. She made no objection when Willie Bain followed her behind the scullery and ran an expert hand down the back of her dress and over her buttocks. Smiling his frank, engaging smile, he assured her that he had not even noticed her face. How thankful she was to him for that, how deep the well of her gratitude.

Damage, the old doctor said in his letter. From *damnum*, 'a loss' or 'a hurt'; *damnare*, 'to inflict a loss'. Lately she has thought of her head injury as the seeding of a malign weed that only years and years later would come poking into the light to start spreading its havoc. But at the time the police-man's baton caused a different kind of loss.

Her discernment is the thing she lost. *Dis*, 'apart', *cernere*, 'to separate'. She could not see past that immense and abasing gratitude to separate what was good for her from what was terribly bad.

In a sheltered shingle cove along the Clyde coast on a blowy Sunday afternoon, the stones cut so sharply into her back that she had to beg Willie Bain to stop. Only fleetingly at first, only flittingly, fleeingly, flyingly, did she become aware of how little he cared if he hurt her. The well of gratitude drained too slowly to save her.

They married when it became clear she was expecting. Willie Bain did his duty by her there, as he never stopped reminding her after. When the joinery work at the big house dried up, he found work in a chair factory, although she never saw much of what he earned there. He moved her into a tenement in the Calton, teeming with disease and too many people, where the bairn was born and the bairn died, and she never sang or composed another word again.

248

For a long time afterwards she tried to remind herself that Willie Bain had been a young man with hopes himself once. He was handy with wood and had schemes to better himself that were always just around the corner, just like hers. But in all the years of marriage she never came to know him. She became expert only in sensing his moods: quicksilver optimism one day and dark broodings on the unfairness of his lot the next. The disappointments that flowed from both were unfailingly spent on his wife.

'Ugly bitch,' he would say when he hit her. 'You're why I'm here.'

One morning he vomited blood over the bed and was dead by evening. She looked at him for a long time before they took him away. In death he looked more pensive and more puzzled than he had let her see in life. Drained of resentment and the viciousness it had bred in him, he seemed younger again. In his grey face she caught a shade of the cocky young joiner who was going to rise in the world, somehow, somewhere, and had taken such a very short time to trace his failures to her.

Her own hopes had evaporated long before in the weary work of keeping bairns alive and her husband at arm's length. Those plans to publish songs, the dreams of bearing witness, they had always been ludicrous anyway.

She stares over her cup at the back of the recess, where candle-light from the bedside stub is chasing itself across the wall.

'Were they ludicrous, the things I wanted to do?'

He drains his own cup. 'What do you mean?'

'Was I daft and deluded all those years in Strathcarron to

249

imagine that if I was just clever enough, which I was once, you know, and resourceful enough, and talented enough, I could amount to something on my own?'

'Well, you're a woman. That was always going to hold you up some.'

See, this is where he's so fly. That is just his way of saying, yes, only the very daft and the very deluded would imagine that a woman on her own would achieve anything at all – never mind one who had just lost her home for the second time, had her brain addled by a baton and been trampled by a policeman's boot.

He puts his cup and saucer on the chair.

'Jamesina, I don't mean to make light of the ambitions you had. There was your class against you, too. It did not come much lower than ours. And you were badly hurt. That's a lot of hurdles to get over.'

'And I married Willie Bain.'

'Well,' he says, 'that also. Nobody gets through a life without mistakes.'

'That was a big one.'

'Sure it was. But even the big mistakes can lead you to a place where a Mr Niall Munro comes calling one day.'

Smug so-and-so.

'And before you think it, I'm not being smug. Not very, at least. Nor am I saying that all you needed was a man.'

'What are you saying, then?'

'That it's never too late. That is all I am saying, Jamesina. It's never too late.'

He takes the cup and saucer from her. 'Would you like another one or do you think you could sleep now?'

'I think I could sleep,' she says.

He puts the crockery on the chair, saucer on saucer, cup inside cup. Then he blows out the candle and draws the bed curtains around them for the second time tonight, patient man that he is.

Wonderingly patient man.

Wanderingly patient.

Wandering lonely as a cloud.

> *A poet could not but be gay,*
> *In such a jocund company.*

Jocund.

From *juvare*, 'to delight'.

Part XIII

The Lawyer

May 1854

27

Donald Ross Esq., St Enoch Square, Glasgow
To John Stoneman Esq., Houlston & Stoneman, bookseller
and publisher, 65, Paternoster Row, London

5 May 1854

Dear sir,

Pursuant to our previous correspondence, I enclose for publication the account of a barbarous act of savagery against defenceless women, perpetrated recently in the Highlands of Scotland. The events herein have already been the subject of letters in my name to the Lord Advocate in Edinburgh, whom I have urged to cause immediate inquiry into the conduct of the Sheriff and the Police Force, and to the Northern Ensign *newspaper.*

I do not hesitate to inform you candidly that the editor of that newspaper has declined to publish my contributions in full, citing his belief that 'they represent the conduct of the Sheriff and its results in such a light as to be almost incredible' and will on that account not be believed by his readers. Pray, sir, do not make the same mistake of concluding that readers should not be acquainted with uncomfortable truths merely because the conduct described is of an order of shamefulness to prompt incredulity in anyone with a shred of humanity.

The background to this disgraceful episode is easily stated. The community of Greenyard in the Strathcarron valley was under threat of removal to make way for a sheep-walk. The twenty-two families to be evicted were the remainder of a population already subject to clearance by the landlord, Major Robertson of Kindeace, some nine years previously. Their record was stainless and they were not one penny in arrears. It is worthy of remark that some of their men are at this very moment serving their country in the 93rd Regiment at Sebastopol, in the Crimea. Such was the population set upon in the most brutal way imaginable on the 31st March of this year by the forces of Her Majesty's constabulary.

Alerted by acquaintances in Ross-shire, I spent two days in Strathcarron, ascertaining the facts I describe with ample particularity in the enclosed papers. Arriving on the 14th April, I set about collecting information from numerous parties and examining the wounded. I conversed at length with those women who were able to speak and with the families of those who were not (and will in all likelihood never speak to anyone again). I also interviewed Dr Gordon of Tain, one of two physicians who attended the patients, and took a careful note of the medical opinions he was kind enough to share with me.

I also made sure to call upon the local tacksman, who continues to maintain that he never applied for or authorised the summonses of removal against his tenants – which assurance, untruthful as it must be assumed to be, emboldened the people of Greenyard to resist delivery of the notices, with the dire consequences that followed.

Please be in no doubt, sir, should further accusations be directed

*at the veracity of my reporting or revulsion expressed at the
shocking detail on which I am obliged to linger, that I am truly
sorry to find myself compelled to write as I do against Sheriff-
substitute Rankin, a gentleman for whom I had hitherto
entertained much respect. But after visiting Strathcarron and
surveying the scene of slaughter, after hearing with my own ears
and seeing with my own eyes the result of his precipitate conduct, I
cannot sufficiently express my indignation.*

*It is my information that Sheriff Rankin did not warn the sixty
or seventy women of his intention to let the police loose on them. He
read no Riot Act. He did not give them time to disperse; but, on the
contrary, the moment he approached with his force he cried out,
stick in hand, 'Clear the way,' and in the next breath, 'Knock them
down,' and immediately a scene ensued which I have called upon
such literary powers as I possess to depict in these papers, although
in truth it defies description.*

*The policemen laid their heavy batons on the heads of the unfor-
tunate females and levelled them to the ground, jumped and
tramped upon them after they were down, and kicked them in
every part of their bodies with savage brutality. The field was soon
covered with blood. The cries of the women, lying weltering in
their blood, was rending the very heavens. Some of the females,
pursued by the policemen, jumped into the deep and rolling Carron,
trusting to its mercies more than that of the policemen or the
Sheriff.*

*There were females who had parcels of their hair torn out by the
batons of the policemen, which hair could be seen in quantities over
the ploughed land. One girl had a piece of flesh, about 7 inches long
by 1¼ inches broad and more than a quarter of an inch thick, torn
off her shoulder by a violent blow with a baton. The ash-wood*

batons that were later recovered from the battlefield had the letters *V.R.* painted in large characters on them. Are people, I might ask in passing, to labour under the impression that Her Majesty sanctions, nay, encourages and authorises such actions?

Another young woman was struck on the forehead and her skull cut open. Such was the force of the blow that it shattered the frontal bone and carried into the fissures pieces of the cap that was on the poor girl's head; the doctor afterwards abstracted a portion of this cap from the wound. She was also kicked in the face and shoulders. When I visited this female a fortnight later at the home of a local Free Church minister, where she was being most tenderly nursed, I found the marks of hobnailed boots still visible on her shoulder and her face bruised and fractured beyond even her mother's recognition.

In Greenyard there was shown to me two tablecloths filled with clothing which the unfortunate victims had on them at the time, and these were dyed red with their blood. There were caps with holes in them where the batons had again carried the thin cotton right into the skulls of the women. Such was the havoc wrought that blood lay pooled upon the ground, the grass and earth were red with it, and the dogs of the district came to lick it up.

It is reported to me that more than twenty females were carried off the field on blankets and litters. At the time of my visit there remained thirteen in a state of great physical distress, including two sisters who both are left with profound alienation of the mental faculties as well as intense pain in the head, vomitings and fever. Three of the women are so ill that their medical attendant had no hope of their recovery. It is my own firm conviction – from the appearance of these females and the dangerous nature of their wounds, coupled with the medical reports I have procured – that not one half of them will recover; and all of them, should they linger on for a time, will bear in their persons sad proofs of the brutality to which they were subjected.

For that reason I consider it proper to entitle this pamphlet 'Massacre of the Rosses', for although every person carried from the field or the river breathed yet, to have inflicted injuries of a gravity which permits no hope of recovery can only be accounted slaughter.

You will see that I have also appended for publication several notes attesting to the moral character and peaceability of the injured women by name. These were sent to me by a number of respectable gentlemen of the parish, who include Mr William Murray, school-master of the parish school at Croick, Reverend John McDonald of the Established Church at Croick, and the minister previously referred to, Reverend Gustavus Aird of the Free Church at Bonar Bridge.

I trust, my dear sir, that I have said enough to induce you to read the enclosed submission with urgency and to publish with haste.

I remain, sir, yours truly,
Donald Ross

Enclosure appended: MASSACRE OF THE ROSSES in Strathcarron, Ross-shire, by Policemen When Serving the Tenants in Strathcarron with Summonses of Removal in March Last. By Donald Ross.

Part XIV

The Soul Healer

Summer 1884

28

'And how are you adapting to your changed role at home, Mr Munro?' Dr Epstein asked. The acrid smell of coffee hung about the workshop.

The doctor was an adroit evader of personal questions himself. While always happy to expound his theories or bemoan the backward treatment of illnesses of the mind, he would not be drawn on his own life at home. However, he was entirely without scruples when it came to encouraging confidences in the other direction.

Niall felt a twinge of disloyalty to be confessing his unease about the difficulties Jamesina had with remembering house-hold tasks and other small confusions. Since she was his wife now and the doctor so obviously qualified to judge his misgivings, these could surely be shared with propriety, but the look on Dr Epstein's face gave him pause. The doctor's eagerness was almost hungry.

'You seem interested, sir?'

'Oh yes indeed. I recognise the signs you describe.' The old man inspected his hands.

'I was not sure,' Niall prompted, 'if they amounted to anything I should be concerned about?'

The old gentleman recovered a brisker air. 'It is not a matter to be considered without my having met your wife. I would be pleased to make an examination of her, Mr Munro, if you have no objection to placing our acquaintance on a more professional footing in that regard?'

'I would like that, Dr Epstein,' he said.

Although it was a task to persuade Jamesina to attend the imposing villa in Mount Pleasant, and a harder one to convince her when they arrived that he had already alerted her twice to where they were going, the consultation fell out tolerably well.

After first glaring at them both and complaining that she had been dragged here without anyone having the courtesy to ask if she wanted her wits checked, she did sit down in the doctor's lofty consulting room when invited and became instantly entranced by his books. Shelves and shelves of them rose behind the gleaming desk. More lay piled on the carpet. Jamesina looked around her with an affectionate gaze. She said she had not been in a room like this since Mr Aird's study.

Dr Epstein smiled. 'Perhaps you could tell me about Mr Aird?' he said.

She answered him beautifully, telling him about her childhood in Glencalvie, the manse in Migdale and the minister who had taught her everything. She talked so fluently and elegantly, and with such excellent powers of insight and recall, that Niall basked in the glow of her.

'Before we proceed further,' Dr Epstein said next, 'pray remind me what you had for luncheon today.' Over the doctor's shoulder she shot Niall a swift, panicked look.

Cold tongue, he longed to mouth across at her. The last of Mr Pinkerton's loaf, remember? They had taken it together.

'Actually, doctor,' his magnificent wife replied haughtily, 'we call it dinner in Anne Street. What did you have yourself?'

Niall grinned at her. He felt like clapping. She caught his admiration and grinned back. They both watched the doctor writing a note.

At the end of the consultation Dr Epstein waved away the maidservant and showed them to the door himself. He smiled at them both jovially and promised to place his thoughts in a letter, along with a tentative diagnosis.

'It has been a delight to meet you, Mrs Munro,' he said with a bow.

Jamesina offered him a regal nod in return and made to go. On the doorstep she turned back, though, and grasped the old gentleman's two hands warmly in hers.

'Thank you,' she said, with a smile of such rare and startling radiance that Niall's heart swooped in his chest to see it.

Looking rather overcome himself, the doctor hurried indoors.

'Fancy the Greeks having the same word for *mind* and *soul*,' she murmured, as they strolled arm in arm down the hill towards Main Street in the sunshine.

It was something Joseph Epstein had mentioned in passing: that the word for the kind of doctor he had become, developing a practice through the sheer compulsion of his interest, was *psychiatrist*, a name derived from both Greek and Latin.

Jamesina had lit up at once. 'What is the derivation?'

'I see why your reverend friend enjoyed teaching you, Mrs Munro,' the doctor had laughed. 'The Latin *psychiatria* comes from the Greek *psykhe*, which in ancient times meant both "mind" and "soul", and *iatreia,* a word for "healing". The term *psychiatry* in English emerged quite early in this century. I believe it was coined by a German physician to describe the medical treatment of the mind.'

'You are a healer of the soul, then,' Jamesina had said thoughtfully.

'You might very well say so, Mrs Munro.'

She practised *psykhe* and *iatreia* all the way home. A vision arose before Niall of his wife striding into MacPhail's next day, basket over arm, to demand a pound of psykhe for the pot. He grinned to himself again.

29

When Dr Epstein came into the workshop the following afternoon, ostensibly to see how his galoshes were coming along,
he made no mention of the consultation, save to apologise that
he had been busy with patients and not yet penned the letter
containing his diagnosis. He wished to take his time over it,
but it would be in the post by the end of the week.

'There is something else I was wondering about, sir,' Niall
said.

'Yes, Mr Munro?'

'I have been thinking that my wife might benefit from a trip
back to Strathcarron. We could go there during the Glasgow
Fair holiday next month, if my savings will stretch to it. I was
thinking that returning might encourage her to be more forthcoming about the course her life took after she was injured,
which she is reluctant to speak about. When I first knew her,
you know, she had so much she wanted to achieve. Perhaps
you had a sense of that ambition and promise when she
described her girlhood to you yesterday? It set her apart among
people who had stopped hoping for anything by then. She went
on to have a difficult life, though, and there is a pain there that
she won't talk about and . . .'

He became aware of saying too much. He had strayed into an area that she would be mortified to think he was discussing. 'That I cannot reach . . .' he tailed off.

'I see.' The doctor regarded him keenly. 'Mr Munro, all I will permit myself to say is that the particular condition I was consulted upon is unlikely to be ameliorated by revisiting scenes associated with a past life. We must be clear on that point.' He paused. 'Emotionally, however, you are right. I dare say it will do no harm at all for you to pay a visit together.'

'That's just what I thought, sir. It might encourage her to open up a little.'

'Ah, but I was not thinking of your wife alone, Mr Munro. Let us talk, you and I, if you will spare me a few minutes, about what I believe happens when harms are done to the *psykhe* – by which I mean the developing mind, the fragile soul – in childhood.'

Niall sighed. Dr Epstein gave him a look that contrived to be both mild and stern at the same time and made him feel twelve again.

'Losing one's home in circumstances of great distress. Witnessing one's mother being savagely beaten. Becoming responsible for nursing and feeding her from a young age while working in conditions of extreme industrial brutality. The child will protect his mind in any way he can, but there is always a cost.'

'You are referring to me, I assume?'

'I see it all the time in my practice,' the doctor said. 'You may go through the whole of your life without suspecting why you are as you are. A word of warning, Mr Munro. If you do return to that place, you should be prepared to feel more than you think you will.'

Dr Epstein poured himself a cup of sludge from the ornate coffee pot he had inveigled into the workshop.

'There is something I have been wondering myself. I know your family were evicted, but how is it that you came to be in New Jersey with only two of them?'

The man did have a way of excavating your soul, no doubt about it. It was highly disconcerting when all you had been thinking about two minutes before were nails in a different kind of sole, one row or two.

It was Mr Aird who had alerted the Munro family to the new danger. Four women had been dragged in handcuffs from Feàrnaich field to the Tolbooth jail in Tain. After helping to secure bail for them, the minister drove them home himself. One of the bailed women was his mother.

Ann Munro had stumbled across the threshold on Mr Aird's arm. As her eyes adjusted from the glare of a spring day, she stared around the room as if she had never seen it before. She was still in her bloodied dress. She had a bandage around her head and her cap was missing. What hair could be seen had formed itself into iron clumps. Iain *Mòr*, catching her in his arms, all but carried her across the floor to her bed.

'Where were you at the time?' Dr Epstein asked.

'Keeping well out of the way. Watching. Ready to run in case I got blamed for something. As, in fact, I was about to be.'

The doctor gave him a dry smile. 'On you go, Mr Munro.'

Mr Aird told them what he had learned from the legal authorities in Tain. It was clear they meant to make an example of Greenyards. In addition to the arrests already made, investigations were to continue into infringements of the law during the two previous attempts to deliver summonses to the tenants of Greenyards. In particular, the boy who had threatened a sheriff's officer with a pistol, a serious offence for which there existed two reputable witnesses, would be sought and brought to justice.

Silence fell on the room. He could feel his brothers' eyes on him.

Later there ensued an uncomfortable family conference around their mother's bed. Niall faced his brothers from the bottom of the pallet, where Anna *Mhòr*'s motionless bulk left a small space for him to perch on the edge. Iain and James stood opposite with their backs to the fire. Douglas was squatting on the floor and Donald lounged in his usual position against the back wall with his hands in his pockets.

The brothers were unanimous in agreeing that Niall alone was responsible for the course the family was now forced to contemplate and should be ashamed of himself.

'And were you?' Dr Epstein asked.

'Not that I can remember. I had only been trying to protect my mother and felt proud of it, as I recall. It had made me quite a hero among the other boys. Anyway, it seemed to me it would be easy to evade arrest. I had visions of haring off to live as an outlaw, existing on berries in a snugly appointed cave. My brothers had more sense. They agreed I had to get away at once – only not to the hills.'

Emigration was an option that every family set to lose home and livelihood by Whitsun was having to examine, but perhaps none so urgently as theirs. Iain had been doing the sums and stated his conclusion baldly that whatever could be raised from the cattle, his share would not stretch to buying a passage for everyone. Niall would have to go, obviously. Everyone glared at him. Their mother should go, too, since she could also find herself in jail, and in any case she would soon have no home. They all glanced at the silent figure in the bed and as quickly away. Iain himself was determined to find another opening in Scotland, supposing he had to walk the length of the country to find it. Douglas would accompany him. That left James and Donald.

In his diffident way James said he thought he would sign up with one of the Highland regiments serving in the Crimea.

Donald assumed the sneer that had possibly, come to think of it, been developed to shore up his position as third among five brothers: torment lest you be tormented.

(Dr Epstein shot Niall a look that said he should leave the analysis to him.)

Anyway, Donald asked what the British state had done to earn the loyalty of any man in Strathcarron, or any man in any Highland glen these past fifty years? What thanks had all his feats at Waterloo gained for old Cameron, a mere onlooker bludgeoned by Her Majesty's Police Force on Feàrnaich field?

James flushed and said that to fight for his country could still let a man stand on his own feet and it had been good enough for their father.

'Aye, off he marched in his feathered bonnet and his bonnie red jacket, and we never saw him again,' Donald said. 'A fine tradition, that.'

To which James replied bitterly that there would be nobody now to notice whether he came back or not, so he could act as he would.

'Well, I hope you manage to shoot straight with your eye off the other way,' put in Donald. James studied the floor.

'Right, that's enough,' Iain had said, taking charge. That was what the eldest did: order everyone around, divert the malice, cuff Niall on an ear when he got in the way.

Talking now, it struck him that he would have liked to know Iain better. That they never had a chance to become acquainted as men came to him suddenly as a loss. They would have got along all right, he thought.

'I'm glad you have no such plans yourself, Donald,' Iain said, 'because you will be the one to take Niall and Mother to America, if you're willing. You have said often enough this place has no future.'

Donald folded his arms and narrowed his eyes at his brother. 'I'm willing all right, Iain *Mòr*,' he said, 'and not a day too soon can it come.'

Iain, James and Douglas. He had not seen any of them again, or heard what became of them. Yes, Dr Epstein, you are right, he thought but did not say. The severance of family was another cost he had never attempted to count up.

The air was wet and warm as the three of them set off from Greenyards for the coast. In heavy silence they made their way west along the Carron through glades of birch and oak. Every tree, as he remembers it, was quivering with birds and young leaves. Donald led the pony that carried their mother. Large-boned but diminished, the flesh on her face hollowed with pain, she drooped over the pony's shaggy neck.

Big Ann had said farewell to three sons, a home and a

community with tears pouring down her cheeks but no words. She had not spoken since she returned from the Tolbooth, nor taken part by sign or expression in the decisions that followed, although they had the impression she understood their import. Her sons had struggled to rid themselves of the expectation that she would leap to her feet at any minute, reach for her apron, demand to know what they were doing hanging around the house when there was work to be done, insult the sheriff and all his works, bustle out to collect the day's news and in general become their mother again. She did none of these things.

As they took their last steps along the banks of the Carron, Donald had his taciturn gaze set on the path ahead and walked without looking to right or left. Their mother's head was bent over the pony, jerking now and then as the beast picked its way through grass and stones, as if she had fallen asleep.

When he could bear the silence no longer, Niall began to sing.

Leaning over the workbench he did so again for Dr Epstein. *Abhainn nan lagan uaine*, he sang, the Gaelic returning without effort, come to him in a rush with the beauty and might of the river and the peerless shine on a salmon's back.

> *River of green places,*
> *river of the mighty surge.*
> *Jewelled salmon in clear water.*
> *How long will you nurture us,*
> *fast-flowing Carron?*

Wind in the birches,
a feather's drift
in white eddies round stones.
Where are the starlings
and when will they rise?

The starlings were Jamesina's way of describing the women. She imagined a multitude of them wheeling about the sky together as starlings sometimes do, acting as one.

'It's a song my wife wrote when Greenyards came under threat of clearance,' he told the doctor. 'It's about the women getting ready to resist the eviction notices.'

What a skill she had in those days. In the song's cadences he could hear something of the music of the Carron itself, but it was also the music of removal, the music of resistance, the music of community, the music of a past he had allowed himself to forget, the music of historical record.

In Coigach the messenger
fared ill for his summons.
Send the man to his boat.
Naked he left them
and never came back.

Dust rises to air
over black Knoydart seas.
The people won't sail.
Frost laces the earth
and bairns burrow.

Flit and remove,
flit and remove.
Dear river, hold us
as women make ready
to resist.

Leaving Greenyards that day, he had been singing only for himself. The song was like a butterfly beating its wings in the cave of your hands: something to replenish the spirits before you let it go.

His mother had raised her head, though, and was listening. He began on the next verse in his reedy voice, which was at the stage of croaking and squeaking when he least wanted it to. Haltingly to start with, his mother joined in. At first she hummed the melody, and then, with growing conviction, she sang out the words.

Donald glanced over at him. Donald's fair skin, as a younger brother watching for danger had ever been alert to observe, always betrayed his feelings. What the sudden whitening around his eyes and the spreading flush told of shock and relief at hearing his mother sing comes now to Niall in belated understanding. Not yet twenty years old, Donald must have been scared of what he had taken on. Beneath the sour insouciance he presented to the world was a man feeling the weight of a responsibility that his nature had not equipped him to handle, and which would all too soon defeat him.

'Jamesina's song,' his mother said. They were the first words she had spoken since crying 'Murder!' on Feàrnaich field.

'You know something?' Niall said to the doctor. At the window the old man leaned forward, his face washed of lines and crinkles in the midsummer light.

'Yes?'

'I am only now realising what it means that my mother and my brother and I all knew that song. All this time Jamesina has been thinking that nobody in Strathcarron heard her music or cared about it. But the truth is, we must all have known it. There were the three of us leaving behind our whole lives and most of our family – and it was not just Iain and James and Douglas, but cousins and second cousins and aunts and uncles and all the generations of Rosses and Munros we had shared that place with – and her song was what we carried with us. My wife's song is what got my mother speaking again. It gave us the spirit to strike out. I have only this moment realised it.'

'You should tell her,' the doctor said quietly.

30

Dr Joseph Epstein, Mount Pleasant, Rutherglen
To Niall Munro Esq., 13, Anne Street, Rutherglen

Friday, 27 June 1884

Dear Mr Munro,

I enclose my bill for your kind attention in respect of the consultation you attended with Mrs Jamesina Munro on the 25th inst. and am pleased to offer my opinion. I suggest you share the contents with Mrs Munro to the extent that you see fit.

Your wife presented with deficiencies in short-term memory, which contrasted with an excellent recall of events and personalities further back in her history. She was lively and engaged throughout the consultation. I attach no significance to her initial reluctance to co-operate with the examination, beyond noting her insistence that she had not received prior notification of the appointment, despite your attesting that you had informed her twice.

May I say by way of preamble that problems associated with memory have not received sufficiently serious medical attention in Great Britain. You and I have discussed this. For this reason I am not in a position to point you towards the literature you expressed an interest in reading yourself on the subject since, in short, there is none, unless you possess a facility in French or German.

At the end of the last century a physician living in Paris by the name of Philippe Pinel classified a number of mental disorders, using the term démence to describe the disorder characterised by a particular kind of memory loss of which Mrs Munro displays, in my opinion, incipient signs. As a hospital clinician M. Pinel is something of a hero of mine. He refused to bleed, purge or blister mentally ill patients in his charge, preferring instead to listen to them. It is an approach I have emulated myself in more than fifty years of clinical observation, although I fear our medical profession today still regards talking and listening to the patient as a profound eccentricity. Should you feel inclined to seek another opinion, I must warn you not to expect validation of my theories.

Let me turn to the areas of concern you brought to me: namely, the difficulty your wife has with remembering to undertake daily tasks, her tendency to repeat the same statement within a short period of time, her struggle on occasion to identify the day of the week, and one particularly distressing experience of finding herself incapable of navigating streets with which she has long been familiar. While occurring inconsistently, these episodes indicate the malfunctioning of a part, or parts, of the brain in which one may assume Memory in its various manifestations to reside. I stress again that assumptions are all one has to go on in this field.

Over the decades of listening to patients, the mental picture I have conceived to guide my own understanding is as follows. Imagine a tall set of bookshelves. The highest shelves contain the most recent memories, the middle ones those which have been formed in mid-life, and close to the floor the memories from *childhood and on through one's twenties. If the bookcase is rocked hard, the books may tumble, and it is then observed that the volumes of memory at the top are the ones to fall first. Those at the bottom remain longest in position, and indeed it is my impression that they are the more eagerly reached for amid the disarray of the other books.*

Might an old injury be the cause of such a dislodgement? It is well established that a head injury may produce a number of immediate effects, these including unconsciousness, inability to recall the event itself, confusion, difficulty with speech, and problems with vision or hearing. When I asked your wife about the head injury she received in March 1854, she acknowledged having experienced many of these symptoms.

You may say to me, 'But she recovered, Dr Epstein.' Mrs Munro was indeed adamant that although severe headaches and what she described as a 'fuzziness' in her mental processes persisted for many months after the injury, she had no difficulty in accessing her most recent memories at that time, except those around the infliction of the injury itself; she had not personally remarked any more substantial change until the last year or so.

However, I have observed that there may be a delay of a great many years before the effects of certain insults to the brain become manifest, having, one would posit, most likely proceeded by imperceptible steps for some time previous. I would therefore postulate a causal connection between an injury to the frontal lobe thirty years ago, observable in the depression and scarring of the forehead, and your wife's present symptoms, which are evidence in my opinion of ancient damage only now manifesting itself.

When we spoke in your workshop yesterday, you mentioned a further concern about the emotional pain occasioned by unspecified events in your wife's past. Here a return to the library analogy may be helpful. Imagine a second bookcase of the brain, in which there exist not memories but emotions. This is a sturdier piece of furniture altogether, so much so that even when shaken robustly the feelings remain. If these be feelings of happiness, love and comfort, the subject will be supported through the cognitive challenges by a sense of security and contentment. However, feelings such as sorrow, anger or self-recrimination, if persistent and unresolved, are likely to exacerbate anxiety and magnify the sense of loss that occurs as previously familiar tasks become difficult and landmarks unreliable.

In such a case, it is my opinion that memories should be encouraged forth and the emotions to which they give rise openly explored, in order that the negative ones may be confronted and as far as possible set aside, and the good ones enjoyed.

In simple terms, therefore, the more secure your wife is in speaking about the pain that still radiates from the life she led before you found each other, the happier she will be; and the happier she is, the better equipped she will be to live with the challenges presented by the damage to her brain. With patience and resourcefulness, Mr Munro, you can help her to be happy.

If you will forgive me for concluding on a less professional note, I will add that I know this to be true from personal experience. I believe you noticed that your description of Mrs Munro's problems occasioned in me a keen degree of interest. What I have never vouchsafed to you is that my own wife became similarly afflicted, although at an older age. You and I are friends, Mr Munro – indeed your friendship has come to mean a great deal to me – and it has not escaped my notice that I have encouraged a greater degree of candour from you than I have been prepared to offer myself.

Therefore I will state it plainly: Sarah was the love of my life.

We were married for fifty-three years and without her this house is the merest shell. I cannot assert strongly enough that such terms as senility *and* lunacy, *which have for too long been carelessly and ignorantly applied by lazy doctors to conditions they make no attempt to understand, did no justice to the complexity of the symptoms I observed in her. Nor did they begin to take account of the great number of skills and attributes that remained to her as others declined; or of the difference that being in receipt of tenderness and understanding made to her continued enjoyment of life. Through her I learned that knowing the time of day is not as important as one might think and that one hour of happiness is worth very much more when it is consciously valued and celebrated.*

Let me say finally that further deterioration in your wife's condition, while to be expected, is likely to proceed slowly and permit the enjoyment of many fruitful years to come. I am supported in this opinion by observing her excellent command of language and her keen interest in the processes of language itself. It is not every patient who is so anxious to remind me that the word doctor *is derived from the Latin for 'teach'; and I congratulate myself on having been able to draw her own attention to the etymology of the modern term* psychiatrist. *I have a feeling your most characterful wife was pleased to learn she was being attended by a 'healer of mind and soul'.*

I should make clear, however, that all I have done is listen. The healing of your wife's soul is in your hands, my friend, as I suspect the healing of your own has already been entrusted to her.

With kind regards,
Joseph E. Epstein

Part XV

The Return

16 to 22 July 1884

31

The route northwards was unexpectedly stirring. He had not imagined finding himself so moved and exhilarated by landscapes of a kind he had not laid eyes on since boyhood: a river with a hint of the Carron about its breadth and confidence; the first pink whisk of heather along a railway embankment; a waste of clouds in a Highland sky, thickening from wisps to masses as they went along, darkening the distant mountains even as flickers of sunshine lit the nearer grasslands.

Jamesina sat opposite, studiedly looking out of the window, her hair swept up and immaculately arranged under her green wedding hat, brows gathered for combat. To underline her stout resistance to coming on the trip, she had chosen to travel with her back to the engine. 'You can tell me what's ahead,' she said. She could see no purpose in seeking out a place where the lives they had known no longer existed and the ending had been so painful. A blast of sea air in Rothesay, she intimated, would have done her fine.

As they rode higher and higher, the landscape paring itself of features with every mile, he was reminded of a tale that had been all over the newspapers some months ago.

'Last winter,' he said, 'a train on this line became snowbound on its way south. I guess it must have been around here. The passengers got themselves out and managed to walk to Dava station before the storm overwhelmed everything. When the train was recovered at last, they found it under sixty feet of snow. Imagine that. Sixty feet.'

She turned from the window. 'Pigs,' she said. He blinked. 'Was there not something about pigs?'

'I don't think so.' He thought furiously. 'Ah, I know what you mean. It was cows.'

She scowled. 'I know it was cows. Obviously I meant cows.'

'You're quite right, then, and here's what you're thinking of. There was also a train coming up the track northwards and it got stuck on the other side of the station. That one had passengers bound for Inverness but also a consignment of cattle. The passengers made their way out and most of them set out on foot for Dava, leaving a few of the men to release the cattle. But those beasts plain refused to move. Try as they might, there was not a thing anybody could do to persuade them away from the shelter of the trucks, and the men were getting cold. You can imagine what it was like, can't you – the wind sweeping across these moors and driving the snow everywhere. So the cattle had to be left there, and when a relief train got through at last they found the snow drifted up around the train and over it and every one of the cattle dead. Suffocated where they stood, poor beasts.'

He shook his head. 'Hardly a surprise, I suppose. A railroad that crosses the mountains as high as this. We're lucky to have it at all. We would have had to come the whole way by carriage not so long ago.'

He had the flat feeling of a man talking to himself.

'Jamesina?'

She flung herself round angrily. 'Why did I say "pigs" there? Tell me. How would your friend the doctor explain that?'

'Well,' he began, thinking, right, sir, what exactly *would* you say? He still carried Dr Epstein's letter in his breast pocket. He had shared those parts of it with Jamesina that he considered, as a magnanimous husband, she ought to know. The word *damage* was what had seemed to strike her hardest. It is a troubling word to hear about the state of your head and she understood its import, no doubt about that. But something else had clearly stirred in her when she heard it. 'Willie Bain did me damage,' she had said quietly. 'Losing my bairns did me damage.' When he pressed her to say more, she had, as ever, no more to say. He did not read her out those parts of the doctor's letter that he regarded as a private message to himself, upon which he was continuing to reflect.

'I guess he might not have tried to explain it,' he said to her, smiling. 'I guess he might ask if you vould be so very kind, Mrs Munro' – Dr Epstein would forgive him for overdoing his very slightly foreign accent – 'to decline for me in Latin ze noun for *cow*.'

'Very amusing,' she said, and turned back to the window.

God help him, had he hit on a Latin word she didn't know?

'*Bos*,' she said to the window. '*Bos, bos, bovem, bovis, bovi, bove*. Third declension, like *nox*. *Bovine*: "pertaining to a cow or an ox", by extension "sluggish or stupid", which I told Mr Aird was very unfair. There was nothing stupid about our cow at Glencalvie. Mind you, those beasts that got stuck at Dava were maybe a bit bovine right enough. Do you want the plural?'

'Jamesina, look at me.'

She looked at him. She was on the way to smiling herself now.

'No,' he said, 'I do not want the plural.'

After that they laughed their way through Latin pigs, seaweed, clouds, gulls and trees. Even the train received the treatment. 'From *trahere*, "to pull",' she announced, eyes alight with memory's triumph as they approached Inverness for their overnight stop.

They were both in good heart next day. As the train for the far north pulled away along the banks of the Beauly Firth, the water was shining like a mirror. When he pointed this out, she told him not to be getting any ideas about mirrors.

He chuckled and shut his eyes. The sun through the glass was warm on his face, the ride more pleasurable than you have a right to expect with so much jolting about. It reminded him of the train journey back from New York on the day he met John Wilson: the heat haze outside the window, the rails rattling and clattering just like this, the hopefulness that had begun to swell in his chest when he promised himself that he would not make a button again on this earth. If he had not hopped aboard that train in Newark for a free excursion in the sunshine, he would not be here today. There's a thought, as Jamesina would say.

Into the station at Tain, the spire of the Tolbooth visible from the train. The arrested women were taken there, his mother among them. His stomach tightened.

They steamed along the side of the Dornoch Firth. The tide was on its way out and the water glassy. Brown wrack seaweed littered the bank almost up to the track. Creamy gulls were pecking in the dark sands. Woodland rushed past. Jamesina pointed out the orange berries on the rowans, ready to ripen soon. Hills and more hills unrolled themselves until, with a commotion of whistling and braking, the train was pulling into their destination and the stationmaster shouting, 'Ardgay!'

The guard hauled down their suitcase from the roof and the train began its wheezing departure. From here it would be heading over the mouth of the Carron, up the kyle to Culrain, across the great iron railway bridge to Invershin, on to Lairg, on in a loop between the empty slopes of Strath Fleet, another valley long denuded of its peoples, and back to the sea. They crossed the road to the inn.

Next day they set off to explore the northern bank of the Carron in a two-wheeled trap pulled by a scraggy brown horse. Jamesina exclaimed at the buttercups and dandelions in the verges, the purple vetch, the white bursts of starwort. Silver braids of water could be glimpsed from the road. Stones that once were houses lay scattered over the braes. Among them, placidly cropping the grass, nosed idiot sheep.

'It's not their fault,' Jamesina demurred comfortably.

She gave no sign of being troubled by the drive through these unpeopled acres, visitors to their past. She felt like a tourist, she said. And she looked it, sitting up pertly and gazing about her as they went along.

He did not feel like a tourist.

At last they came to a place where the river ran close enough to the road for them to see straight across to the other side. The Carron here ran broad and fast. On the other side, above a beach of pale stones, could be seen a sloping, uneven field of grass, thinly patched with woodland. He pulled the horse up and they sat in silence, looking across together at Feàrnaich field.

'Do you feel all right?' he said.

'Better than I thought I would, yes. Do you?'

He was still staring across the river. It's a field, Munro. It's just a field.

'Thank you for asking, *mo chridhe*. I don't know what I'm feeling. I can see the clump of trees I was hiding in that day, and the place my mother fell. I —'

'What did you call me?'

'I don't know. What did I call you?'

'I think you called me *mo chridhe*. Your heart. You have never called me that before.'

'I believe it has never come to me before this minute. Do you like being called that?'

'I do,' she said slowly. 'It makes me feel' – she hesitated – 'happy.'

Happy among the rubbled walls of Greenyards? Happy within sight of Feàrnaich field? This he had not expected.

And what was he feeling? Not that.

Looking about him under the big Strathcarron sky, across the tumbled river, he was remembering his mother. But not the way she was in Greenyards, not the way she had come back to him when Dr Epstein began asking questions about his childhood. What he was seeing now was not Ann Munro ordering her sons around like a sergeant major, talking nineteen to the dozen with Christy Ross over the kiln, sitting in the byre with her face to a warm flank and singing lullabies to the cow to encourage the milk to flow. No, what he remembered was his mother in Newark with her dress on back to front and nothing in her eyes. His mother with the imposing spread of her body reduced to sagging folds and her mind gone to a place from which there was no bringing her back, or none that he could discover. His mother gazing at him wordlessly from the chair she lived in, her face twisted into a grimace of silent weeping, her blue Ross eyes leaking the losses she had no other way to express.

One summer's morning, preparing to leave for work, he had set by her bed two slices of bread and a soft tomato, which would not trouble her to chew. Then he bent to say goodbye. His mother was still asleep, her face tipped into the pillow and turned to the grey wall. Tucking the sheet around her shoulders, he leaned in to kiss her cheek. It was wax-pale and far too cold. He saw that again too, three thousand miles away with a pair of reins loose in his hands.

'Be aware that memory is powerful,' the doctor had told him. Perhaps he should also have mentioned that once untethered, it may stray anywhere.

He thought about his brothers. The trees further up the burn reminded him of Douglas and how the two youngest boys used to hide there when their mother was on the warpath. Round the far bend was where James had fished him out of the river once. And was that not the inlet where Iain, sitting him down at the water's edge, had taught him to whistle?

And Donald. Suddenly he was saying in a strangled whisper that sounded strange to himself and must have sounded stranger to her, 'Donald never wrote to us after he left for New York. He never wrote once, not once, though I looked for that letter. I never stopped looking out for it. I never knew what happened to Donald.'

She took his hand from the reins and stroked it. There was comfort in the rhythm of her fingers sweeping back and forth, back and forth, skin to skin, as they both continued to look across the river. Then she said briskly, 'Come on, then. Let's go and find a place for our picnic.'

'*Mo chridhe*,' he asked, 'what picnic would that be?'

Doubt streaked across her face. He knew she had meant to order food from the inn. She had even asked him what kind of pie he had a fancy for. She had gone to seek out the innkeeper's wife for that very purpose. Afterwards he had checked, as he was in the habit of checking everything.

He blew her a kiss. 'Tantara,' he announced, and produced a basket from under his feet in the well of the carriage.

'No need to look so pleased with yourself,' she said.

They drove past the falls, where the Carron exploded through the gorge between huge primeval slabs, trees clinging to the sides. There were orchids littering the grass and great puddles in the marsh.

'"Lochans full of broken sky,"' Jamesina murmured. 'I put that in a poem once.'

Here was the Black Water rushing in to join the Carron, black alder and birches greened with lichen along the bank, heather tufted in clefts of rock. The river was hustled by the wind and disturbed by stone. He noticed a tiny feather drifting on the surface in aimless circles.

Wind in the birches,
a feather's drift
in white eddies around stones.
Where are the starlings
And when will they rise?

He sang a few lines out loud, as he had for the doctor. 'Remember this? Of course you do. You made it.'

He seized her hand. 'And others will remember it too. Do you realise that, Jamesina? Your music became part of us, just as the strains of the pibroch did, or those bleak, beautiful Psalms that were sung each Sunday on the hillside, though I fidgeted through every one of them at the time. I thought all those experiences gone, and I believed I was the better for losing them. But now these empty slopes are pouring song wherever I look. Music stays, Jamesina. And if it's within me yet, it will lie still within others. Do you see?'

It was a long and passionate speech for him, and for a moment she only gazed in surprise. Then, slowly, she nodded.

The rain stayed off long enough for them to spread their picnic on the grass. She scolded him for stuffing sandwiches into his mouth two at a time, and he protested that you never got over being the youngest in a family: you have to grab what you can and eat like the wind before it is whipped from under your nose. She said she'd have thought he would have learned some manners in the years since. He said she might have learned a few more herself. She laughed and said he might be right at that.

Birdsong came to them from among the trees, and he put

a finger to his lips. They listened together. It might or might not have been a blackbird, but it reminded him anyway.

'"After the rain the blackbird sings,"' he began. 'Come on, help me out here.'

She gave him a dark look.

'Jamesina, I know what that song means to you. I would only suggest that you are better not hiding from it.'

'It means I failed,' she said, picking at the grass, beheading a buttercup. 'I wrote it when we were losing Greenyards, when I still thought I could make a life afterwards. I truly did. A life of words and truth-telling. Somehow or other I was going to do it.'

'Go on.'

'I thought I would make poems about being an inferior race in your own country. I thought I would make songs about women fighting back.'

The buttercups were getting massacred.

'I thought I would get so many folk singing my songs, or reading my words, that nobody would forget what was done to people in these Highland glens or try to excuse it in the name of improvement.'

More beheadings.

'And what did I become? A washerwoman. What did I write? Nothing.'

He got to his feet and offered her a hand up.

'You know, Jamesina, there are battles to be fought yet. I look at this place and I think, yes, Greenyards is gone, Glencalvie is gone, but the laws that permitted what happened here are not changed. There are crofters on Skye refusing to pay rent right now. There's a Highland Land League formed to campaign for our rights to the land. There's a Royal Commission been going round the country asking questions.'

'*Our* rights, you say? I didn't know you were so interested.'

She was interested herself, he could tell: Jamesina normally made a better stab at sarcasm. And she was right to wonder about him. There were thoughts crystallising here in his home valley that he had never attempted to put words to, though they had been forming for months. And it was possible that the thoughts were not unconnected to his learning what it is to feel. He had lived on the surface for a very long time before becoming the lodger of Jamesina Ross.

'Do you know what is different now from the days when townships like ours were on their own, worn out and worn down, men away in the army, women who made a stand getting their heads beaten in and nobody answering for it? Sure there were newspapers who took an interest, and there was public sympathy for a time, and there were ministers like Mr Aird who did their best to help, but it was never enough. I'll tell you what's different now.'

She is on her feet now, listening.

'Organisation. It's not just the Land League. Supporters in the Lowlands are involving themselves in protest – mostly Highlanders who've had to move to the cities, I would guess. They're gathering at ceilidhs in Glasgow to share music and ideas. They're setting up Celtic societies to celebrate the culture. All sorts of people are writing pamphlets and making speeches and sending letters to the newspapers.

'And composing songs, Jamesina. The songs that people sing matter. Those Highland crofters need to know that the starlings still rose at Greenyards when there was none to help.'

She did not say anything. That might be accounted a start, at least.

Along the road as far as Croick they went in the bouncing trap. There was nothing very different about the lone kirk by the Black Water, except the unnerving quiet of a place without people. She led him around the side to the furthest corner of the graveyard. There was no stone to mark John Gillespie's resting place, but Jamesina said she knew exactly where her grandfather was buried. Niall took off his hat and bowed his head.

'You would have liked each other,' she said.

On Sunday, the last day of their holiday, the horse laboured gamely up the hill above the Bonar bridge. Niall had never been to Migdale before and found the setting enchanting. The church stood next to a schoolhouse and there was a sturdy manse nearby, with fine views across to the hills and down to the kyle below. Jamesina was more excited and agitated to visit here than anywhere else. As they settled into a pew, she confessed to doubting that Gustavus Aird would recognise her.

'You didn't know who I was. Why should I expect it of Mr Aird?'

'Ah, but I was only a boy and Mr Aird knew you after you were injured. All he will think is how well and handsome you look now.' Niall would be putting particular effort into praying that this was so.

The minister did recognise her. He most certainly did. He saw her from the pulpit, perhaps alerted by the unusual intensity of the gaze directed towards him from beneath the jaunty green hat in the back row. With the vigour of a man half his age he came striding towards them at the end of the service. He was a little stooped and his hair was thin and whiter than Dr Epstein's, but his voice was resonant as ever. He clasped her hands in both of his and exclaimed, 'Young Jamesina Ross, can it really be you?'

But Niall's own attention was elsewhere. From early in the service he had been staring at the back of a bulky man towering over the congregation a few rows in front. Surely he recognised the massive shoulders and the shape of that head. The fair hair was peppered with white but still indisputably familiar. He knew that figure. He knew that man.

Leaving his wife and the minister beaming at each other, he slipped into the milling congregation. There were so many people exchanging Sabbath greetings on their way out of the church that he began to fear he would lose him.

'Excuse me,' he said. 'Pardon me if I push past you, ma'am. Excuse me, please.'

Only a few heads remained between them.

'Iain!' he shouted. The figure turned and it was him all right, weathered by the years, leaner and redder in the cheeks, quite a deal larger in the nose.

'Iain *Mòr*, it's you.'

'Is this Niall *Beag* with the deep voice?'

'It is, brother. *Is mise Niall.*'

With a shout of laughter Iain strode across the last couple of feet and folded him into his great arms.

'*Fàilte air ais, mo bhràthair*,' he said. 'Welcome back, my brother. It has been a very long time. Let me call over my wife.'

'Let me call over *my* wife,' said Niall, craning to see if Jamesina was still talking to Mr Aird and wondering how she would react to this different category of surprise.

But already a woman had arrived at Iain's side. She was tall and merry-eyed and not nearly as wispily thin as he remembered. She looked from one man to the other in astonishment.

'Ah, there you are, Grace,' said Iain. 'Look who this is, come back to us at last.'

Part XVI

The Kitchen Bed

Morning
Thursday, 24 July 1884

32

The room is full of light. Waking up after not nearly enough sleep, she leans across his cool slice of bed to see what he's up to. Dressed already (nice clean shirt and necktie, brown waistcoat), he is nipping around with a frying pan. Hard to imagine Thomas Langton doing that, or any other man come to that. He says he learned his way around a griddle when his mother depended on him and has never done other than look after himself. It's handy, of course, but it does make her feel useless sometimes. It even makes her feel just that wee bit *like* his mother, especially when he goes asking if she would like to take her breakfast in bed. What kind of invalid does he think she is?

She must have said that out loud because 'Jamesina,' says he, a bit impatiently for him, lifting the plates down, 'I am not suggesting you're ill. I thought you could do with more rest and I have my work to go to. May I not bring you a plate over?'

He is looking tired himself. Weary puddles under his eyes.

'It makes me feel like your mother.'

'My mother?' He lays the plates slowly on the table and comes over to the bed. Stands in front of her, arms folded. 'What are you talking about?'

There is a speck of shaving soap on his chin. He could do with a mirror.

'The way you used to look after her. You said you used to bring her food before you went to work. I don't want to be another old woman you're feeling sorry for.'

There. Said it.

His lip does that twitchy thing it does when he is deciding not to say something. But this time he says it anyway, or maybe it's a different something.

'Right, you can come and get it at the table, then. I'm going to get started.'

He forks some bacon into a roll and sits down at the table to eat it with his back to the bed. And here she is, wondering how to get out of this with dignity, because really it would have been nice to be brought breakfast on a tray for once in her life (is there even a tray in the house? has she ever had a tray? when did she last see a tray?), so what made her say that?

Why does she always have to fight him?

Why does she not know what to do with happiness when it's in front of her nose?

Out behind the shipbuilder's scullery, dizzy with desire. Skirts up to her waist and Willie Bain's breath in her ear, promising he would take her to London, what a place London was, all their dreams would come to pass, he would see to it when they were married.

The ravenous sensation of lust. The exquisite sensation of being lusted after.

Was that happiness?

Exquisit, past participle, from *ex* plus *quaerere*, 'sought out'. Sought out excitement.

Not the same as being able to laugh when you have said 'pig' instead of 'cow', even as you spit out your frustration at the person least to blame.

Not the same as the caress of a punctured thumb on your broken face.

Nothing like the exasperated affection that is filling her up as she lies on her side here, looking at the back of his head (really that hair is getting too long), and smelling the bacon, and knowing, knowing deep and sure, that her husband is not brooding and boiling himself to a rage behind the averted back; knowing that whatever she goes and says next, or does not think to say, this one is not going to stand up abruptly, send the chair flying, lurch across to the bed and tighten a hand around her throat.

No, this man will turn when she asks him to, and he will smile and maybe raise an eyebrow and say something like, 'Cold bacon isn't up to much, is it?', which won't exactly mean he is letting her win whatever point she was making – what point was she making? – and actually he'll be laughing at her when you think, but it will be done with love.

And maybe that is what happiness is.

Felicitas.

Knowing it will all be done with love.

Grace looked happy when they saw her. My goodness, the shock of seeing her standing in the kirk beside Iain, who was looking just that bit raddled after all this time, nothing like as beautiful as his brother, although he did seem pleased to see her and there was no awkwardness at all. She did wonder in

303

those first moments how he would react, but then she was so amazed to see who was by his side, so shocked, thrilled, stunned, dumbfounded, from *confundere*, 'mix up', so mixed up you can hardly speak, that she forgot all about Iain.

'I thought you were dead,' she murmured in a daze.

It was always a dead Grace in her thoughts and her dreams, a dead Grace with her head beaten in, a thin wrist motionless in the bloodied grass. Even in the night just passed, when the horror of Feàrnaich field came back to her as it had not when she was right across the river from it, she could not make Grace open her eyes. It took Niall to calm her down and make her a cup of tea and remind her that Grace was alive and farming with Iain – and how many children did he say? – on a piece of land the other side of Migdale.

Oh, but she was lovely to look at in the kirk, nicely plumped out and her hair in a neat bun under her Sunday hat, and not a thing to show for that terrible day but a wee bash in her right temple, just above the ear.

'I do tricks for the grandchildren,' she said. 'I fit a ha'penny in and they see how long I can wave my head around without it falling out.' Grace was laughing as she talked. Such a gay, cheerful laugh. 'I've made a rod for my own back, mind. These bairns are demanding I produce a ha'penny every five minutes.'

'Were you not hurt that day?'

'I was. Folk carried me across the river and I lay in bed for I don't know how long. I mended, though.'

'And Iain? Where did he come in?'

'We met here in the kirk. I was working at the inn by then for my bed and board. He had been all over the place looking for land and in the end he found it where he started.'

She tried to think of a careful way of asking about the dead bairn, and the boy who left her violated. 'And your old trouble?' is how she put it.

'Was never mentioned between us. There were no wifies to stop us and Iain was very respectful of me. He asked and I accepted. I was always very fond of Iain *Mòr*.'

'I remember,' she smiled.

Grace linked an arm in hers. 'And I'll tell you this,' she whispered. 'I had no need of any mirror.'

The pair of them, two matrons in their Sunday best who would not be seeing fifty again, began to laugh. They nearly doubled themselves over with laughter. They kissed each other and they laughed again. They wiped their streaming eyes and they scarcely knew what kind of tears they were.

Happy. Happy. Happy.

Happy to see Grace.

Happy to see Niall Munro eating a roll in the kitchen with his back to her, making that little slurpy sound with his tea.

There were times with her children when she was happy. Weren't there? Must have been. Why can't she remember them, then?

She can remember dread setting up home in the pit of her stomach and hardly ever leaving. She can remember joy. Fierce, hot joy, a great blaze of it when she nursed Archie through a crisis and watched him from the parlour window making his way along the road to school again, his wrists poking from the freshly washed jumper that was too small for him but would have to do. And delight. Plenty of that. Just to count his freckles filled her up with delight; just to hear one breath following the next.

None of it was happiness.

His arms and legs became so spider-thin, even as his body was growing into manhood, that it tore at her to see them. Night sweats began, and she sat with him hour after hour, trying to convince herself that this stage too would pass. He lay here, where she is now, just where she is now, wracked by coughing, his fair hair slick with perspiration. When she lay down herself in the parlour bed, she heard him through the wall. Many a night she stayed in the chair by the range, poking up the fire to keep some heat in the room. In the morning she crept over to look at the colour of the spit on his hanky. Lovely white handkerchiefs she made sure he had, washed in the sink every day and dried over the fire. And each time that she saw there was blood, her own ran to ice.

Sometimes, especially if she had forgotten to open the window, she would catch a smell of decay coming off him. Whatever else this hobbled mind of hers stops her remembering, the fetid reek from the lungs of her golden boy will surely accompany her to the grave.

She was forgetting a few things by then. Little things at first, like not opening the window when she meant to. Silly things. Nothing things, like . . . Hah, if she could remember them now, she would likely not have forgotten them in the first place. She can remember the dawning terror, though, that in the middle of losing her boy she was also losing her mind. Fear in her gut. The dread that she might become ill too and he would have nobody. The nights crying out to be spared for his sake. Let me not die, because he needs me. Let him not die, because I cannot bear to lose him. Only he's gone now, and I need him back. How can I go on being alive if I don't have him back?

And now she is crying.

'What is it, *mo chridhe*?'

He has come. He is on the edge of the bed, where she used to sit when she was stroking the boy's damp brow, his hair so dark with sweat.

'Archie,' she says in her agony.

She turns her face to the wall, her body to the wall, curling like a baby into the sobs that have arrived at last from a long way away.

He lays a hand on her back, feeling each ripple of a departing sob under his own skin. One by one he sucks the finger-tips of his other hand, where specks of loose flour have engrained themselves in the tiny holes.

She becomes conscious of a light pressure just below her shoulder blades. Not a stroking, not a patting. Just the flat of his palm resting there.

Soon she will tell him what it is like to watch a heart ceasing that once beat under your own. She will. It is time. And what it is like to hold fast to a limp hand and wait for a bairn's last breath, and then to will another one to come, to beg, implore, beseech and finally command – this is what you do – you command one more breath to come, even as another treacherous part of you is only longing for it to be over. She will tell him it does not matter how old they are when their breath stops. She will tell him it does not matter how often it happens, or how many other mothers it happens to, because it happens all the time: nothing out of the ordinary in children being slain by want and disease. Still, she will tell him, it rips lumps out of you. Do you understand, Niall? Lumps, stumps. In time it leaves you with a stump of a heart.

She will tell him that her firstborn was called John for her grandfather and her second Iain. He will like to know that. She will tell him about Constance having eyebrows that could not be laid at the feet of the Gillespies. She will tell him about the babe who never breathed, and the colour of him, violet: a violet by a mossy stone, fair as a star. And about little frail William, thin and silent as an old man but with soft mouse-cheeks that fitted into your hand, whose whole short life was a dying. She will tell him about Archie.

Not now, though. Not yet.

His hand on her back through the nightgown.

Later.

He is becoming conscious of a small but insistent pulse of impatience. Nothing as direct and shaming as a wish that Jamesina would hurry up and finish crying, but the fact is, he is late. Mrs Montgomery will be at the workshop any minute to collect her pumps, and he will have to explain about the shank piece. Being late offends him, and it leaves a bad impression. He is going to have to get away.

A beam of morning sunshine has reached the bed. There is sun on her hair now. Long, shining strands of silver, wires of gold and copper among them. Beautiful.

To know the time of day is not as important as you think.

But the problem, Dr Epstein, is that I know the time of this particular day only too well and I am late.

One hour of happiness is worth more when it is valued.

But what is Mrs Montgomery's happiness worth? The sum is not inconsiderable, my old friend, and payment of your bill may depend on it.

One last shiver. Her face still buried in the pillow.

Two hurt people learning how to take care of another soul.

Do this for her, Niall Munro.

She must have been sleeping. She can feel sunshine on her face and her mind is clear as glass. Sore eyes, though.

He is still here, just sitting on the bed quite the thing, smoking his pipe. How long has he been watching her like this?

She puts a hand over her eyes, like some daft bairnie who thinks you won't see it if it can't see you. He takes the hand away and encases it in his own.

'I'm glad you slept, *mo chridhe*.'

'How long have I—?' Her voice comes out thick and snuffly.

'Long enough to let me do some thinking.' He pauses. Wry smile. 'And I now have something to say.'

Oh-oh.

'I'll start with one or two points in regard to what you were saying earlier.'

Dear Lord, what was she saying earlier?

'First, you are not an invalid.'

Ah, that.

'You were injured a long time ago and your mind is feeling the effects of that injury. But it is still a wonderful mind. A mite irascible, I grant you.'

Good word. From *ira*, 'anger'.

'But fortunately you find yourself sharing your life with an even-tempered, mostly patient and generally exemplary specimen of manhood who barely notices.'

'Not to mention smug.'

'Not, as you say, to mention smug. And secondly, you do not remind me of my mother.'

Did she really admit to that? She tries to draw her hand away. He holds it fast.

'Yes, both you and my mother received head injuries in similar circumstances. Both your lives were affected by these, and mine too in another way, as I understand better now.'

She pulls herself up on the pillow so that their faces are level.

'But believe me, Jamesina, it is not my mother who has mined this shallow heart of mine for feelings I didn't know it was capable of. You are going to have to take my word for this, but I hope to emphasise the point shortly when I return to bed.'

'The workshop?' she asks faintly.

'Will remain closed for the day. After we have explored the aforementioned issue to your complete satisfaction, I would like us, if you're willing, to stroll to the churchyard in the sunshine and you can start to tell me about your children.'

'How did you know?' she says. Grumbles, it might be true to say. 'Have I been talking in my sleep?'

'I have been thinking you might be ready, that's all. I would like it very much if you are. And when we come back we can start planning the ceilidh I intend to hold here a week on Saturday, so you might want to start seeing how many of your songs you can remember.'

'A ceilidh here? With only one chair in the parlour?'

'It's time we got involved. Both of us. People need your music, Jamesina. I hope you can see that. And as for me, I may not be ready to lead a riot yet, but I do reckon I can manage a ceilidh.' He gets to his feet, adding airily, 'Just something I read once. I'll explain another time.'

'And what do you think you're doing now?'

'I am removing my waistcoat, which I intend to drape very neatly over this chair. There we are. Soon to be followed by the rest of my clothing. And while I'm doing that, I am going to sing something. Please feel at liberty to join in.'

The Gaelic words taste strange to her after all this time and they come out a bit tremulous. But the melody carries them. Carries her, too. Lifts her and carries her in a flood of images as she sings. Fresh, damp earth, a boy in a glade of alders, a thumb rubbing her forehead, a bowl of snowdrops.

> *She bides in the undergrowth,*
> *wombing her voice,*
> *she who may one day sing too*
> *of life and promise*
> *at the end of the rains.*

*

She moves over, pulls aside the sheet and reaches out an arm.

'By the way,' he says, easing himself into the bed. 'I have been meaning to ask you. That mirror.'

'What mirror?' Her arm freezes.

'Bessie MacKinnon's mirror. I've been wondering, did it get my moustache?'

'No,' she says, laughing. 'I am desolate to say it did not get your moustache.'

'Are you sure?'

She can't tell if he's serious. His eyes are smiling all right, but this is a sensitive area.

'Niall Munro,' she says, 'there was not a shadow, not a hint, not the slightest suspicion of a growth on the upper lip of my silver man. And since you've raised the subject, I really do think you should take that as a sign.'

'Of?'

'Of the close-shaven good looks of the true love I was led by the spirits of All Hallows' Eve to expect.'

'Ah,' he says, lips very close, tobacco on his breath, which is not entirely free of bacon and strong tea either. 'In that case, I guess I'm going to need a mirror to aid the removal of this magnificent piece. It's a delicate task, you know.'

It is possible he has just won again.

Also possible that she is content to let him.

Contenta, 'satisfied', past participle (feminine) of *continere*, *con* plus *tenere*, 'to hold together'.

Contentment. The state of being held together.

'Come here, *mo chridhe*,' she says.

Her face in a mirror.

Why not?

312

Historical Note

This novel was inspired by actual events in the Ross-shire townships of Glencalvie and Greenyards (also known at the time as Greenyard) in the 1840s and 1850s; by the efforts of journalists and Free Church of Scotland ministers to raise awareness of what was happening; by the little-known role of women in leading community resistance; and by aspects of my own great-grandmother's experience in Rutherglen, decades after her own family were evicted from another part of the Scottish Highlands.

Dispossession from the land has taken many and complex forms in Scotland, and the reasons for, and social consequences of, the mass removals of people in the eighteenth and nineteenth centuries that became known as the Clearances remain the subject of debate. But the shockingly heavy battering the women of Greenyards received from the batons of charging policemen during the delivery of eviction notices in March 1854 is beyond argument. Eric Richards, a leading historian of the period, has described Greenyards as 'the last great confrontation and the last great clearance' before the more famous Crofters' War of the 1880s.

The injuries inflicted on the women at Feàrnaich field

were documented in minute medical detail by the crusading journalist-lawyer Donald Ross, who travelled to Strathcarron two weeks later, on 14 April, spoke to doctors and conducted dozens of eye-witness interviews. Although his anger can lead him into hyperbole and many were suspicious of his florid style, Ross's pamphlet, 'Massacre of the Rosses', remains a disturbing read. Newspaper accounts of the encounter, drawn largely from more official sources, tend to be less censorious of the way the authorities acted, but the volume and severity of the one-sided injuries is not in dispute. Neither is the determination of the law to put a final stop to women's resistance in general, which was proving embarrassing.

While opting for the creative freedom of different names and fictional personas, I have drawn on Ross's account for the description of how this encounter, and those earlier in the month, unfolded and for what happened to individuals on 31 March 1854, including the specific injuries of the fictional Jamesina Ross. Sheriff-substitute Rankin's letter is based on correspondence between the lawmen involved at the time, Sheriff-substitute Taylor and his superior Sheriff Mackenzie, and reports from Mackenzie to his boss, the Lord Advocate of Scotland.

Four women were arrested on Feàrnaich field and removed in handcuffs to jail in Tain. On the intercession of Gustavus Aird and others, they were released on bail. Only one of the females, named as Ann Ross, subsequently faced trial, along with one male, Peter Ross, for his involvement in the deforcement of sheriff officers earlier that month. The pair were accused of 'mobbing and rioting, breach of the peace, and assault on officers of the law in execution of their duty'. After pleading guilty to breach of the peace, a modified charge accepted by the prosecution, Ann Ross was sentenced to twelve months in jail and Peter Ross to eighteen months with hard labour.

The longer-term physical and mental effects on the women of Greenyards are in almost every case unknown, although it is certain that many of the injuries were of life-altering gravity. One exception is a young woman by the name of Grace Ross. The experience of the fictional Grace Graham of being bludgeoned and then chased halfway across the river reflects Donald Ross's description of what happened to Grace Ross on Feàrnaich field. Grace's great-grandson Alastair McIntyre, who still lives in Strathcarron, tells me that she recovered from her injuries but retained a deep dent in her right temple, which for the rest of her long life she would demonstrate by placing a coin in it.

In 1845, nine years before the Greenyards battle, *The Times* of London printed a series of articles amounting to a thorough indictment of the Highland Clearances and the Scottish poor laws. They were penned by an unnamed 'special commissioner', who was sent north to investigate after Gustavus Aird and his fundraising committee requested aid for the ninety people of Glencalvie seeking sanctuary in the graveyard of Croick church. A number of the commissioner's descriptions and sentiments found their way into the letters of the novel's Thomas Langton.

The Times article describing the exodus to the graveyard can be read at Croick itself, a beautiful little church nestling at the western end of the Strathcarron valley and easily accessible today along the road Thomas Telford built to reach it. Etched on panes of glass in a church window, near where the booths were erected, are short messages in English, purporting to have been written by the people of Glencalvie when they resided there in May 1845. These remain a haunting reminder of that desperate period for all who visit Croick today.

One Glencalvie woman is known anecdotally to have given birth to a baby boy in the graveyard. Her son lived for most of his life in Ardgay, and has descendants in the wider area.

The Reverend Gustavus Aird was a constant supporter of the people of Strathcarron, and others, in their struggles with the authorities, as indeed were many of the Free Church ministers who had broken away from the established Church of Scotland. While remaining faithful to the outlines of his early life as a minister, his physical characteristics and the tenor of his correspondence, I have imagined a great deal else. I hope the character that emerges in the novel captures something of the fire and the grace this man clearly exuded in life. I did think about acknowledging artistic licence by calling him something different, but I do think the real Gustavus Aird deserves to be remembered. (Also, it's an excellent name.) His evidence in October 1883 to the important Royal Commission of Inquiry into the Condition of Crofters and Cottars in the Highlands and Islands, chaired by Lord Napier, shows him in later life still fighting for human value in a depopulated Highlands given over to sheep and deer.

My feisty Gaelic-speaking great-grandmother, Annie McKechnie Baird, was sent into domestic service in Glasgow as a girl, after her township of Ardmore on the isle of Mull was emptied in the clearances that swept that island too. Little is known of Annie's first marriage, which I have no reason to believe was other than tranquil, but she did lose every one of her children to consumption (tuberculosis), with the sole exception of my grandfather, John Baird, who lived his whole life in terror of catching it. She took in washing to make ends meet and in later life rented out part of her room-and-kitchen flat in Rutherglen to a far-travelled younger man, whom she later married. My mother, who came to know this step-grandfather as Papa, never forgot his description of working in a lethal button factory in Newark, nor the shoes he made for them all.

The unmentionable subjects affecting the lives of women (in the case of the menopause only now becoming acceptable subjects of conversation) have always interested me. Women undergoing the multiple childbirths common in Victorian times are likely to have suffered, in addition, eye-watering internal wear and tear, which absolutely nobody seems to have talked about. Queen Victoria's prolapsed uterus was discovered only after her death, during an examination by her personal physician, Sir James Reid.

Rutherglen, an ancient royal burgh now all but absorbed into Scotland's largest city, is where I grew up. By the middle of the 19th century it had embarked on the transition from a country village with a proud history to the adjunct of Glasgow it later became. Although you will not find the name in any archive, 13, Anne Street is inspired by the tenement life that my mother and her mother remembered in Rutherglen. Last time I checked, older residents of the town were still declaring roundly that, despite appearances, Rutherglen is not a part of Glasgow.

Acknowledgements

Thank you to historians James Hunter, whose many books on the Highlands and Islands I warmly commend, and Elizabeth Ritchie, whose research into Gaelic schooling and women's lives was also invaluable. Both shared their expertise and their time with immense generosity.

Thanks also to Catriona Mackinnon for hours of help with Gaelic. And to Alastair McIntyre, Iain Robertson, Joanna Storrar, William Storrar and Kirsteen Macdonald; to Wendy Mitchell, whose moving memoir *Somebody I Used to Know* alerted me to the 'bookcase of the mind' analogy; and to Greg Guderian, Special Collections Associate at Newark Public Library, who cheerfully endured many emails about buttons.

Thank you also to Two Roads publisher Lisa Highton, who set the book going and was a treasured mentor throughout her time there; to publisher and editor Jocasta Hamilton at John Murray Press, who enthusiastically supported it across the finish line; to my agent Jenny Brown, who was there to pick me up along the way; and to copy-editor Hilary Hammond, whose thoughtful rigour I have much appreciated.

My long-suffering sisters, Margaret and Anna Magnusson, for whom the phrase 'constructive criticism' could have been coined, will be in receipt of red wine for life.